Murder at the House of Funerals

A Tracy Brubaker Mystery

Murder at the House of Funerals

A Tracy Brubaker Mystery

John Carter Stell

ARPress
45 Dan Road Suite 5
Canton MA 02021

Hotline: 1(888) 821-0229
Fax: 1(508) 545-7580

Ordering Information:
Quantity sales. Special discounts are available on quantity purchases by corporations, associations, and others. For details, contact the publisher at the address above.

Printed in the United States of America.
ISBN-13:   Softcover   979-8-89330-231-8
              eBook   979-8-89330-230-1
              Hardcover   979-8-89330-232-5

Library of Congress Control Number: 2024901473

CONTENTS

DEDICATION

For George "Ghost Host" Lewis and Richard "Count Gore De Vol" Dyszel for all those wonderful Saturday Nights.

If we're honest with ourselves, we have to admit we enjoy our tears just as much as we enjoy our laughter. The only moments of life that are a bore are when we don't care one way or another.

— Vincent Price

CHAPTER 1

"I want a pink one!" Nicole Shane told her mother enthusiastically. She was pointing at the grinning pumpkin that would serve as her bedroom nightlight for the Halloween season.

Tracy Brubaker Shane smiled as she reached for it, pushing aside the orange and green plastic gourds that sat on either side of her target.

"I thought your favorite color was green," the mother commented.

"NO!" Nicole shouted firmly as she jumped up and down.

The almost-three-year-old girl's father was pushing the shopping cart that held her 10-month-old brother Peter. Peter was looking at his sister and smiling, his eyes following her as she danced her way through the aisles. Brian Shane, on the other hand, scowled.

"A pink pumpkin?" he asked his wife as she added the intended purchase to the cart. "How about an orange one instead?"

"She wants a pink one," Tracy said calmly.

"Weren't *you* the one who didn't want to promote gender stereotypes? What do you think this is doing?"

"Oh. calm down, Brian," Tracy grinned. "She picked it out herself. I didn't encourage her one way or the other. And you know I'm no big fan of pink anyway."

"Can I pick Petaw's?" Nicole asked her mother.

"Better let Daddy do that," Tracy smiled.

"I want to hold it," Nicole said as she stared into the cart, her fingers wrapped around the thin, steely bars. "She's sad in there."

"I'll let you hold it in the car," Brian told her.

Nicole said nothing in response. She instead went to look at a series of "cute" skulls that adorned a nearby shelf.

"How about this smiling *orange* one for Peter?" Tracy asked her husband. She brought the decoration up to Brian's face, so man and squash were eye to eye.

"Fine," Brian said.

Tracy frowned. She added Peter's pumpkin to the cart. "What's wrong? Where's your Halloween spirit?"

"September's not even done," Brian mumbled. "What's the hurry?"

"Brian, the craft stores have been selling spooky stuff since August. Halloween ornaments came out in July. They'll start selling Christmas stuff in October. It's been that way for years, honey."

The father just shook his head. "Well, that's just nuts."

A big smile stretched across Tracy's face. "Speaking of food…where are they hiding the candy corn, I wonder? Yummy, yummy, yummy…" She started looking around lightly clapping her hands together.

"Let's wait on getting the trick or treat candy. It would be over a month old by the time Halloween came."

"Ahem. You seem to be under the impression I'm buying for others. You are *gravely* mistaken." She leaned towards Brian and grinned. "Get it? See what I did there?"

Brian chuckled. "All right then."

Nicole returned to the cart. "I want this too, Mommy."

She was now holding an otherwise traditional looking off-white skull — except for the blood oozing from its empty eye sockets. Tracy made a mock-horrified expression which started Nicole giggling.

"Where are we going to put *that*?"

"In *my* room. It's for Bonkahs."

Brian sighed. "Dogs don't care about that stuff, sweetheart. Bonkers might lick the red stuff off it and get sick."

Tracy took the item from her daughter. "Well, we'll just put it where he can't get at it then." She gave Brian one of her "stop being a spoil sport" looks.

"Thank you, Mommy!" Nicole shouted as she hugged Tracy's legs.

"You're welcome, dear-heart. Now, Daddy is going to take you to pick out a bag of candy corn."

"AND PUMCANS TOO?"

"Sure. A bag of mellow creme pumpkins too."

Nicole started hopping up and down while Tracy took control of the cart.

"And where are *you* going?" Brian asked suspiciously.

"I want one of those lawn blow-up thingies."

"Tracy…"

"What? I love those things. And maybe some other stuff too; make our front lawn really Halloweeny. It'll be fun."

"And whose *fun* will it be putting all that up — and, more importantly, taking it all down?"

"Oh, stop being a pumpkin pooper. *I'll* do it. I *can* handle things like that, you know — even though I'm just a *girl*."

"I didn't mean it like that."

"Then how did you mean it?"

Brian sighed. "It'll be a miracle if everything gets taken down before Christmas."

"Very funny not."

"It's perfectly acceptable to keep Christmas decorations up for weeks after Christmas. But if you're still plugging in your blow-up ghost a week after Halloween, the neighbors will get nervous."

Tracy laughed. "Our neighbors are probably *already* nervous, honey."

"My point exactly."

Nicole was pulling on her father's hand. "Come on, Daddy, come on! Candy corn!"

Brian smiled and lifted his older child. "All right. Some sweet pumpkins for my sweet pumpkin."

"I'm not a pumcan, Daddy."

"I used to call you that all the time when you were little. I guess you're too much of a big girl for that now, huh?"

Nicole put her arms around her father's neck and hugged him. Then the two headed towards the most dangerous part of the store.

Tracy smiled at Peter, who was looking at the hanging mini monstrosities. "Aren't they scary, honey?" She leaned over and kissed his head. "But they're all just pretend." Peter made no comment; he just kept on looking.

"Peter's too little for candy pumpkins and corn," Tracy explained. "He has only a couple of teeth and he could choke. We don't want that, do we?"

Nicole shook her head violently. "No, Mommy. I *love* baby Petaw." Her daughter's sentiment almost brought a tear to Tracy's eye.

"We'll give Peter a different kind of treat, okay?"

"OKAY!"

Tracy started laughing. Her daughter's ability to bring enthusiasm to almost every aspect of day-to-day life was a constant source of delight for the happy mom. Now mother and daughter were snacking on sweet treats while Brian Shane was putting his son down for an early afternoon nap. Nicole's would come shortly. The sitting Bonkers— the family's Irish setter who was just a few months older than Nicole — stared enviously at the nibblers.

Tracy saw the look in Nicole's eyes. "Nicole, dear, Bonkers can't have one. Sugar can make him sick."

"But he hungry."

"I'll let you give him a doggie treat. Okay?"

"OKAY!"

Bonkers understood what was happening. He came to all four paws and started wagging his tail, and then followed Tracy towards the cabinet that held *them*. Bonkers let out a joyful bark when Tracy removed the box. Then she handed Nicole two biscuits.

"One at a time," Tracy reminded her daughter.

Nicole giggled as the doggie gently took the first of his snacks from her small fingers. In mere seconds, he was back for the second.

"See, Mommy. Bonkahs *so* hungry."

"He's always willing to eat *something*," Tracy told her.

"Just like someone *else* I know," Brian said as he returned. He was grinning at his wife.

"Watch it, mister," Tracy grinned in response. "Want some?"

"Doggie treats or candy?"

"Daddy's silly," Nicole giggled.

He grinned at his daughter. Then he looked at Tracy.

"No thank you. My teeth are rotting just looking at that stuff."

"Daddy! You should brush your teef!"

The parents started laughing. "Daddy was just kidding," Tracy assured the mildly alarmed-looking tyke.

"We will have to brush *your* teeth extra special tonight," Brian said as they all returned to the dining room table.

"What do you think you would like to be for Halloween?" Tracy asked Nicole.

"A mommy."

"A mommy?" Tracy asked, feeling rather moved.

"Yes! I can use toilet papah!"

Brian started laughing. "I think you meant mummy."

Tracy frowned. "Mm. What do you know about mummies, Nicole?"

"Daddy told me all about them, Mommy. They're cute!"

"You'd make the cutest mummy ever," the mother agreed.

"What mummy?" Violetta Brubaker asked as she joined the others.

"Hi Grammaw!" Nicole shouted happily. "Want some pumcans?"

Violetta just smiled and gave her granddaughter a kiss on the head.

"No, dear child. Grandma will just sit down."

"Whatcha been doing Gram*maw*?" Tracy grinned.

"Reading yesterday's paper. I didn't have time yesterday."

"Anything interesting?"

"You might like this."

It was then that Tracy realized her mother was in fact holding a newspaper. Violetta handed the daily to her daughter.

"It's on the first page of the Entertainment section."

Tracy looked at her mother curiously as she accepted the item. She quickly found the recommended story. And then she started smiling.

"What is it?" Brian asked.

"Dr. Mort Itchin," Tracy answered, almost inaudibly. She was suddenly swept up in nostalgia.

"Dr. who?"

"Not Dr. Who. Dr. Mort Itchin."

"I don't—"

"Dr. Mort Itchin and his *House of Funerals*."

Brian's eyes suddenly widened. "Wait a minute. He was one of the area's horror show hosts from the 1970s and 1980s, right?"

"Right."

He looked at Tracy confused. "But he got cancelled in the mid or late eighties. You'd have been way too young to be watching that stuff."

Tracy looked at Brian. "My dad taped them. One thing he splurged for was a VCR back when they cost a pretty penny. A lot of the old horror movies he watched growing up weren't on home video yet. So, he taped the show, commercials, and all. He showed me some of them when I was seven or eight because I really liked the old mystery movies that I watched with him."

"Ah," Brian said. "That explains it. I wish I'd have been old enough to watch horror hosted movies. I was one generation too late."

"They've made something of a comeback though."

"Yeah, but I think you had to grow up with it for it to really mean something."

"Maybe," Tracy sighed. "Dad really liked Dr. Mort. He had this sidekick — Nagging Skeleton."

Brian chuckled. "Nagging Skeleton?"

"Yeah," Tracy grinned. "He was the only neighbor that lived beneath the funeral parlor that ever visited. You see, the premise was that after this funeral home closed for business each night, the disgraced Dr. Mort Itchin would come back from the dead, wanting to continue his life's work of trying to bring the dead back to life — which was weird, because the doctor had somehow come back from the dead on his own already. I pointed this oddity out to my father, and he just laughed. 'It's just a TV show' he'd tell me."

"Yeah," Brian chuckled.

"Well, every Saturday night the show would open with a pre-filmed sequence of the doctor emerging from his coffin and making his way — via a secret entrance — to the basement of the funeral home. Then he'd plan some grand experiment, presumably using one of the upstairs' corpses as his guinea pig. He never did succeed from what Dad told me."

"I want to go play!" Nicole interrupted.

"Come on," a smiling Violetta said while rising. "Grandma will take you to the playroom. We can play before your nap."

"OKAY!"

Nicole quickly headed in the room's direction, with Bonkers following right behind her. Tracy and Brian smiled at the admittedly familiar sight.

"Anyway," Tracy continued, "the funeral home's basement was supposedly littered with failed experiments. The only partially successful experiment was Nagging Skeleton. And he would visit regularly and annoy the heck out of the doctor. Those host segments always made me laugh when I was little."

Brian was nodding. "How did they handle the skeleton? Was he a guy dressed up or something?"

"No. It was moved by strings and such. It was very low-tech and clumsy of course. But I still loved it."

"I can tell," Brian grinned.

Tracy stuck out her tongue. She looked back at the article. "This story says Richard George is going to play the character again for a Halloween show they're doing. And the hook is that — for the first time ever — Dr. Mort Itchin will be successful in his experiments."

Brian smiled broadly. "Sounds pretty cool. Everything old is new again, as the saying goes."

"Listen to this promo," Tracy said. "Whether you're five or a hundred and five; whether you're dead or alive; whether you care or not, join us *live* this Halloween night at 8:00 p.m. for a special misrepresentation of Dr. Mort Itchin and his *House of Funerals*! The not-so-good doctor — who haunted the Baltimore airwaves from 1971 through 1985 — will be your host once again for this once-in-a-*death*time opportunity! And he'll be joined by his sidekick, Nagging Skeleton! Dr. Itchin will present the classic *Abbott and Costello Meet Frankenstein* while he once again dabbles in dread with the dead. See it live! More details will soon follow!" Tracy put the paper down. "It's going to air live on channel 42. And they're going to have a live studio audience too and be giving away tickets over the next couple of weeks."

"That sounds like a lot of fun."

Tracy smacked her lips. "I want to go."

Brian chuckled. "I guessed you did."

"I'll pull my own skeleton strings if I have to, but I want to go. You and me. We'll take Nicole out early for trick-or-treating and then hightail it to the studio."

"And leave a sugar-upped kid with your mother?"

"Mom will be fine. Besides, Mom's the one most likely to let Nicole indulge in sweets rather than you or me. That's part of a grandmother's job, isn't it?"

"You have a point."

"So, if I could get tickets, would you be my date?"

Brian grinned. "Sure."

"Supreme! I'm going to start making calls on Monday." Tracy pondered a moment. "You know I still have all of Dad's videotapes."

"Upstairs in boxes I bet."

"Yeah. I think I'll go look through some of those boxes; see what I can find."

"I thought you were hell bent on setting up your air-blow ghost."

"It's a ghost coming out of a pumpkin."

"Whatever."

"I'll do it later."

"All right."

"Can you hook up a VCR to the first floor's TV? I know a tape would look crappy on your home theater set-up, but it probably would look OK on the other TV."

Brian smiled warmly. "Sure, I can do that. You thinking of watching some Dr. Mort, huh?"

"Maybe a little, assuming I can find those tapes. I'm pretty sure Dad didn't tape over them. I know I didn't."

"I'll set it up right now; shouldn't take long."

"Thanks, honey," Tracy said gratefully.

"Then I'll join you upstairs."

"Fine. I'll be the weepy woman you find. Thinking about how simple things seemed once upon a time always does that to me."

Brian kissed her before they each went their separate ways. And Tracy couldn't resist grabbing a handful of candy corn for the journey.

"Daddy! Daddy! Daddy!" Nicole Shane shouted as she came through the front door.

"What is it?" he grinned.

"Mommy put up a ghost! It's *so* cute!"

He chuckled. "She got it working, huh?"

"Come on, Daddy!"

"All right."

Brian followed the hopping moppet into the front yard. He looked around. There was more than just an inflatable ghost and pumpkin inhabiting his lawn. Tracy had erected tombstones; staked skeleton parts in the ground; donned the gutters with orange and purple lights; and was now securing a witch to a tree trunk so that it looked as though the poor dear crashed into it.

Nicole was standing next to the ghost, which stood several inches taller than she. "Look Daddy! Look!"

"I see, I see."

"Be careful, Nicole," Tracy said as she approached. "There are all kinds of things in the ground you can trip over. So don't run around on the grass."

"OKAY, MOMMY!" She then started running around on the grass.

"Nicole!" her father called sternly. She stopped, looked at him a moment, and then decided to just sit down and look around. It wasn't long before she was rolling around in the grass.

"Now she'll need a bath," Brian grumbled.

Tracy grinned. "What do you think?"

"Spooky."

"Maybe we should get some more stuff; really go all out."

"Some more what?"

"I don't know. I'll just look around the stores and see what tickles my fancy."

"Great."

"Maybe put some spider webs in the tree branches or hang some things from them."

"What's come over you? You never were so gung-ho about Halloween before."

"The Halloween spirit, I guess. Halloween should be fun. On Thanksgiving we should be appreciative and on Christmas we should be reverent. But Halloween should be a blast."

"Ah."

"I want Nicole and Peter to have happy holiday memories, Brian. I want them to remember how much fun they had during the holidays. I want to be Fun Mom!"

He stared chuckling. "Well, you *are* Fun Wife…" She hugged him.

"You say the cutest things, Linus."

"Linus?"

"Maybe we can fool around in a pumpkin patch or something. *It's the Great Humpkin, Brian Shane!*"

"Will you stop that?!' Brian scolded while trying not to laugh. "Nicole's right there."

"She doesn't know a hump from a pump…But *I* do."

"Tracy, I think we need to get you inside — quickly."

"Good evening, my fellow seekers of knowledge," Dr. Mort Itchin greeted. "It is I, once again, Doctor Mort Itchin! I have returned from the underworld to continue my work! And you will all be witnesses!" The doctor started laughing maniacally, throwing his gray-wigged head back in a most melodramatic fashion, while pointing at the camera. The sound of thunder was suddenly heard throughout the makeshift laboratory. A cat could be heard screeching also.

The doctor was a rather sorry looking sight. His outfit was a wrinkled, dust-covered tuxedo which had lost all sense of form. There were various stains covering it, each of a different color. What were obviously splotches of paint were meant to be remnants of the various multi-colored liquids which were bubbling and spilling in the background. His face was pale, with some black shoe polish added around his eyes to make him look extra sinister. But the hot lights had already caused some polish to streak. Nevertheless, the black streaks resembling tears achieved the desired effect.

After he was done cackling, he straightened. He removed a pair of surgical gloves from his pocket. As he was putting them on, he again addressed his viewers.

"Tonight, my friends, we will be conducting an experiment using my favorite creature of the night: the vampire bat!" Again, there was maniacal laughter.

"Good grief this is cheesy," Brian opined.

"It's *supposed* to be cheesy," Tracy said while not-so-gently elbowing Brian's ribs. "Now shush or go away."

"As you all know — since you're watching this show — vampires live forever! So tonight, I will try harnessing the life essence of the vampire bat, and then transfer it to a human body! If I succeed, I will have discovered the secret of—"

"Oh, hey doc," a Bugs Bunny-esque, off-camera voice suddenly called out without much enthusiasm. The camera not so smoothly panned right to reveal the top half of a skeleton. The bottom half was obscured by the coffin he was standing behind, which also conveniently concealed the puppeteer. "What're you doing over there?"

"Will you go away?" Dr. Itchin not so much asked as ordered.

"Sorry Doc," the boney guest said. "But I have a *femur* to ask of you."

Dr. Mort Itchin glared at Nagging Skeleton. Then he glared at the camera. Tracy started chuckling.

"Get it doc?" the skeleton asked, starting to move his hand up and down while laughing. "Femur? *Favor?*"

"Go away."

"I'm telling you, doc, I would kill me if I weren't already *kilt.*"

At this point, an off-screen assistant tossed a primarily blood-red colored kilt so that it landed on the coffin. Again, Tracy giggled as the mad medico scowled at the camera.

"Our funeral tonight is — appropriately enough — *The Vampire Bat*, staring Doctor X himself — Lionel Atwill — and the guy who played Renfield, Dwight Frye. And the beautiful damsel is Fay Wray, who would be King Kong's girlfriend soon enough. Oh, there's also some award-winning guy named Melvyn Douglas. Meanwhile, I'll grab my own *bite* before we begin."

"Hey doc," the skeleton called out. One of his arms was extended outward with his palm facing upward.

"What is it now?"

"Come over here and give me some skin, baby. I mean really, give me some skin. It's cold in here."

The doctor smiled. "I know a nice, warm place you can lay down. It will heat you up — permanently!"

"Hey, you tried that once before."

"I did?"

"Yeah. Don't make me have to kick your *ash*, doc."

Then the bones jangled once again as the skeleton howled at his pun. The camera faded on the doctor as he was shaking his head.

"That was awful," Brian said. "So, this Nagging Skeleton just made terrible puns and bone jokes all the time? Just how many bone jokes can you make?"

"Feel free to leave then," Tracy said, clearly annoyed.

"Actually, I'd like to watch the movie. I've never seen it."

"Then stop putting down my pleasant memories. Stop screwing with my nostalgia, buddy."

"I'm sorry. I wasn't putting you down for liking it."

"My dad liked it too."

"I got it. I'll not say another negative word about it."

Tracy grinned. "Did you know Nagging Skeleton came out with his own board game?"

"Really?"

"Yeah. It was called *Tibial* Pursuit."

Brian shook his head. "Stop it. Please just stop now."

"I mean it, Brian. I wouldn't fibula."

"Tracy, have mercy."

"Brian, you have absolutely no sense of humerus."

At this point Tracy started laughing, prompted by the scowl on her husband's face that was growing in intensity with each ticking second. He reminded her of Dr. Mort Itchin.

"Can we just watch the movie now?" Brian asked.

Tracy just nodded as she leaned against her sour-faced spouse. But he put his arm around her and kissed the top of her head. How could he resist her? She was, after all, his one and ulna.

It was almost midnight when Brian Shane's first exposure to Dr. Mort Itchin and his *House of Funerals* came to end. As Tracy had warned him, the doctor's experiment failed. Instead of restoring life, what Dr. Itchin actually did was create a corpse that woke up every five minutes wanting a drink of water, his thirst unquenchable.

"Well," the scientist sighed, "my thirst for knowledge has been turned against me in a most cruel way." He looked upward and shook his first. "Darn you, you hoarders of life's mysteries! I will one day discover your greedily-held secrets!"

"I'm *so* parched," a voice moaned. The body it was coming from was covered by a blood-spattered sheet. "I'm *living* of thirst."

"Just *shut* up," the doctor ordered. He then looked at the camera. "I'll deal with this freak later; probably will have to sew his mouth shut."

"Just give me a sponge to suck on! I *beg* of *YOU!*"

Dr. Mort shook his head. "Next week we'll visit *Horror Hotel* here at the *House of Funerals*. Until then, keep your labs clean!"

"Hey doc," Nagging Skeleton called out.

"Good Hades, what is it now?"

"You won't believe this. I'm locked out of my coffin. Ain't *that* ironic?"

Again, Dr. Mort Itchin just shook his noggin. And then the credits rolled.

Now Brian shook *his* head. "Now how many kids would have gotten that last joke?" he challenged. "How many kids would know what a skeleton key is?"

"That was great," Tracy said as she stood up from the couch, a smile on her face. "Admit it, Brian. It was fun."

"I liked the movie okay. But I don't know about the doctor."

"Brian, try and appreciate what you just saw. An independent TV station bought a package of movies that had some horror stuff. They corral some employees and tell them they have to come up with some something or other and host these movies. There's no money and no time to rehearse. They're just trying to have some fun. Can't you appreciate that?"

"Sure, I get it. And back in the days before home video when this was the only way to see this stuff, I'd have probably watched."

"I think I want to watch another one."

"It's midnight."

"Mm. Well, maybe next Saturday then. It could be a new Saturday night thing for us — at least until we've gone through all of Dad's old tapes."

"Marvelous."

"Jeez. Some guys would love to have a woman who would watch stuff like this with them. You're a real square dude." Tracy ejected the videotape and shut down the television. "When Nicole's a little older, I'd like *her* opinion on this."

Brian smiled and shook his head. "Give her popcorn, I bet she'd watch anything."

"Just like her dad…" Tracy grinned. "I'm going to bed. And I'm going to get tickets to the upcoming revival. Who knows? If it goes really well, maybe they'll bring him back for more. Wouldn't that be cool?"

Brian nodded unenthusiastically. Tracy frowned appropriately. Then the couple began retirement exercises for the evening. Climbing the stairs, they started giggling quietly over their mock argument and were hand in hand by the time they arrived at the bedroom door.

"I need a favor, Meesh," Tracy said into the receiver early Monday. "I need to get my hands on two tickets to the Dr. Mort Itchin show. I won't take no for an answer."

Michelle Balder started laughing. "You're kidding me," the client said finally.

"Nope. Deadly serious. Can you help me?"

"Sure," Michelle said after a few more chuckles. "We've advertised on WMFT long enough I'm sure I can hook you up. Are you a fan or something, or are these for your husband's benefit?"

"My dad was a fan and he showed me some episodes now and again. When I saw that article this past weekend, the nostalgia was overwhelming. I even made Brian watch an old tape with me."

"Well, you know what they say about nostalgia."

"I *live* dangerously, babe," Tracy said. Michelle started guffawing again. "But seriously, if you could call your pal at Channel 42, I'd be eternally grateful."

"Consider it done, Tracy. I'll call him right now."

"Supreme! Call me right back, would you? I won't be able to handle the suspense."

"Tracy, you are just *too* adorable sometimes. I'll call you back; promise."

"Thanks so much, Meesh!"

"Sure," Michelle chuckled.

As Tracy looked up from her desk after ending her call, she saw her associate Neal Bennett grinning at her. "Dr. Mort Itchin, huh?"

"You a fan?"

"Sure; I remember him."

"Oh! Should I order more tickets then? We could make it a double date! It's been so long since I've seen Sara."

Neal chuckled. "No, that's okay. I like him okay but watching the live show from the comfort of my own *extraordinarily* comfy couch will be fine."

"Your loss," Tracy smiled. "Maybe you'll see me and Brian in the audience." She closed her eyes tightly and started waving her fists back and forth. "Oh, this is so *exciting*!"

Neal laughed heartily. "I wouldn't have believed it had I not seen it," he said finally. "All this over a—"

"You better choose you next words carefully, Bennett," Tracy said.

"What's going on?" Keandra Moore, Tracy's newest associate, asked.

"I'm going to be in the live studio audience at the Dr. Mort Itchin Halloween extravaganza! Isn't that just too awesome for words?"

Keandra started laughing. She had a loud, joyous laugh, and Tracy had the ability to bring it out. The joyful sound was especially striking because Keandra Moore was only five foot three and 115 pounds, which made for an odd pairing. Although Tracy had not yet met Keandra's husband, she had seen his picture in Keandra's office. The handsome Daryn Moore was six-one and all smiles. Tracy felt she and Brian and the Moores would have a great time on the town together someday.

Keandra Moore had been with Tracy only since August 5. But the new attorney and Tracy had, as they say, hit it off famously. In many ways, Keandra reminded Tracy of Rita Tanner, wife of Elias Tanner, Sr., the former partner of Tracy's late father, who now did occasional investigative work for the law firm. Never mind Tanner was supposed to be enjoying his retirement.

But Keandra, who was five years Tracy's senior, was no one to laugh *at*. Her impeccable resume had showed much experience in the areas where Tracy most needed help — mainly in corporate work. Tracy's clients had taken an instant liking to Keandra too, and the new attorney's personality fit perfectly with the family atmosphere of Tracy Brubaker Shane & Associates, Attorneys at Law. Even Neal — who had wanted another male to even the gender makeup — liked Keandra Moore almost immediately. It had been a very happy two months.

"Should I try to get tickets for you and your hubby, Keandra?"

"Thanks, but no thanks. We already are going to a party that night at my sister's. The cousins will play while the adults will…play too, I guess."

"Sounds supreme!" Tracy smiled.

"Michelle Balder on line one, Tracy," Rebecca Dietz, the firm's secretary and much more, announced.

"Ooh! Goody!" Tracy chirped. Neal and Keandra left the boss' office laughing. "Hi Meesh! Make me happy!"

After Michelle ceased her chortling, she said, "I'm going to make you so much more than happy, Tracy."

"How's that?"

"How would you like to stop by the studio and watch some rehearsals; actually meet Richard 'Dr. Mort Itchin' George in person?"

Tracy's eyes widened. "Oh, Meesh, I think I'm going to cry."

"You don't have to do *that*, Tracy. I'm going to give you a phone number for a man named Steve Dante. He's producing the show and knows who you are, as do most people who work in local television. You, my dear Tracy, will be something of a guest of honor. You might even get to make a cameo appearance or something."

"I'm not sure I'm up for *that*," Tracy said, still with a huge smile on her face. "But I'll do what I gotta do, I guess. I'll take that number now."

So, Michelle Balder gave Tracy Steve Dante's phone number. And Tracy wasted no time dialing that number. Soon she was making plans for her first visit to Channel 42, future home to the newly resurrected Dr. Mort Itchin and his *House of Funerals*.

Chapter 2

"I'm really excited you'll be with us," Steve Dante told Tracy as they sat in his office. "It's amazing how excited everyone around here is over this."

Tracy just smiled. "I know *I* am. I want to tell Richard George how much he meant to my father and me. I have such wonderful memories watching that show with my dad, even if it was after it officially left the air. Dad treasured those tapes he made."

"Will your father be joining us too then?"

The smile weakened. "No. He passed away many years ago."

"Oh; I'm sorry."

"Thank you. But that's why my memories of him are so precious to me. So, please tell me a little bit about yourself, Steve."

"Sure. I've been with the station six years now. I've produced quite a few in-depth pieces for our newscasts; got some local awards for it too."

"Supreme! Belated congrats to you."

Dante chuckled. "Thanks. Of course, we became part of the Speigel Broadcasting Company long before I settled here, so I wasn't here when the Dr. Mort Itchin show originally aired."

"I know a lot of independent stations became affiliated with new networks in the eighties and nineties. And a lot of local programming was lost because of it. I miss those evening magazine-style shows a lot of stations used to run."

Dante nodded. "Right. A lot of changes happened in the eighties. The cable and home video industries simultaneously exploded and, as you said, there were new networks with original programming. Not too many stations run old movies anymore, so they don't need horror hosts and the like. The specialty cable channels pretty much handle all that now. So, when Speigel bought Channel 42 in 1985, they started making immediate changes to compete with cable and VCRs. And sadly, getting rid of the bad doctor was one of them."

"What, may I ask, brought this revival on then?"

"Me. You can't help but notice that people who grew up in the seventies and eighties are feeling nostalgic about those times. Just look at the movies — horror movies especially — being remade from those decades, everything from *Halloween* to *A Nightmare on Elm Street*. And Universal is trying to bring back their classic monsters too. And then there's the horror TV series programming which is still pretty big. So, I thought why not see if there was interest in bringing Mort back. We conducted some informal polls, and the response was incredible. So here we are."

"I think it's awesome. I think it will be beyond fun."

Dante nodded. "That's what we are hoping a lot of people think. And we were able to license a very good movie to go with it; perfect for the family."

"I'm not sure my almost-three-year-old is quite ready for all those monsters, even with the comedy stuff."

"Ah. You're bringing your husband with you I take it?"

"Yup. Have you started building the sets or anything?"

"We officially begin production October 2. The station needs the space for something else through the first. Then it's all ours. I take it you'd like to come and see us at work?"

"If at all possible, I'd love to. But I'd have to work it around my schedule; maybe come by on a Saturday."

"Sure; we can probably do that. I'll have to check on exactly what our designer's plans are. As for meeting Richard George, I'll have to see about his schedule too."

Tracy beamed. "I'll carve out time to meet Mr. George regardless. Is there anything I can do to thank you for this, Steve?"

"Actually, I was hoping you might be willing to record some public service announcements for us."

"Sure! What are they for?"

"Victims of domestic violence who are afraid to come forward."

Tracy nodded. "Of course, I'll do that, Steve."

"Well then this will work very well for everyone. If you don't mind, let me know when you're available for a few hours and I'll have Megan Wallace get a hold of you. She's coordinating and overseeing these PSAs, as well as serving as co-producer for the live show."

"Okay. Usually Saturdays are good for me. I try to avoid working on weekends these days."

"That's great, Tracy. Thank you."

"Sure, Steve."

"You'll like Megan. She'll be handling most of the day-to-day producing duties and will probably be your main contact."

"Sounds supreme!"

"The ticketing will be done via email, so you'll probably have your four waiting for you before you even get back to your office."

"Four? I only wanted two."

"I thought you might like to invite some other couple you think would be interested. If you decide two is really all you need just let me know. We'll have no problem finding someone else to give them to. The studio will have room for only 80 or so people."

Tracy couldn't help but give Steve Dante another warm smile. "Ok, I'll let you know."

"Great!" Dante stood. "I guess I'll see you in a couple of weeks. Just give me a call."

Tracy rose also. "You bet. Thank you so much. This means a lot to me."

"No problem. Let me show you out."

"You don't have to. I remember the way."

They shook hands and then Tracy left to find her way.

"Sorry I'm a little late," Tracy told her family as she came towards the dining area. She was holding Nicole, who had personally greeted her at the mudroom door. Bonkers was circling her, wagging his tale.

"Ma!" Peter shouted, pointing at Tracy. He was already in his highchair.

"So much love in this room," Tracy observed with a broad smile on her face.

She walked towards the table and then secured Nicole in her booster seat. Next, she moved towards where her son was seated and lowered herself, so they were eye to eye. She kissed each cheek which started him giggling. Lastly, she allowed herself to fall onto the floor so Bonkers could get his share of affection.

"Bonkahs kiss Mommy!' Nicole laughed.

"Tracy!" Violetta scolded. "Don't let that dog lick your face like that!"

"It's okay, Mom," Tracy countered. "I've had all my shots — and so has Bonkers."

"Go away!" Violetta shouted at the family pet.

"I'm going, I'm going," Tracy said while rising, pretending to be hurt.

Violetta just snorted and returned to the kitchen. There were still more serving dishes that needed to be retrieved. Tracy winked at Nicole and then took Peter out of his chair.

"You're coming upstairs with me little man," she told him.

"Petaw nurse, Mommy?"

"Yes, sweetie. Mommy and Peter will be back very soon. You, Daddy, and Grandma can start eating."

"OKAY!"

"Where is Daddy, by the way?"

"Daddy take a showa. He cut a grass."

"Oh, Daddy cut the grass today? I hope he didn't run over our decorations." Tracy looked at Peter. "Let's go say 'hi' to Daddy upstairs."

Tracy waited until her mother had come back into the dining room until she moved towards the staircase. She didn't want Nicole to be left all by herself. Once upstairs, Tracy entered the bedroom to find Brian pulling on a sweatshirt over his head.

"Looks like I missed the show," she grinned.

Brian grinned back once the shirt was secured. "They'll be an encore tonight."

"Uh-huh."

He formally welcomed her home with a kiss. "How'd your ticket thing go?"

"Supreme! We're in. All they want in return are some PSAs for a very worthy cause. Steve Dante seemed really nice."

"*Everyone* you meet seems 'really nice'."

"Oh, stop that. Why didn't you turn on the lights and ghost?"

"That's your thing."

"Sheesh, Brian. You're getting a lump of coal in your treat bag this year — or a rock maybe."

Brian chuckled. "I just didn't think about it."

"Even after you cut the grass?"

"Yeah. By the way, thanks for the obstacle course."

"Sorry, Brian. You didn't hurt any of my beasties, did you?"

"No, everything's fine, relatively speaking."

"Supreme!"

"Uh-huh."

"Oh, I actually got *four* tickets to the Dr. Mort show. I was thinking about asking Crys and El-J."

Brian frowned. "Great. My sister can pick on me all night."

"Oh, Brian…"

"Can't you ask someone else?"

By now Tracy was sitting on the bed and nursing the appreciative Peter Shane. "She probably can't make it anyway. Her schedule isn't as flexible as mine. And El-J works weird hours anyway."

"Exactly. How about I ask Ben and Lisa?"

Tracy frowned. "The Falcones? I don't like Ben, Brian. He's a jerk."

"He's a friend of mine and he's *not* a jerk. You two don't share the same sense of humor is all."

"He's foul-mouthed and sexist."

Brian folded his arms. "He's not that bad. Lisa always laughs at his jokes."

"I like Lisa, but I think she laughs at anything."

"Yeah, she laughs at *your* jokes all the time too."

Tracy snorted. "Very funny — not. Look, Brian. I appreciate he's your friend and all that. But I can't pretend he doesn't make me feel uncomfortable. First thing he looks at every time he sees me are my boobs. He does more than just look, actually. Haven't you noticed that?"

Brian cleared his throat. "Well…They have gotten bigger since you've been nursing."

"What does that have to do with anything?"

"I'm just saying…"

"What *are* you saying? Are you saying you're perfectly all right with another man leering at your wife's breasts?"

Brian sighed. "I think leering is a strong word."

"Give me a break."

"Fine. But there aren't too many of my old friends who don't drink, or at least have the courtesy not to when I hang out with them. Ben's the only one."

Tracy blinked. With some concern in her voice she asked, "Are you saying that seeing others drink is starting to bother you? I thought it didn't."

"Well…Sometimes it does. I had some real good times with my friends when I was drinking. I'm not saying I want to start up drinking again. But I don't want to put myself in a position where I'm tempted either."

"Tempted? Is something bothering you that you haven't told me about?"

"No…not really."

Tracy frowned as she moved Peter to her other breast. "It sounds like something is bothering you. Please tell me what it is."

"You'll think it's stupid," Brian muttered.

"How can you say that? That's not fair to me."

"Tracy, I need to get out of this house more than I do."

"Oh," Tracy said quietly. "We don't go out enough?"

"We don't. You work five full days, sometimes part of the weekend. Saturdays you like to spend mostly with the kids. Maybe we go shopping together. Of course, there's church on Sunday. But if we have company, it's usually Crystal and her family. I have to admit it's all getting a little old."

"Being a stay-at-home dad is getting old for you?"

Brian shook his head. "That's not what I meant. But I do need some time for myself. And by that I just mean to do something that's totally relaxing and not obligatory. That's the best way I can explain it."

Tracy sighed. "I'm sorry, Brian. It's just with hiring a new person and catching up on the backlog—"

"I'm not trying to blame you for this. I'm not blaming anyone. And it's really not the big deal I may be making it sound like it is. You asked, so I told you."

Tracy looked at Peter. He released his mother and smiled at her. "Are you done, little man? I bet Grandma has something good to eat downstairs." Tracy stood up. "Let Daddy take you downstairs while Mommy gets changed."

Brian looked sympathetically at his wife while he took Peter. "I didn't mean to upset you. It's really no big deal."

Tracy forced a smile. "Even if it isn't now, it will be eventually. That's how these things work. And you're right. You're here practically seven days a week and you rarely hang out with your friends."

"I get to hang out with my best friend everyday though," Brian smiled.

"Shucks," Tracy grinned. "Okay, Brian. If you want to ask Ben and Lisa to this thing, go ahead. But I'm not sitting next to him."

Brian laughed. "And I'll say something if I catch him leering."

Tracy chuckled. "Deal. Now go see how Nicole is doing while I change into my play clothes."

"Can't I stay and leer?"

"Good grief."

"All right, all right. We're leaving."

Brian gave his wife another smile as he headed towards the door. After they had left and she had donned her comfy attire, Tracy sat on the bed and sighed. Was this just the beginning of something with Brian? Was he getting restless? Maybe she should ask if he'd like to go back to work. She liked having him at home with their children but if he was starting to resent it…She shook her head and stood up. If she was going to be worrying over this not-so "big deal," she'd rather do it on a full stomach.

Tracy and Violetta where cleaning up after dinner while Brian entertained the youngest family members in the playroom. Bonkers — torn between potential food and play — decided to be optimistic and stay in the kitchen.

"Nicole is very excited about Halloween this year," Tracy told her mother. "She said she wanted to be wrapped up in toilet paper, but I think a cute ballerina outfit is the way to go."

"Toilet paper is expensive," Violetta said.

"Well, so is a Halloween costume. It might actually be cheaper to buy TP and we'd have some left over." Tracy grinned. "I know some Halloween-type things we can do with the extra paper."

Violetta stopped washing the serving tray and looked at her daughter. "Don't you cause any trouble."

"Who? *Me*?" Tracy pressed her fingers against her chest and tried looking angelic.

Violetta shook her head and resumed her washing. "I think a ballerina is nice."

"Me too." Tracy moved towards the sink and stood next to her mother. "What did I go as when I started trick-or-treating? I can't remember."

"A monkey," Violetta answered quickly.

"No."

"Yes. I'm sure I have some pictures in my albums upstairs."

"A monkey? How'd that happen?"

"You thought monkeys were cute. You thought snakes were cute."

Tracy chuckled. "Even then I could see beauty in everything, huh Mom?"

Violetta smiled. "You jumped around the house making monkey noises all night. You tried playing on the furniture, but I put a stop to *that*."

"Did I have a costume or what?"

"You father got you one from the store; just some plastic thing in a box."

"I'd like to see some of those pictures, Mom."

"They're in boxes in the spare bedroom somewhere."

"Mm. What other things was I?"

"A princess a few times; a bride." Violetta shook her head.

"What's wrong?"

"You got chocolate all over that nice white dress. I told you to get changed before you ate but you didn't listen. Then you made a mess."

Tracy chuckled again. "Is it too late to say I'm sorry?"

Violetta smiled and shook her head. "You and Elias, Jr. started going out together when you two were older. But you never got into any trouble."

"Of course not, Mom. Our dads were cops."

"Well, don't start getting into trouble now."

"Good grief. You know I was kidding about the toilet paper."

"I never know with you."

"Gee, thanks." Tracy wrapped around her arms around her mother's neck and kissed her cheek. "I'm going to see what the kids are up to." Tracy looked at Bonkers. "Sorry, fella. Nothing for you tonight."

The family pooch put his head down, looking disappointed. Better luck next time. He followed Tracy as she left the kitchen.

"How are you doing, Beck?" Tracy asked her secretary the next morning. It was early and the office hadn't yet officially opened.

"Just fine."

"How's life without your daughter living with you anymore?"

Rebecca smiled. "I'm fine, Tracy."

"You had Georgina when you were like 23 or something?"

"Right."

"How's your man dealing with his little girl being out in the world?"

Rebecca laughed. "It's getting better. I've got him down to calling her just four times a day now."

Tracy smiled and nodded. "And you guys are still young, too: mid-forties. I bet the good times will roll after some more time passes."

Rebecca frowned. "What's wrong, Tracy? Can I help you with something?"

Tracy didn't hesitate. "Brian's getting restless. He's spending all his time at the house with the kids."

"Now he knows what most women felt like once upon a time."

"When you were doing the stay-at-home-mom thing, did you get antsy? Or did Andre make sure he took you out enough?"

"Of course, there were days when I wanted to just hand Georgina to Andre and do my own thing. That's perfectly normal. But a lot of that was because of money — or rather, lack thereof. But Andre was very creative. We did things at parks; he'd set up his old Boy Scout tent in the backyard during the summer and we'd improvise a camping trip; anytime it snowed he made sure we all played outside and then he'd make hot cocoa; and probably a dozen other things like that."

"They all sound like great things, Beck."

Rebecca nodded. "They were. But what was nicer was realizing he was always thinking about things that we could all do together." Rebecca sighed. "Funny. Once I started working again when Georgina became the latchkey kid, we of course had more money. So, we went out to dinner and the movies and other things like that more than we ever had before. But, if truth be told, I think I liked the other stuff better. They made for better memories."

"Yeah. It's, of course, not about the money with us. It's time and a certain degree of exhaustion."

"Your kids are small. Naturally, they wear you guys out. But it really is important that you go out on dates."

"I'm not sure I'm the person he wants to be with though."

"What?"

"I think he wants to hang out with the guys, you know? We've been back together over four years now and the novelty has worn off for him I think."

Rebecca shook her head. "Tracy, Brian is crazy about you. Maybe it's just that with you working so much and then wanting to spend time with your kids, he feels a little left out. It could be a male ego thing with him. I don't see how anyone could get bored with *you*."

Tracy laughed appreciatively. "Just what is it you think I do when I leave here, Beck, perform at open-mike nights across the city?"

"Don't you?"

Both women laughed. "I'm just afraid," Tracy said finally.

"Afraid of what?"

"That Brian will…Well, I probably shouldn't go into all of it."

Rebecca started nodding. "Is he still struggling, Tracy?"

"Huh?"

"With the drinking. That's what you didn't want to bring up, right?"

"Well…I'm not sure I should say anything."

"I won't tell anyone, boss; promise."

Tracy gulped. "He just made a passing comment. It's probably no big deal."

"But it has you worried. I can tell."

"Yeah, I'm a little worried. I'm afraid if he keeps feeling suffocated or whatever you want to call it, he might start drinking. I'm afraid if he starts going out with his friends, they might offer him a drink that he won't turn down. And the one friend who *is* considerate about Brian's past, is a real jerk."

Rebecca stood up from her desk and then embraced her employer.

"I'm sorry, Tracy."

"Me too," the employer responded. "I think I need to talk to Brian about how I'm feeling."

"I think that's a good idea."

"He might get mad though."

"But if this is really bothering you then you should let him know. This isn't just for you, either. You have those two little angels to think about too."

"Yeah, my angels." Tracy sighed as Rebecca pulled away. "Thanks, Beck. I think I'll have to talk to him about this. I'm just not sure when."

"Soon, Tracy. I don't like seeing you worried."

Tracy managed a smile. "I'm always worried about *something*, Beck."

"Not like this you're not."

"No. No, I guess not."

Later that same afternoon, Rebecca announced, "Megan Wallace is on line two for you, Tracy."

"Got it, Beck. Thanks." After Tracy had it, she said, "Hi Megan. Steve told me you'd be in touch."

"Am I calling at a bad time?" Megan asked. Tracy thought the woman sounded as if she were five years old.

"Now is fine."

"Oh, great. First, I want to thank you for doing this for us."

"It's the least I can do."

"Okay. Second, would Saturday be too soon to do this?"

Tracy paused. Given what she learned last night about Brian, she wanted her weekend free. She decided to hedge her bets. "I think so. But I need to check with my husband first."

"Of course. I'm not sure if Steve told you, but we're going to be filming several of these PSAs with local celebrities. Richard George is going to be here Saturday and Steve told me you were a fan. I thought you might like to meet him and do the PSA at the same time."

"Hey, that does sound great. What time would you need me there?"

"Is 9:00 a.m. too early?"

"No. My kids are early birds — especially on Saturdays."

"All right. Well just let me know either way. If you can't make it, we'll do it another time."

"Supreme! I promise to talk to Brian tonight, and I'll let you know tomorrow."

"Great! Thanks again, Tracy. I look forward to meeting you — whenever that turns out to be."

"Thank you, Megan. I look forward to meeting you too."

Tracy hung up the phone with a smile on her face. Then the smile left her. She didn't think Brian, Nicole, or Peter would be happy if she weren't around most of Saturday morning. Maybe she could figure how to put a positive spin on this before she talked to Brian. Maybe.

"And how long would this all take?" Brian asked, sounding mildly irritated. They were sitting next to each on the bed, prepared to retire for the night.

"Probably just a couple of hours. These are just minute-or-two things, Brian. And it's all for a very good cause."

"I get that. But Nicole, more than anyone, is going to be upset. You guys have your marathon story time on Saturday mornings."

Tracy looked at her hands. "I know. I figure you could do something special with her Saturday to make her forget about me."

"Come again?"

"What if we all went out to breakfast early — as soon as Nicole gets up? Then I can go off and do my thing. Maybe you can even drop me off and then I can call you to come pick me up."

"Or we could just take two cars to the restaurant."

"Or that."

"And what about your mother?"

"She can come with us or stay home; her choice."

"I guess that would be okay," Brian said, sighing.

"But you're not happy about it."

"I just like having you home on the weekends."

Tracy put her arms around Brian, who was still looking forward, and kissed his cheek. "It's just for few hours, honey. I'll make sure to let them know I have to leave by 11:30 a.m. I'll be home for lunch and that will be that."

Brian looked at her and smiled. "Okay. It *is* for a good cause, after all."

"It is." Their lips met. Then she said, "Brian, I'd like to talk about something."

"What's that?"

"What you said last night. I've been thinking about it ever since."

He sighed. "It's really no big deal, Tracy. I shouldn't have said anything."

"I think you should have. And I need to know if there's anything I can do to help you."

Brian put his hand against her cheek. "I'm sorry I worried you. I overdid it. I'm not in danger of taking a drink."

"Are you sure? I'm a little scared."

He embraced her. "Listen. I love you. I love our kids. I'm not going to do anything to jeopardize any of that. Maybe I've been feeling sorry for myself or something but I'm really okay. Please believe me."

They were rubbing each other's backs. "All right, Brian. I'll try not to worry."

"I'm sorry I worried you. I never meant to do that. I guess that sounds like a stupid thing to say though."

"No. I think understand what you're going through. Don't be afraid to plan a night out with the guys every once in a while. I'm not your warden or something."

Brian started laughing. "I know that. But I know you like me around when you're here and I like being around."

"I *do* like you around," Tracy whispered. "I like you all kinds of ways." She started kissing his cheek.

"Hey, this isn't fair," Brian said, not meaning a word of it.

"What's not fair?" She worked her hand underneath his pajama top.

"You're taking advantage of my biggest weakness."

"I am?" She moved her hand south.

"This would never work the other way around. It's not fair."

"Should I stop?"

"Of course not."

Tracy laughed softly. "I love you, Brian. Remember that whenever you're out with your guy friends. Remember who is waiting for your return — your *safe* return."

"You do things like this so I won't *want* to leave," he said, starting to unbutton her top.

"That's not true. But again, I'll ask, should I stop?"

"Too late for that now, Tracy."

Tracy just smiled. She knew Brian liked when she initiated things. And she wanted to make sure he would never forget there were things only she could provide for him; things he'd never want to go without. She wrapped her arms tightly around him to let *him* know there were things only *he* could provide for *her*; things that *she* didn't want to lose. In moments such as these, all her fears left her, scattering like frightened cats. Halloween wasn't too far away, but at present she suddenly wasn't the least bit scared about anything.

CHAPTER 3

She thought it silly, but Tracy Brubaker Shane had butterflies in her stomach. As she pulled open the entrance door to WMFT Channel 42 this Saturday morning, her heart started racing. Here she was — a woman of 36 — feeling like a little kid meeting her idol. But Dr. Mort Itchin — or rather, Richard George — was not really an idol of *hers*. But she was excited and nervous just the same. Megan Wallace smiled when Tracy appeared in her doorway.

"Here I am!" the attorney said cheerfully.

Megan laughed. "Well let's go to the studio then. I think they're still setting up. So, you'll have time to talk to Mr. George."

"Here's here already?" Tracy asked, her eyes getting a little wider.

"Oh, yes. Follow me."

Megan smiled as she came from behind her desk and moved towards the hallway. Tracy followed her. As Tracy entered the studio, there was a man, hands on hips, with his back to her shouting at someone she couldn't see.

"I'm not as spry as I used to be!" he was calling out. "Don't make anything too complicated!"

"No, sir," a voice responded.

"This is going to be live. I don't want to fall on my ass!"

Tracy started chuckling, more out of nervousness than anything else. The figure turned to see whom he had amused. Tracy suddenly felt warmth in her cheeks.

"Hello, Mr. George," Megan said as she moved towards him. "Is Andy treating you okay?"

"I'd like to be sitting in a chair that has arms, not one of those damned metal things. They're uncomfortable and I might fall off of it."

"No problem," Megan said emphatically. Then she called out, "Hear that, Andy? A comfortable chair for Mr. George!"

"Yeah, I got it," Andy answered back, although Tracy still could not see him. She was now standing next to Megan.

"Mr. George, I want you to meet Tracy Shane. She'll be doing some PSAs today too."

The up-until-now crotchety-sounding Richard George smiled broadly. He was a man in his mid-seventies, with a full head of white hair and a gray moustache. He was about two inches taller than the five-foot five attorney.

"Have we met before?" he asked while offering his hand. "Your name is very familiar — and your face is too."

"Tracy's an attorney," Megan continued. "She's cracked some big local cases."

"OF COURSE!" George shouted. "It's a pleasure to meet you!" George gripped and shook Tracy's hand.

She was smiling broadly. "And I want to say how great it is to meet you, Mr. George. It really is. I hope we have some time to talk."

"We have time now," he said, still smiling but finally releasing her hand. "They're still working some things out; damned lights or something. And those chairs? You can use the comfy one too when I'm done with it."

Tracy chuckled. "You bet."

"I'll see what's going on," Megan offered. She left the pair alone.

Tracy continued, "My father was a huge fan of yours. He taped your show all the time and showed it to me when he thought I was old enough to handle the movies."

George continued smiling. "Taped the show? Now *that's* a fan. Is your father coming to the show?"

Tracy kept her smile when she said, "My father passed about 16 years ago."

"Oh," George said, his smile uprooted. "I'm very sorry."

"Thank you. I just wanted to make sure I let you know what a fan he was — that I am — of yours. I recently watched one of your old shows — the one with *The Vampire Bat*. It brought back a lot of great memories."

The smile returned. "Thank you, young lady. It's nice to be remembered."

"You are, Mr. George."

"Call me Richard, please."

"Okay," Tracy said softly.

"*You* are coming to the show then?"

"Oh my, yes! I'm bringing my husband."

"Marvelous!"

"I understand Nagging Skeleton will be there too."

The smile left again. Tracy felt a chill in the air when George said, "Yes, he will be."

Tracy gulped. "I'm really looking forward to it."

George nodded, and then the smile returned for its encore. "It will certainly be…interesting."

"Ready for you, Mr. George," Megan said as she moved towards the duo. "Follow me, please. And you can come too, Tracy, and watch. This is pretty much how it will be for you, too."

"Okay!" Tracy chirped, echoing Nicole's enthusiasm over almost anything.

Tracy then followed behind Richard George, who was tailing Megan Wallace. The attorney found a seat — a hideous, rusted- looking metal one that used to be all brown-colored — to rest her laurels while George completed his segments. The poor director, Andrew Honeywell, was having a hard time keeping the irascible Richard George happy. The lights were too hot; his cushioned chair wasn't comfortable enough; the teleprompter was too hard to read; and on and on. Tracy just watched, knowing how much Honeywell was going to *love* her, since she would be so much easier to deal with. But just how much was today an indicator of how rehearsals were going to go, never mind the show itself? It might be a horror show in more ways than the obvious one.

"So how was it?" Brian asked after Tracy kissed her children hello. While Nicole went back to whatever she was doing before her mother returned, Peter wanted to be held. She lifted her son and moved towards the living room sofa.

"It was great!" she said. "I got my stuff done in less than half an hour."

"Really? Then why are you home so late?"

"Richard George didn't think it was all that great," Tracy explained while making funny faces at her giggling son. "He took three times as long as I did. I'm not sure this show is going to come off."

Brian sat down next to her. "What was the problem?"

"Probl*ems*, you mean." She gave a quick overview. "To tell you the truth, Brian, I'm not sure why he's doing this."

"Was he that way with everybody?"

"Not with me. He was as nice as could be. But I don't think he likes this Andy guy — who *is* going to be directing the live show. And then there's…"

"There's what?"

"There's something about Carl Jeffries, the guy who plays Nagging Skeleton. You should have seen the look on his face when I brought *him* up."

"Oh?"

"I didn't ask anything further. It's really none of my business." And when she saw the grin spreading across Brian's face she quickly added, "And if you say, 'that never stopped you before' I'm going to stick my foot up your butt."

He laughed. "You're so violent."

Tracy just grinned and then went back to amusing Peter. His giggling told her he was quite enjoying whatever it was his parents were engaged in.

"Mommy! Mommy! Mommy!" an excited Nicole Shane cried out as she came sprinting into the room.

"Whaty? Whaty? Whaty?" the mother asked.

"Grammaw say we have to eat now."

"Oh, yes. We should listen to Grandma, so we don't get in trouble."

Tracy stood up and watched as Nicole ran back to the kitchen, where Violetta Brubaker was finishing the lunch preparations. With her work for the day behind her, Tracy could now look forward to spending the rest of her weekend with her family. They always made her feel like the star of the show.

"Brian, do you have any pictures from Halloweens long ago?"

"I'm sure I do. But they would be at Crystal's. I have no idea where they might be though. Attic, maybe."

"I'd like to see you all dressed up when you were little."

"You would, huh?"

Tracy grinned and vigorously nodded. "Mom says she has some pictures of me in some boxes."

"I guess I could call Crystal and ask about them."

"Supreme!" She kissed him. "Do you remember some of the costumes you wore?"

"Some. I know one year we went as Luke and Leia."

Tracy smiled. "Really? That's very fitting, don't you think?"

"I suppose. My mom always came up with suitable pairs for us to go as. So, it was Luke and Leia, and Ernie and Bert."

Tracy let out a laugh. "You and Crys were made up like Ernie and Bert? Oh, I just *have to* see that. Which one were you?"

"Can't you guess?"

Tracy nodded. "You had to be Bert."

"Yes, I was Bert."

"And were you a happy Bert or a sour Bert?"

"No comment."

Tracy giggled. "Did you carry around a paper clip collection? Did Crys carry around a rubber ducky?"

"Not that I recall."

Tracy was very much in Brian's face, a large grin on hers. "What else? This is just so adorable."

"I don't know. I think we were Thing 1 and Thing 2 one year and Mom dressed up like the Cat in the Hat."

"I LOVE IT!"

"Stop," Brian chuckled.

"Did you guys have crazy wigs on?"

"Yes, and red pajamas."

"Nicole and Peter have to go as Thing 1 and Thing 2 next year. It will be *so* cute."

"And you'll dress up as the Cat?"

"Sure!"

"Mm."

"You can be the grumpy fish."

"Gee thanks."

"Anything else?"

Brian sighed. "I do remember one year I was a magician and Crystal was dressed up as my assistant."

"That's neat."

Brian grinned. "I kept hitting Crystal with my wand."

"Brian! You were such a mean big brother."

"I'm sure I had a good reason."

Tracy chuckled. "Do you have any of your old costumes by any chance? Maybe Nicole and Peter can dress up in them."

"I doubt it."

"Too bad." Tracy yawned as she stood. "Goodnight, Brian. I'm beat."

"I thought you wanted to watch one of those old tapes."

"I did. But I'm just too tired. Maybe next week." Tracy kissed him before heading towards the stairs.

Brian was sitting on the couch by his lonesome. He could now do anything he wanted: watch a movie in his home theater, read, surf the net, have a snack — whatever he desired. But what he desired had just retired for the evening. So, he followed his desire's example and prepared to turn in for the night.

Both Steve Dante and Megan Wallace made it a point to let Tracy know she could visit WMFT on Saturday, October 5. Sets were being built and rehearsals were underway, and Tracy wanted to see what she could. She wasn't sure how long she could or would stay, but she arrived just before 9:30 that Saturday morning. A security guard who went by Corky showed her to where the action was. She thanked him as he left her.

The set designers had already finished the backdrop that was secured at the rear of the stage. Standing at what must have been almost 20 feet tall were the doctor's laboratory walls. The display consisted mostly of gray-painted bricks, some with dark edges. On the left side, a myriad of beakers, tubes, and whatnot had been sketched. But it was the center that captured Tracy's attention. Above the painted doorway was a large circle of bright green. At its center was a hideous portrait of Dr. Mort Itchin. His eyes were red with madness; his hair was white, unkempt, and stringy; his lips were pulled back in the evilest of grins. Just below the circle's bottom, Tracy could see the doctor's hands, rendered to make it look as though he was reaching out to strangle whoever was in reach. Lastly, at the top and above the doctor's head, "House of Funerals" was written in blood-red letters so that it formed a semi-circle.

The lighting crew was, at present, testing how various colored lights would look against the backdrop. Occasionally the entire studio would go dark as various beams were projected: purples, blacks, and blues. Some of the paint used must have been neon, Tracy thought, given the way certain areas of the display glistened. It was quite a sight. Sure, it was low budget stuff. But Tracy thought it created the needed mood perfectly.

"Would you people *please* warn us when you're going to turn the lights out?!" Tracy heard a familiar voice cry out. "I can't find the john in the dark!"

"Calm down, you old fart," an unfamiliar voice called back. "It's in the same place it was when you worked here. Surely, you can't have forgotten."

"Shut the hell up!" George responded.

"All right!" someone else said as the lights came up. "Mr. George is right. We need to give everyone a heads up when we go dark."

Tracy thought *that* voice belonged to the beleaguered Andy Honeywell. She was correct.

"Don't let him treat you like that," the man with the unfamiliar voice said as he approached the director. "*You're* the director. And *he* ain't no Tom Cruise."

And it was then that Tracy *did* recognize the voice as belonging to Nagging Skeleton himself, Carl Jeffries.

Now, George approached Honeywell also. "You just mind your own," George said angrily, waving his finger in Jeffries' amused face. "*You* aren't the director either."

Tracy noted the looks by the crew as they observed the heated exchange. Some shook their heads; others rolled their eyes; and some others whispered to the ones standing closest. Apparently, scenes like this had been going on for the last few days.

"Will you two please try and get along?" Honeywell's exasperated voice begged. "This is supposed to be fun! We're not making high art here!"

"And *that*, young man, is your problem," George snarled, now looking at Honeywell. "I take everything I do seriously. *You* and this moron obviously do NOT!"

"Of course, I take this seriously," Honeywell countered angrily. "But *I* also am able to keep this in perspective, something *you* obviously can NOT!"

There was now total silence in the studio. People were looking at each other in shock. This must have been the first time young Honeywell had dared talk back to Richard George. Everyone was preparing themselves for George's response. Would he walk off the set? Would he slug the director in the puss?

But Richard George surprised everyone. Instead of lashing out, he smiled and then boomed, "It's about damned time you showed some balls, kid! Now, show 'em during the rest of this thing and maybe we can get some damn work done!" Then George looked at Jeffries. "And as for *you*, you little pipsqueak, you better stay outta my way, if you know what's good for you!" George didn't wait for a response; he turned and marched to the back of the studio.

"You know better than to talk to me that way!" Jeffries shouted. Then he added, after George was no longer visible, "That guy's nuts!"

He looked at Honeywell. "Let me host the show! I can do it! *I'm* the one who always got the laughs anyway!"

"I don't think so, Carl."

"Come on, Andy."

"Let's all take five," Honeywell announced while ignoring Jeffries' additional plea. "I need to use the head myself."

Jeffries just stared at Honeywell as the director went in search of relief.

Tracy Brubaker Shane decided it was time to meet Carl Jeffries, even though her first impression of him was anything but favorable. Jeffries appeared confused as she approached him.

"Hi, Mr. Jeffries," she greeted. After she introduced herself, she said, "My father and I used to watch you and Mr. George. It's great to meet you."

She was smiling at him, so he smiled back. "It's great to meet you too. Do you want an autograph or something?"

"Oh no, that's okay," she told him.

"Oh," he said, sounding disappointed.

Carl Jeffries was, as Richard George had suggested, on the small side. He was maybe five foot three. But what really was giving Tracy trouble was *not* staring at whatever it was that was on his head. Calling it a toupee would be an insult to toupees since they can look fairly decent if worn correctly. But this thing? A *very* angry squirrel must be running amuck looking for his coat and tail. Jeffries had done little to blend the unnatural-looking brown carpet slice with his fully gray sideburns. And even though Carl Jeffries was about 15 years younger than Richard George, the opposite appeared to be true. Tracy didn't know if it was booze, drugs, or too many hours in the sun. Jeffries' face was hard, wrinkled, and haggard.

"So, you're a lawyer, huh?" Jeffries asked while looking Tracy over.

"Yes," the attorney responded, not liking being looked over.

"You know anything about copyright infringement?"

"Some. I've never worked on such a case though. But I know some lawyers who have."

"I bet it's expensive."

"It can get to be."

"Why?"

"Why what?"

"Why you lawyers charge so much?"

"Lots of reasons."

"Like what?"

Tracy sighed. "Okay. First, before you can even take the bar exam you have to go to law school and get your degree. That costs money, which of course is in addition to basic college tuition. Most people have large loans that need paying off before they've even really started their career. Then of course there's the fact you need a special skill set to practice; not everyone can be a lawyer. You need to get licensed and keep up with current regulations through continuing legal education classes. Maryland doesn't require CLE, but other states do. That costs money. Some of the money you pay in legal fees flows to other people, such as experts an attorney may hire to help with her case. Sometimes I use a private detective in my work, and I have to pay him. Those are some of the factors, anyway."

Jeffries blinked. "Oh. Still seems expensive though."

"The better the attorney, the higher the fees, Mr. Jeffries, just like the better the actor the more money she gets per picture, or the better the football player the higher his paycheck. It's capitalism, Mr. Jeffries."

Jeffries grinned. "Oh, I understand capitalism just fine."

"DAD!" a voice called out. Tracy turned to see Megan Wallace entering the studio. And she did *not* look happy. "I need to talk to you!" she snapped. "NOW!"

"I'm *talking* to a fan," Jeffries snarled.

Megan looked at Tracy, then back at her father.

"Huh. A fan? She must not know you very well. Now, come *here*!"

"I'll see you later, Mr. Jeffries," Tracy said, starting to move away.

Then Megan Wallace grabbed Jeffries arm and started pulling him towards the entrance way. Jeffries appeared in danger of having his limb torn from its socket. Tracy couldn't help but overhear the exchange.

"Did you hear that? *Mister* Jeffries, she called me," Jeffries began.

"That's because she doesn't know what a complete and total *asshole* you can be!"

"Don't talk to me like that! I'm your *father*!"

"Screwing my mother doesn't make you my father! Now, I told you to stay off Richard's back and I meant it." The two came to a stop just in front of the entrance doors.

"He won't be able to handle this. He can't remember his lines and he can't see the teleprompter. If you let this go on, you'll be a laughingstock! Is that what you want?"

"He'll be fine!"

"He won't be! Let me help you! I'm your father. I can do this! Won't you let me? I'm your father!"

"Just shut up about that, would you? Stop reminding me!"

"Just 'cause *you* don't like it doesn't change the fact that I'm your—"

"Look! I'm warning you. If you don't leave Richard alone, I'm going to insist they *fire* you!"

"You wouldn't! You wouldn't do that to your own flesh and blood!"

"The hell I wouldn't! I never wanted you to be part of this to begin with! That's Steve Dante's doing. But if you keep this up, I swear I'll make sure you're shown the door. Anybody — and I mean anybody — can spout those lame jokes of yours while hiding behind a coffin. You understand me…*Dad?*"

"You have NO right to talk to me like this. And after all—"

"…You've done for me? Is that what you were gonna say? Don't you *dare* even think that. I'm here because of my own merits — not because of who my sperm donor was."

"SPERM DONOR?!"

"Yeah! SPERM DONOR. I shouldn't even call you 'Dad.' I should call you SD. Or 'the prick,' maybe."

"How *dare* you—"

"I'm done talking to you. *I'm* the boss here, *not* you. You leave Richard George alone…or *else!*"

And with that, Megan Wallace turned and left the studio, leaving her father huffing and puffing, full of fury if not sound. Tracy also quickly turned, lest Carl Jeffries realize she had, without really meaning to, witnessed the unpleasantness in its entirety. She wanted to spare Jeffries and herself the embarrassment. Then, a voice behind her spoke.

"Quite a show, huh?"

Tracy turned around to see Andy Honeywell seated in his director's chair, staring at a clipboard in his lap.

"And we've only been working on this thing since Wednesday."

Tracy gulped; she hadn't escaped Camp Embarrassment after all. "I didn't mean to…I tried to leave but I just…"

Honeywell looked an her and smiled. "Hey, don't worry about it, Tracy; really. No one has shied away from sharing their feelings around here — especially Megan. It's well known what she thinks of her father."

Tracy took the liberty of sitting next to Honeywell. "Megan doesn't have the same last name. Is that because she's married? I didn't notice a wedding ring on her finger."

"Megan's parents were never married," Honeywell said glumly. "Jeffries had a fling with Megan's mother and then was pretty much out of the picture. He went to Hollywood a few years after *House of Funerals* was cancelled thinking he'd become some big star. And he burned a lot of bridges when he left. Of course, he never did become that star. So, when he came back, he had few places to go."

"You mean Megan's mother took him back after he abandoned her?"

"Yup. I'll never understand why, or what she saw in him. Megan was like 14 or 15 at the time Jeffries came into her life. You can see how things turned out."

"Yeah," Tracy sighed.

"Jeffries thought he'd build up some good will when he found out his daughter was interested in television production; her parents were both TV people, after all. He got her an interview here; at least he made a phone call. But that's all he got her. She's done well because she knows her stuff and she busts her ass. He likes to think it was all because of him."

Tracy nodded. "So, Steve Dante doesn't care that practically no one likes this guy?"

Honeywell started chuckling. "I think Steve believed all the stories were exaggerated and that everything would be fine. Megan was so mad when he asked her to reach out to her father. But she did it anyway. And she's been looking for a way to *undo* it ever since."

"Jeez. Can I ask something else?"

"Sure."

"Why is Megan so found of Richard George? I thought he had retired from here before Megan stared working at WMFT."

Honeywell leaned back in his chair. "You're a smart one from what I hear. I bet you could make a good guess."

Tracy gave Honeywell a quizzical look. But she guessed just the same.

"Did Mr. George help out Megan's mother or something? Is that why Jeffries dislikes Richard so much?"

"You got it. Megan's mother worked here as a production assistant; everyone liked Carrie Wallace. When Jeffries took off and left Carrie alone, Richard tried to help her. When Megan was born, Richard and his wife let Carrie and Megan stay with them for a while since Carrie's partial pay wouldn't cover all her expenses and rent."

"I see," Tracy said. "And with all that's happened, Carl Jeffries hasn't tried to change or make amends."

"Carl Jeffries thinks that Carl Jeffries is the one who is owed apologies: that Richard George deliberately alienated him from his daughter; that he should have been star of the program when it ran originally and that he should be the main attraction for the reunion. He lives in his own fantasyland. He may have good comic timing, but that's about it. He did very little of the writing, even though he makes it sound as though he wrote all the jokes. I've seen some of the original scripts and who got the credit. It wasn't Jeffries."

"They had scripts?" Tracy grinned, trying to lighten the mood a tad.

It worked. Honeywell laughed heartily. "That's very good. Maybe *you* should write for this damned thing."

"I don't think so. I have it on my mother's authority I am the un-funniest creature to ever walk the earth. Maybe I should introduce her to Carl Jeffries."

"If you have any love for your mother, Tracy…"

"I was kidding, Andy."

"Good."

Tracy stood up. "One last question…"

"What's that?"

"You know an awful lot of the back story."

"Yes; I do."

"May I guess how you learned it?"

Honeywell looked up at Tracy and smiled. "Yes, Megan and I are lovers. More than that, really. It's yet another poorly kept secret around here."

Tracy nodded. "I think it's been more than five minutes," she grinned.

"So, it has…" Honeywell said as he stood. "I guess it's, as they say, on with the show."

Tracy returned from having put Peter to bed. Even though he was still nursing, he was sleeping through the night and thus had his own room. Brian Shane liked his bedroom to consist of only two occupants.

"I'm telling you, Brian," Tracy said after sharing details of her Saturday, "it's a regular soap opera over there. Absentee fathers, employee-lovers, resentment and hostility...all the while filming a horror show where nobody really gets along."

"Are you going back?"

"Of course!"

Brian laughed. "Don't want to miss the next episode, huh?"

"Next Saturday they're going to do some dress rehearsals. I hear the makeup guy they got for this is really good."

"Ah."

She was leaning on her side, her head propped up. "Seriously Brian, it's really something over there. I can *feel* it."

"Feel it? What 'it' are you feeling?"

"It's only a few days into the production, and everyone is already on edge. And it's not the show itself but rather the people who are putting it on. In other words, it ain't gonna get any better."

"How about you feel something else for tonight?"

"Oh, you're cute," Tracy grinned. Then she reached over and kissed him. "I love that you still flirt with me like that, you naughty boy."

"It's not naughty now that we're married."

"We can pretend it is though..."

Brian started to move closer to her. Then she suddenly shook her head.

"I don't know, Brian..."

"Don't know what?"

"About this whole reunion thing. I know you're going to be mad at me for saying this..."

"I'm already mad about you..."

"But I have the uneasy feeling that if things don't change over there, there very well may be a murder at the House of Funerals."

CHAPTER 4

"How's that feel, Mr. George?" Tom Kramer asked.

"It feels fine. I'm more concerned how I'm going to feel getting this gunk *off*."

"I'll help you with that," Kramer laughed mildly. "It shouldn't be too bad."

George said nothing. He stood up from his chair and moved towards Andy Honeywell.

"All right, where should I stand?"

"You look awful!" Honeywell smiled. "It's perfect."

"Hooray," George mumbled.

"Just go on stage and stand on the right side of the table. Then we'll test the lighting; see how it looks."

Kramer sat down so he could observe how his makeup fared when lit. The woman he was now sitting next to said, "That looks terror- ific!"

He turned and smiled at her. "Thank you."

"I'm Tracy," she told him, smiling.

His eyes widened. "Oh, are you the Tracy who's playing the bride?"

Now Tracy's eyes expanded. "What?"

"Someone told me I was going to have another subject to work on. He said the bride's name was Tracy."

"Must be some other Tracy then," the attorney said nervously. "I'm already married."

Kramer laughed. "They didn't tell you? That figures."

A man, holding a digital camera, approached Kramer and Tracy. "Tom, tell us how exciting it is to be working on this project! What's it like working with local legend Richard George? What changes have you made to the original makeup?"

"Seriously, Ned?"

Ned Topolski put the camera down. "Megan wants me to put together some behind the scenes stuff that we can use to promote this thing. Live television is hardly done anymore, and this is a big risk. So, we need to promote the hell out of this thing."

"All right," Kramer sighed. "I'll play."

Topolski smiled as he repositioned his camera.

"I'm thrilled to be part of bringing back Dr. Mort Itchin," Karmer began, "It's been a joy working with everyone here, especially Mr. Richard George. It's clear everyone is so excited to be part of—"

"THOMAS!" a voice cried out. Then a figure approached him.

"Goddamn it, Larry!" Topolski shouted. "Can't you see I was interviewing here?"

"What?" Larry Peachtree asked reflexively. Then he fixed his gaze on Kramer. "Where is it?"

"Where's what, Larry?"

"My nail gun!"

"How the hell am I supposed to know where your nail gun is?"

"Someone said they saw you with it," Peachtree said accusingly.

"Someone is mistaken. What would *I* need with your nail gun?"

Peachtree blinked. Then he snorted. Then he just turned and left Kramer, Topolski, and Tracy, while mumbling under his breath.

"Who was *that*?" Tracy asked.

"He's props and production design, more or less," Kramer told her.

"He's a little obsessive about his things," Topolski added. Then he looked at Tracy curiously. "Say, I don't think I've met you."

"*This* is Tracy," Kramer said quickly.

Topolski smiled broadly. "It is? Hey that's great. I bet you're excited, huh?"

Tracy gave him a confused look. Clearly there was something they — and maybe several others — knew that she didn't. "I…"

"Have you done any makeup tests on her yet, Tom?" Topolski asked.

"Not yet."

"Makeup tests?" Tracy asked.

Topolski added, "I've seen the stakes. They look perfect."

"Stakes?"

Topolski gave Kramer a confused look. "Isn't she the vampire bride?"

"The *what*?!" Tracy shouted.

Kramer started laughing. "I don't think anybody told her, Ned. She doesn't know."

"Oh," Topolski said.

Tracy had had enough. "Will one of you two gentlemen please tell me what you *think* it is I'm supposed to be doing?"

"Dr. Mort is supposed to revive his long-dead wife— *you*," Kramer answered.

"Uh-uh," Tracy said while shaking her head.

"It's going to be incredible!" Topolski said excitedly. "He revives her, but it turns out she's a vampire. So, he has to destroy her, stake through the heart and everything."

"A *what* through my *what*?"

"Where are you going to put the blood packet, Tom?"

"Gentlemen, I'm afraid there has been a horrific misunderstanding here. I'm just going to watch the show. I'm getting my behind-the-scenes peeks because I did some PSAs. I'm not here because I'm playing Bride of Itchin."

"But you're the only Tracy around here," Topolski protested. "So, it must be you I'm hearing about."

"Be that as it may, I'm no vampire bride."

"Then who's the bride?" Topolski asked Kramer, sounding upset.

"Easy there, Ned. It will all work out. Megan had originally volunteered to do it so if Tracy doesn't want to…"

"Hard at work all of you, I see," Carl Jeffries said sarcastically as he approached the trio. Then he looked from Topolski to Kramer. "You want to come to the stage instead of chit-chatting over here?"

"Blow it out your ass," Topolski snapped. Jeffries, shocked by the insult, just snorted before turning and leaving.

"That guy is going to get his butt handed to him if he doesn't let up," Kramer chuckled. "Now, he thinks he's the director too."

Tracy couldn't help but smile as she shook her head.

"I guess Andy is looking for us," Topolski said. "We better go see what's up." He looked at Tracy. "Nice meeting you, Tracy. Sorry about the confusion."

"No problem, Ned. Nice meeting you too."

"Did one of you take my paint roller?" Larry Peachtree, having snuck up on everyone, blurted. "It's not where I left it."

"No, Larry," Tom Kramer said flatly.

"I saw Carl playing with it," Ned Topolski said.

"*Him*? The nerve!" Peachtree turned so he could hunt down Jeffries.

Topolski started laughing. Kramer looked at him.

"That was BS about Carl, wasn't it?"

Topolski didn't answer. Instead, he started moving towards the stage.

"Let me at least show you the coffin," Andy Honeywell pleaded.

"You can show me the coffin, Andy. But I don't want to be in the show. I just want to watch it."

"I thought you'd love the opportunity."

"I'm afraid you thought wrong. I'm no actress."

"Actress? You just need to lie in the coffin; sit up and bare your fangs; then lay back down when George shows you the cross. That's it."

"And get a stake through my heart."

"Just an effect. The stake will be pounded into a part of the coffin next to you. From the audience's perspective though, it will look as though it's actually going *into* you."

"Sorry, not interested. Besides, I have to take my daughter trick-or- treating so it's going to be hard enough to get here in time for the show. There's no way I could get here early enough to get into makeup and all of that."

Honeywell frowned. "That's too bad."

"I appreciate the thought…I think."

He chuckled. "All right then; no hard feelings. Come on. I'll show you the coffin anyway."

"Supreme!"

Tracy followed Honeywell onto the stage. The lab table had been placed on the stage's left side, the coffin on its right. The casket was positioned on a table so that it would align with Richard George's waist. It was seven feet long and black, with a red-colored interior.

Honeywell smiled. "Doesn't this look great? Peachtree and his team did a very nice job, didn't they?"

"They sure did," Tracy said smiling.

"Oh! And let me show you these." Honeywell went to the lab table, lifted the white lab coat that was resting on it, and removed what the coat had been concealing. He came back with a stake and mallet. He smiled at Tracy. "Pretty terrific, huh?"

Her eyes widened. "That looks real," she said while studying the wooden shaft.

"It is. When the point punctures the blood pack, we should see a spurt of blood. We still have to test that out though. But I doubt we'll do that today."

"Good grief," Tracy said with alarm. "Isn't that dangerous? What if Mr. George misses his mark and hurts whoever is playing the bride?"

Honeywell shook his head. "Richard is a professional and has done this kind of thing before. Besides, that's why we have rehearsals."

"Mm..." Tracy mumbled skeptically.

Honeywell grinned. "Let's go to the lunchroom. The sandwiches should be here by now."

"Now *that* I will do," Tracy said.

"It was an accident, Carl," Andy Honeywell insisted.

"The hell it was!" Jeffries shouted. "I want whoever worked on this damn thing fired!"

Larry Peachtree came onto the stage with a fire-breathing dragon's disposition. He glared at Jeffries.

"What did you do to my coffin?!"

"What did *I* do?" Jeffries responded indignantly. "You got a nerve! The thing almost crushed me to death!"

"You kicked it!" Peachtree countered. "It would have stayed right where it was if you hadn't kicked it!"

"I didn't!"

"You DID!"

Megan Wallace, having been summoned by Andy Honeywell, came to the stage.

"Just what the hell is it *now*, Dad?"

Waving a finger at Peachtree he answered, "There's shoddy workmanship going on here, that's what! The table holding this coffin collapsed and I nearly died!"

"LIAR!" Peachtree countered. "You kicked the table leg when you were under there and the coffin came down!"

"What, your poorly built crap table can't take a little poke?"

Not surprisingly, Megan did not take Jeffries' side.

"Stop abusing the props, Dad."

"*Abusing the—*"

"Yes. That table was holding a two-hundred-pound coffin just fine until you messed with it." Megan looked at Peachtree. "Larry, please have someone from your team take a look at the table and reinforce the leg that collapsed."

"Certainly."

"Thanks, Larry." Looking at Jeffries again Megan said, "Be more careful next time, Dad. Luckily, nobody got hurt." Megan said nothing further as she prepared to return to her office.

Jeffries looked around. He saw Tracy looking in his direction. "Did you see what just happened?" he asked her. "Can I sue for that?"

Tracy shook her head. "You kicked the table leg, Mr. Jeffries," Tracy answered flatly. "I saw you."

Jeffries stared at her. "You didn't," he challenged.

"Oh, but I did. I'm just not sure if you did it accidentally or on purpose."

"I'm not interested in your *opinion*," he snapped.

"You're not? Then why did you just ask me a question?"

"Well..."

"For the record, I have 20/20 vision and don't wear contacts or glasses. So, if I were asked to give testimony in a lawsuit, I would have to say I saw you kick the leg."

Jeffries looked at Tracy as if she'd run over his puppy dog. "What did I ever do to you?"

"Nothing, Mr. Jeffries. *Nobody* here has done anything to me. That's why I'd make such a good witness. I have no biases."

Andy Honeywell approached the nearly wounded thespian. "I need you off the stage, Carl."

"What?"

"Let these guys fix the table and repair the damage to the coffin. I'll let you know when you can come back, and we'll let you play with your bones then."

Jeffries scowled. "*Play with my bones?* If you don't watch it, sonny, I'll have *you* fired." Then Jeffries quickly exited the platform.

Honeywell stretched out his arms and placed his clasped hands behind his neck. He leaned back slightly and let out a loud sigh. Then he shook his head and left the stage.

Tracy rubbed her eyes. Why did Jeffries kick that leg? She was sure he did it deliberately. The first thought that came to her mind was lawsuit. He wanted to sue the studio and collect. Unfortunately for him no one took his side. Or was that it? Was this some test to see how people would react if he were almost hurt? Was Carl Jeffries up to something? Too bad Ned Topolski hadn't been here with his camera to catch all of this. Of course, if he had been, maybe there would never have been an accident.

Even though Carl Jeffries seemed to annoy everyone on the *House of Funerals* set, nearly the entire crew was watching as he finally assumed his position behind the coffin and brought Nagging Skeleton back to life. He gripped the wire attached to one of the boney prop's arms and waved at his onlookers. Everyone chuckled, including Tracy.

"Can you see any of me?" Jeffries asked Honeywell.

"No. You're perfect."

"Say everyone, how do skeletons get to work every day?"

People started looking at each other, some chuckling in anticipation of the horrendous punch line.

"They carpals," Nagging Skeleton announced.

The small crowd burst out in laughter. Some even applauded. Tracy giggled as she shook her head.

"I guess that's a keeper," Jeffries called out.

"Don't you mean crypt keeper?" Honeywell asked.

After a few minutes of silence Jeffries said, "Leave the jokes to me, sonny boy."

"Deal. And you'll leave the directing to me."

Jeffries didn't respond. He instead stood up and left the stage, taking his skeleton with him.

Andy Honeywell looked at his watch. "All right folks it's after 6:00 p.m. Let's call it a day. Everyone did really well today. Enjoy tomorrow and we'll see each other on Monday."

"And make sure you put everything back where you found it!" Larry Peachtree called out. "I still am missing one of my paint brushes."

"I'll buy you a new one," Topolski grumbled.

Honeywell sighed. "Larry's right. Let's not leave everything a mess."

"And I want some interviews if I didn't talk to you already," Ned Topolski added. He was once again recording while moving about. When he approached Peachtree, the busy designer scowled.

"Get that out of my face. I'm still at work here."

"Just some positive words for our potential audience," Topolski pleaded, as Peachtree continued loading assorted items in drawers.

"Not now; maybe later. Find someone else."

"Megan won't be happy about this."

"What, you're going to *tell* on me?" Peachtree snorted as he slammed a metal drawer closed. He then turned and moved quickly elsewhere.

"What is it with people around here?" Topolski asked aloud. Then he shook his head.

Tracy watched as people started evacuating the studio. Despite the long day she wanted to sit a while and gaze at the stage. There was something eerie about a place that is busy most of the day, and then goes completely quiet at night. High school hallways were what Tracy was thinking about. Sometimes she'd stay late after school to get her homework done, and then she'd have to walk the silent halls to the parking lot. It gave her the creeps.

Tracy was putting on her jacket when she saw Richard George heading towards her, or rather, he was moving towards the studio's entrance doors. She smiled at him.

"An exciting day, Mr. George," she said.

"That's one word for it," he said pleasantly.

"What are you doing now?"

"Going home. I need to start dinner."

"Oh. Cooking for one?"

"No, my wife will join me when she gets home."

"That sounds nice," Tracy grinned.

"Mm. She's with our grandson and his parents. Today was their annual trip to the pumpkin patch."

Tracy nodded. "I've never taken my kids to a pumpkin patch. That sounds like it could be fun."

He smiled. "I guess I'll see you next Saturday?"

Tracy shook her head. "I think I've seen enough, and my family's already wondering why I'm not yet home yet. Besides, I want to save some surprises for when I watch the live show."

"Ah."

"I got two Saturdays worth of behind-the-scenes glimpses. I'm good."

"Well then, make sure you say hello to me on Halloween."

"I will. I really enjoyed meeting you, Mr. George. This has all been very exciting for me."

George smiled warmly. "After this is all done, perhaps you and your family could be my guests for dinner one night."

Tracy beamed. "I'd love that!"

He chuckled. "I will look forward to it. Goodnight then." He smiled and turned.

"Oh, Mr. George?"

"Yes?"

"You have some white stuff behind your ear. I guess Tom missed that."

"Mm. Thank you. I'll take care of that at home. Goodnight."

"Goodnight."

Tracy watched as George left the studio. Dinner with the Georges? She smiled again at the thought.

"I'm about to lock up," Andy Honeywell said as he approached Tracy. "I think everyone else is gone."

"Oh, okay," she said.

"Enjoy yourself today?"

"Very much, thanks."

"Great."

"You said you're locking up the studio. Is it top secret or something?" Tracy asked as the two started moving, side by side.

"We don't want curious people wandering in and out. And some of Dr. Mort's fans…"

"What do you mean?"

"Corky already has had to send people away. We've had people show up demanding tickets, and not taking 'no' for an answer."

"Oh."

"Weird, right?"

Tracy and Honeywell were now outside of the studio. The latter locked the doors while Tracy waited.

Megan Wallace approached and asked, "All done?" She was smiling at Honeywell.

"Yes," he said, and then gave her a quick kiss. "How was Dad today after the whole coffin thing?"

"He was okay. And when the time came, he really did just slip back into character, as they say. I think everything will be fine."

"Thank God," Megan sighed. She looked at Tracy. "Can I talk to you for a few moments, Tracy?"

"Sure," the attorney chirped.

"I'll see you soon," Andy told Megan. He turned and left her.

As the women began walking, Ned Topolski approached. "I got some good stuff here, Megan."

"I'll look at it tomorrow, Ned. I'm leaving soon."

"Oh, okay." Topolski sounded disappointed.

"Thanks for getting the footage, Ned. Steve and I appreciate it."

He smiled. "No problem."

When Topolski had left them, Megan turned to Tracy. "I'm really sorry about that mix up."

Tracy started laughing. "Oh, that's okay."

"I mentioned to Andy that you might want to be part of the show being you were a fan. And things I guess got all confused."

Tracy was still chuckling. "I do appreciate the offer. But I really just want to watch and enjoy the show. And I'll be on a date with my husband."

"I get it," Megan smiled.

"Does that mean *you'll* be the bride?"

"Yes. I did some theater back in the day, so I know how all this works."

"You prefer things behind the scenes now, I take it."

"Yes. But I think this could be fun."

"You're a braver woman than I. Aren't you nervous about…that stake?"

Megan laughed softly. "It'll be fine."

Tracy nodded. "I'm not sure if I'll be back. I've gotten my fill of the behind-the-scenes stuff. I want to thank you so much for letting me spy."

Megan smiled as the women shook hands. "It was a pleasure having you. I look forward to seeing you again on Halloween."

"Good luck with everything, Megan. Everything looks great — and it's not even all finished yet. I can't wait."

Tracy headed towards the exit as people bearing rubber gloves, trash cans, and mops started filing the station. But she knew of one place in here these people wouldn't be cleaning.

"I missed you, Mommy," Nicole said as she hugged her mother's legs.

"I missed you too, sweetheart," Tracy responded. "Did you have fun without me?"

"I play with Daddy and with Petaw and with Grammaw and with Bonkahs and with Baby Susie."

"That sounds like a busy, fun day!"

"Petaw needs a dolly, Mommy. He want a play with Baby Susie."

"Oh? Did you share?"

"Yeah. But he wouldn't give back when it my turn."

Tracy was sitting on the couch with Nicole on her lap. "That was very nice of you to share Baby Susie with your brother. He's a little too young to understand sharing though. I'll talk to Daddy about getting Peter his own doll."

"Okay!"

"Did you have dinner yet?"

She shook her head. "Mommy, what's stubert?"

"Stubert?"

"Yeah. Grammaw was talking to Daddy about you being home. Daddy didn't know."

"Oh, Grandma probably was asking Daddy what time I'd be home so she could have dinner ready. And Daddy might not have known what time to tell her."

"That's what Daddy say. He say, 'I don't know' and Grammaw got mad."

"Mad?"

"She said you were stubert. What's stubert, Mommy?"

Tracy thought a moment, and then started chuckling. "Maybe Grandma said 'stubborn'."

Nicole nodded. "Yeah!"

"Stubborn means you won't change something about yourself. Like you won't change your mind or the way you do something. Grandma thinks Mommy likes to do things her own way."

Nicole blinked. "Oh. I want to be stubert too!"

Tracy chuckled. "Stubborn is not always a good thing, sweetheart. I think Grandma wanted Mommy to stay home today but Mommy went out anyway. I guess Grandma was a little angry with Mommy."

"You get a time out from Grammaw?"

"Not anymore," Tracy grinned. "Let's see if we can help Grandma with dinner. That will make her happy."

"OKAY!"

Nicole hopped off her mother's lap and charged towards the kitchen. Tracy laughed at the sight. Then she frowned. It was Grandma who was in danger of getting a time out.

"Look, Mom," Tracy said as she loaded the last dish into the washer. "You need to be careful what you say in front of Nicole. You can think what you want about me. But I don't want you knocking me in front of Nicole. It confuses her."

"What knock?"

"Calling me stubborn."

"You *are* stubborn."

"And so are you. Maybe that's where I get it from." Tracy, hands on hips, looked at her mother. "Regardless, I don't want you, or me, or Brian saying anything negative about another adult in front of the children. Adults should be authority figures and respected. If we badmouth each other Nicole will eventually seize on that to play one against the other. And I don't want that to happen. Okay?"

Violetta Brubaker gave her daughter a hurt expression, as she usually did when her own child scolded her. And, as she also usually did, she just shrugged her shoulders and went about her business.

Tracy frowned and rolled her eyes. After drying her hands, she left the kitchen and headed to the first-floor play area where the children were waiting, already dressed for bed. Over the next hour stories were read, teeth were brushed, children were tucked in, and goodnight kisses were exchanged. After nursing Peter to sleep, Tracy joined Brian in the bedroom.

"Mom's mad at me," Tracy said as she started to undress.

"I knew something was up. What happened?"

Tracy told him. "You agree with me, right?"

"Yes, I do. Nicole was very confused about the whole thing. She could tell your mother took a dig at you."

Tracy frowned. "Terrific." She finished her change into pajamas and joined her husband in the bed. "I want to know if she does that again. Hopefully, though, I made my point."

"I always get a kick out of hearing the two of you call each other stubborn. I just haven't figured out who's the pot and who's the kettle."

"Did you just call me a pot?"

"Er…"

Tracy playfully punched Brian's nose. "If it's a question of genetics, mister, then it's not my fault, any more than my being how tall I am is my fault."

Brian chuckled. "And I wouldn't change a thing."

"Nice recovery," Tracy said as she gently kissed Brian goodnight.

Originally, she wanted to run another *House of Funerals* episode this Saturday night. But, given the animosity she had seen on display, she didn't think a trip down memory lane would give her the warm and fuzzies. So, she instead snuggled next to her husband to get those warm and fuzzies, and a few other things as well. She was asleep almost instantly.

"Tracy, wake up," Violetta said while shaking her daughter.

"What is it?" Tracy groggily asked. "What's wrong?"

"The phone wouldn't stop ringing so I answered it."

"Huh?"

"Someone kept calling and calling."

"Who?"

"I don't know. Get up and come talk to this person so I can go back to sleep."

Tracy sat up and yawned. "Okay, Mom. I'm coming."

"You need a phone in this bedroom."

"Brian doesn't want a phone or TV in the bedroom."

"Bah!"

Violetta exited Tracy's sleeping quarters. Tracy soon followed, noting the clock-radio said 12:07 a.m. Once downstairs she picked up the receiver.

"This is Tracy," she said.

"Oh, Tracy," the voice said, sounding relieved. "I can't tell you how sorry I am for disturbing you and your mother."

"Who is this?" Tracy asked.

"Oh. Richard George."

"Mr. George? What's wrong?"

"I'm at the studio. Carl Jeffries is dead."

"*What*?!"

"Yeah. Somebody drove a stake right through his black heart. And they did a pretty damn good job of it too."

CHAPTER 5

"Well, if it isn't Tracy Brubaker…" Detective Deborah Price said.

"Hi, Detective," Tracy smiled.

"But it's Tracy Shane now. You hadn't been married too long, the last time I saw you."

"It *has* been a while."

Detective Price motioned to the man standing next to her. "You remember Detective Mike Simmons…"

"Sure." Tracy shook both of their hands. "Richard George called me."

"Yes," Detective Price nodded. "He's with some of the staff right now."

"Is he a suspect? I couldn't get a clear answer over the phone."

"Everyone's a suspect right now. Nobody seemed to like this Jeffries person."

"Mm…" Tracy pursed her lips. "Mr. George said he got a stake through his heart."

"While in the prop coffin, no less…"

"You're kidding."

Detective Price sighed. "Happy Halloween."

"Can you tell me what happened?"

"Security guard found him."

"Making his rounds?"

The detectives exchanged glances and then Detective Price said, "Not exactly. I get the impression he just came in here to take a look around — curiosity, I mean. The place had been locked up from what I understand."

Tracy nodded. "That's right. I left earlier tonight — or yesterday I guess — when Andy Honeywell was locking things up. I guess the guard had keys."

"Yes, he did. Anyway, he found the body and called 911. Most of the people working on the show today have come back."

"Why?"

"We asked them to. We want to know if anything's been disturbed or tampered with in this studio."

"You're thinking robbery?"

"Not likely given how Jeffries was killed, and there's no evidence of forced entry. But you never know."

Tracy frowned. "I wonder why Carl Jeffries came back here. I wonder who came back with him."

"Good wonders," Price agreed. "Since Jeffries wasn't on staff anymore, I assume he didn't have his own set of keys, which means the person he came back with did. That would suggest somebody on staff killed Jeffries."

"Carl Jeffries irritated a lot of people," Tracy confirmed. "But murder seems to be a rather extreme reaction to what I saw Jeffries do."

"Tracy, I heard there was an accident here today. Carl Jeffries almost got hurt."

The attorney shook her head. "That's a nonstarter, Detective. I was here and saw what happened: Jeffries kicked that table leg as he was preparing to puppet his skeleton."

"Kicked it?"

"And pretty hard too."

"Why?"

"I don't know. But one of the first things he asked when he saw me was if he could sue the studio."

"How'd he know you were a lawyer?"

"I'd met him; he knew what I did."

"And you think he was trying to get himself hurt?"

"I'm not sure. And I really don't want to hazard any guesses given what's happened. But I saw what I saw when I saw it."

Price grinned. "All right. Your eyewitness testimony has been noted."

"Can I talk to Mr. George now?"

"Sure. I'll walk you over to him." Detective Price then smiled and said, "I know I don't have to tell you to keep your hands to yourself."

"I'll be good," Tracy smiled back.

The detective and Tracy were soon approaching the small group of likely suspects. When Richard George spotted the woman whose sleep he had interrupted, he quickly moved towards her.

"Thank you so much for coming here," he told the attorney, an appreciative smile on his face.

"You're welcome. How are you holding up?"

He didn't answer her. He instead looked at Detective Price, who took his gaze to mean he wanted privacy. So, she left George, Tracy, and the group to resume her own detecting.

"Let's go over here," George said, "away from the others."

"Of course," Tracy agreed.

After they were about 10 feet away from the crowd George whispered, "I'm worried about Megan."

Tracy pursed her lips. "Why do you think Megan is any more a suspect than the rest of them?"

"The killer had to have keys to get inside the studio."

"It would seem so."

"And the cops know about Megan's shouting matches with her father."

"But that wasn't unusual for Jeffries," Tracy said. "He argued with everybody."

"But people don't kill people over arguments — not like this anyway."

"Ah," Tracy said. "You think the murder was symbolic in some way."

George shook his head. "I don't know."

"Then why are you worried about Megan specifically?"

"They've just been asking us so many questions about her: how well we knew her; what fights we witnessed; were threats made; the history of her relationship with Jeffries; you get the idea."

"I do. Who called you about the murder?"

"Megan. She was very upset. I came here in case she needed me."

"The police didn't ask you to come?"

"No. I think they're focused on employees right now."

"Of course," Tracy agreed.

"THIEF!" a voice suddenly called out. "IT'S ROBBERY!"

Tracy and George turned to see Larry Peachtree moving hurriedly towards Detective Price. Tracy looked at George, shrugged her shoulders, and then decided she'd follow the panicky prop master.

"Calm down, Mr. Peachtree," Tracy heard Detective Price telling him. "Now, what's been stolen?"

"My tape!"

"Your…tape…"

"Yes! My black electrical tape. It's not where I left it. I distinctly remember leaving it on the lab table on stage. And now it's gone! Who knows what else has been stolen?!"

Detective Price twisted her lips. "Why would someone steal your tape, Mr. Peachtree? Is it rare or valuable or something?"

"What? How the hell should I know?!"

"You need to calm down," Detective Mike Simmons said sternly.

"Look. I was asked here to see if I could identify anything that may have been stolen, and now I have, and now you…Well…." Peachtree's face was red.

"Have you checked the entire studio?" Detective Price calmly asked.

"I think so. No! Wait! I haven't looked in my drawers!"

Detective Price raised an eyebrow. "Your…drawers?"

"Yes. I have a set of drawers – a set on wheels, you know – where I keep some of my things. I haven't looked in there yet. But there's nothing of value of in them."

"Yet you think someone committed murder over your missing tape."

Peachtree scowled. "I never said that! Stop being ridiculous."

At this point Tracy had to turn lest Peachtree see the smile on her face. The man who was losing it over an easily replaced item was calling someone *else* ridiculous?

"Why don't you see if the tape is in one of those drawers?" Detective Price continued.

"But I didn't leave it there," Peachtree protested.

"Humor me."

Peachtree snorted, twisted his lips, shouted, "Very well!" and then moved towards his portable organizer. The detectives, Tracy, and George followed. It was in the third drawer from the top that Peachtree found his "missing" electrical tape. He stared, looking dumbfounded.

"Is that your tape?" Detective Price asked.

"I don't understand it. I *know* I left it on the table."

"Looks like we have a notorious organizer on our hands then," Detective Price said humorlessly. "Let me know if you're missing anything else, Mr. Peachtree." The detective then left the perplexed Peachtree.

Tracy, again, had to stifle some laughter. She liked Detective Deborah Price very much. They had become fast friends when they met about three and half years ago. Tracy had been attending a magic show on her birthday with her then-fiancé, Brian, when murder stole the spotlight. Tracy worked with the police to help unmask the culprit. They collaborated again when Tracy "ear-witnessed" the murder of a potential whistleblower. The last time she had seen the detective, however, they did not get a chance to exchange words. It had been at the funeral of Detective Price's former partner, Jim Lucas. A friendly catch-up chat did not seem appropriate at the time.

"I guess it wasn't robbery after all," George snickered.

Peachtree stopped looking through the remaining drawers long enough to glare at the amused former horror host. But Peachtree had no further accusations to make.

Tracy grinned at George. "What can you tell me about tonight, Mr. George?"

"Please call me Richard."

"Okay."

George sighed. "Megan called me around 10:30 p.m. She had gotten the call from Corky that Jeffries had been killed. He had called *her* right after notifying the police."

"Okay."

"The police and Megan were already here when I arrived."

Tracy frowned. "Didn't Andy Honeywell come with her?"

"I think she had left him a message at his place. I didn't ask why they weren't together tonight."

"I see." Then she frowned again. "Actually, I don't see."

George looked at her quizzically. "How's that?"

"Exactly. How did Jeffries end up in that coffin? Did he get in there voluntarily? Was his body placed there after he'd been killed? And why *did* the killer choose to use the stake? Maybe it was symbolic. Jeffries *was* sucking all the fun out of this thing, wasn't he?"

"But murder — over *that*?"

Tracy nodded. "And that's why you think Megan's in trouble. She had a very personal reason to hate her in-name-only father."

"She never wanted him here," George added. "Everyone knows it."

Tracy sighed. "So, I take it you want me to be Megan's lawyer if she needs one."

He nodded. "Would you?"

"That would really be up to Megan."

"But I can tell her to call you if she needs help."

"Maybe I can talk to her now."

"I'm not sure where she is. I think she's with Steve Dante, in his office."

"Of course. They need to figure out what happens with the show now."

George sighed. "As much as I hate to admit it, Jeffries — or rather Nagging Skeleton — has his fans. The emails have proved it."

"Emails?"

"Fan mail of the modern age. Plenty of people have let it be known they don't want Mort without that damned skeleton. And then they sign their names with monikers ranging from 'NSFan#1' to 'Blood Licker'. And we never even showed gory movies."

Tracy chuckled. "But you didn't get anyone making threats, did you?"

"I don't think so."

"Moot point though. A fan would have no way of getting in here after hours."

"I guess you're right."

"As for Nagging, I guess someone could try to imitate his voice," Tracy offered.

"Still won't be the same. There's a certain wise guy tone that Carl had down really well. He was actually great to work with in the beginning.

I think he joined the show about seven years after it started. But all the praise he got went to his head. Then he became the jerk he remained being the rest of his life."

"Was he the one who came up with Nagging Skeleton?"

George shook his head. "No. I don't remember exactly who suggested Dr. Mort needed a sidekick. And they didn't want some hunchback lab assistant since it seemed everyone had one of those. So, we came up with this idea for a skeleton partner. We thought we'd name him after Boris Karloff or Bela Lugosi or Vincent Price. But I was the one who came up with the name."

Tracy smiled. "How'd you do that?"

"You ever hear of Skelton Knaggs?"

"I don't think so."

"You'd probably remember him if I showed you a picture. He had a very unique face, perfect for horror movies. He was short with a pock-marked face; he was British and did Shakespeare before coming to America. He never did hit it really big here, and he died young; 43, I think. If you've seen a lot of Universal horror movies you would have seen him."

"I think my dad showed me all those Frankenstein and Dracula movies."

"In *House of Dracula* he plays the brother of one of the victims and leads the attack on the mad doctor's laboratory."

Tracy started nodding. "Yeah. I think I remember him now. He was also in one of the Sherlock Holmes movies."

"That's right! *Terror By Night*."

"So, Skelton Knaggs became Nagging Skeleton."

"Yup. Everyone thought it was a great idea, so we went with it. And Carl was great. We even thought about having a Skeleton Knaggs doll made, one that Nagging could take to bed with him. But we couldn't seem to track down the rights we needed to make the likeness. So, it never happened."

"That would have been so cute."

George sighed. He looked in the direction of the stage. Tracy followed his gaze. There were still forensics personnel in the area, although it looked as though they were wrapping up. Jeffries body had been removed earlier.

"I used to really like Carl. We had a lot of fun the first few years we worked together. I really hate how some people think, because they have the ability to perform or whatever you want to call it, that they are better than other people. I met some professional actors through my years in local television. Most were nice; some were pricks just like Carl. I don't think I could have survived in Hollywood. Too many egos."

Tracy just nodded. She had never met anyone in the entertainment field who wasn't a local. All she knew about Hollywood was what she read in the papers or saw on the television. But she shared George's sentiments for the most part.

"If the movie industry suddenly went away," she began, "people would still have plenty of places to find entertainment: theater, books, museums, local playhouses. People mistake the money they make for how important they are. My dad was a police detective. He didn't make much. But he was the star in *my* show."

George smiled. "Well, that's capitalism for you." He looked to the floor, and then back at Tracy. "Let's go talk to Megan. I'm really worried about her."

After getting permission from Detective Price, Tracy and George moved towards the office of Steve Dante, the driving force behind the *House of Funerals* reunion. Megan Wallace was still with him.

"Come in," Dante told his unannounced visitors.

"I'm really sorry about all this," Tracy told them. "It's so awful." Megan and Dante thanked her.

"I just can't believe it," Dante said. "I knew Carl was irritating people. But *this*?"

Megan twisted her lips. "Mom is going to be so upset."

"She doesn't know yet?" Tracy asked.

"No; I haven't called her. I don't know how I'm going to tell her."

George moved so he could put a comforting arm around Megan.

"I still think we should do the show, though," Dante continued. "It can be a tribute to the late Carl Jeffries.

George stared at Dante. "Are you sure that's such a good idea? How are we supposed to pull this together when we're all murder suspects? I don't think I'd be comfortable working under such conditions. What if the killer isn't done?"

George's direct assessment of the situation caused Megan Wallace to start crying. Dante looked mildly shocked.

"Let's not pretend this isn't what it is," George continued. "He didn't *accidentally* stake himself."

"Richard," Dante said in a scolding tone. "I really don't think…"

George looked at Megan. "I'm sorry if I sound cold, my dear."

She shook her head. "That's okay. I know neither of us liked him. But I didn't want something like this to happen."

"None of us did."

"*Somebody* did," Tracy thought. She kept that thought to herself, however. "Megan," she said instead, "can I talk to you alone for a few minutes?"

Megan wiped the tears from her eyes and nodded. "Sure. We can go to my office; it's just a couple doors down."

Soon Tracy was taking a seat in Megan Wallace's office as the latter was closing the door.

"I think I know what this is about," Megan began as she looked at Tracy. "Richard is worried about me."

Tracy nodded. "The police know you hated your father; that you had keys to the locked studio; and, as I understand it, you don't have an alibi."

Megan sighed. "Andy and I picked the wrong night to have an argument." She shook her head.

"So that's why you guys weren't together? I thought you were going out when I left."

"Andy isn't having a good time doing this. And he said part of the problem was me because I wouldn't make nice with Dad. Me showing up to chew out Dad was hurting his position as an authority figure. Well, I just wasn't in the mood to hear all *that*. Then we both agreed we were each very tired, and we called it a night, before we even *had* a night."

Tracy sighed. "I'm sorry, Megan."

Megan waved a hand. "It's okay; it's always stressful when you're up against a firm deadline. Egos clash. Andy and I will be fine."

Tracy smiled. "I'm glad. I like Andy and I like you."

The expressed sentiment brought a smile to Megan Wallace's face — and more tears to her eyes. "I didn't kill him. I could never do something like that, even to him." Megan sat behind her desk.

"Do you think the police really think you did?"

Megan shook her head. "I have no idea. I told them about my activities since leaving the studio and that's been it."

Tracy nodded. "I'm curious to know if the body was moved. No offense, but you don't look like you could have picked up your father and put his body in the coffin. I guess you had already changed into your pajamas when you got the call."

Megan blinked. "How did you know that?"

"Oh, simple. You're not wearing what you were wearing earlier. So, you had already changed for bed when you found out what happened, and then threw on something more comfortable before you came back here."

Megan nodded. "Or got blood all over my clothes when I moved Dad's body."

"Is that what the police asked?" Tracy asked, mildly surprised.

Megan sighed. "It's what I thought myself. But I don't think the body *was* moved. From what I've been able to overhear, the amount of blood in the coffin and on the stage suggest he was killed in the coffin."

"Oh," Tracy said, very appreciative of the information. "Then that makes things even weirder."

"Weirder?"

"For what reason did Carl Jeffries lay down in that coffin? Did he think he was rehearsing a scene? Was he threatened and, if so, with what? And, more importantly, what reason did his killer give for wanting to meet him here? And why would Carl have even agreed to such a meeting? Unless he was kidnapped or something. It's all very strange."

Megan nodded. "I see what you're saying now. But I don't have any answers."

"I never thought you would. I was just thinking out loud."

"Yeah." Megan looked at her desk. "Richard thinks the police think I came back here after my fight with Andy; to have it out once and for all with my father. I told him he's worried over nothing. I know enough to know there has to be evidence to back up a theory. And since I'm innocent there can't be any evidence." Megan looked back at Tracy. "Isn't that all true?"

Tracy sighed. "In theory, yes. But police have arrested people based on circumstantial evidence. In this case, they have a motive for you; you have no alibi; and you had access to the studio and the murder weapon. I think you need to have someone in your corner when they question you formally."

"Question me?"

"You'll have to give an official statement at some point. There may be more questions too. If the studio has a lawyer on retainer, you should use him or her, just to protect yourself."

Megan forced a smile. "I'd rather have you with me, if it comes to that."

Tracy smiled in return. "Sure, Megan. Just let me know after the police contact you, and I'll make time in my schedule."

Megan smiled sheepishly. "Thank you, Tracy."

As the women looked at each other, there was a knock on the office door.

"Come in," Megan called out. When Andy Honeywell entered, he moved immediately toward Megan Wallace. Megan stood and the couple embraced.

"God, Megan, how are you?"

"I'm fine."

"I'm so sorry."

"Thank you."

"Do the police have any ideas what happened?"

"I don't really know."

"Okay. Have you told your mother yet?"

"No."

Tracy stood, deciding it was time to leave. Her movements did not go unnoticed.

"Oh, Tracy," Megan said, breaking her embrace. "You don't have to go."

Tracy smiled. "You two should have your private time. I won't leave tonight without saying goodbye." Then the attorney continued, this time successfully, to make her exit.

Tracy Brubaker Shane was not one to meddle — most of the time. She had no real client at this point, so she had no cause to be playing either lawyer or detective. But, after exiting Megan Wallace's office and seeing Corky sitting at the security desk by his lonesome, she wasn't about to ignore an opportunity.

"Hi, Corky," she greeted.

The security guard turned and smiled. "Oh, hi," he responded. "What a night, huh?"

"Yeah," Tracy agreed. "It must have been awful for you, finding the body and all."

Corky nodded. "I thought it was just a prop at first — a very realistic one. Then I realized…. Christ, I almost slipped in the blood." He shook his head.

"There was blood on the stage, huh."

"Yes, some. And his hands…"

"His hands?"

"They were grabbing the stake, like maybe he was trying to pull it out, or at least stop it from going in. That look on his face…" Corky again shook his head.

Tracy gulped. "I'm sorry, Corky."

"Thanks."

"Was the door locked when you came inside?"

"Yeah." He rubbed his eyes. "I never intended to go in; honest. I just checked the door because I knew Ms. Wallace wanted the studio locked up. So, I check it and it's locked. But, God forgive me, I got curious."

Tracy nodded and placed a hand on the distraught guard's shoulder. "Were the lights out?"

He nodded. "I turned them on. I went to the stage. I wish I never did."

"It's actually a good thing you did that, Corky. It's possible the body wouldn't have been found until Monday morning. That would have been much, much worse for all kinds of reasons."

"I guess so," Corky said unconvinced. "I wouldn't have found him Sunday; that's my day off. I just work weeknights and a full day Saturday."

"How long have you worked here?"

"Almost four and a half years. I like my job. I hope I don't lose it over this."

Tracy squeezed his shoulder. "I doubt you will. Nobody is blaming you for this from what I've heard."

"I was at my desk all the time unless I was doing rounds. I didn't even leave to take a leak."

Tracy snuffed. "Do you check the outside at any point?"

He shook his head. "The doors are all locked."

"So, you can't get in without a key."

"Yeah. And if you come through the front, I'll see you. I guess Mr. Jeffries and whoever killed him came through one of the back or side doors."

"I'm sure you're right," Tracy agreed. She looked at the guard's desk. She was looking for video monitors; she didn't see any. "You don't have live monitoring?"

"What?" he asked appearing momentarily confused. "Oh, no, we don't have anything like that. We've never had anything bad happen at this place before now." He shook his head yet again.

"I'm sorry."

"Thanks," he said, looking up at her. But before he could say anything else, both he and Tracy were distracted by the sudden noise coming from the hallway. Tracy turned in its direction.

Megan Wallace was again crying and trying to gain the attention of Detective Deborah Price.

"There must be some mistake!" Megan cried out. "There *has* to be!"

A confused look came over the attorney's face when she saw Richard George being led towards the exit doors — in handcuffs. She moved quickly so she was in the pathway of Detective Price.

"Please let us pass, Tracy," the detective ordered.

"What's going on here?" Tracy demanded.

"He's been arrested," Megan answered tearfully.

"Why?"

Detective Price stopped. "Look Tracy, stay away from this one. This is a done deal."

"What the hell does that mean?" Tracy asked defiantly.

"Richard George killed Carl Jeffries. There's no doubt about it."

"Can't be…" Tracy countered.

"Tracy, the murder was recorded, and the victim identified Richard George as his killer. And since you don't defend murderers, I suggest you go home."

CHAPTER 6

"They don't want to show it to me, Richard," Tracy told George. "They claim it's too upsetting and disturbing. But I'll insist on seeing it."

George looked at Tracy. They were seated in a small room awaiting George's transportation to his jail cell, where he'd remain unless he made bail at his bail review hearing, which would most likely be Monday.

"They *can't* have me killing Carl on film; they just can't."

Tracy gulped. "I'm no technology expert. But I've seen enough DVD special features to know you can manipulate camera images, put a person's face on another's body."

George's eyes widened. "You think that's what happened?"

"They say they have video of you killing Carl. You say it can't be you. What other explanation could there be?"

George shook his head. "I don't know."

The two remained quiet for the next few minutes until a knock on the door disturbed the silence. Detective Deborah Price entered.

"It's time for Mr. George to go to his cell," she announced.

Attorney and client rose.

"I'll see you tomorrow at your hearing," Tracy said while gently touching George's forearm.

George forced a smile as a uniformed officer escorted him out of the room.

Detective Price shook her head. "You're defending him?"

"I can't believe he killed that man."

"He did it, Tracy."

"I want to see that video. As his attorney I have a right to see it."

The detective sighed. "All right. But it's very upsetting…and graphic."

"I saw a man put a gun to his head and blow his brains out, Detective. I've had a gun aimed at me more than once. I've given birth twice. I think I can handle it."

"Very well. Follow me."

Detective Price turned and Tracy followed. Soon they were entering an interview room where a small digital recorder had been plugged into a large video monitor.

"You guys watch baseball games on this thing?" Tracy asked while taking a seat.

The other person in the room, Detective Michael Simmons, grinned slightly. Then Detective Price told him to start the video.

The first thing Tracy saw was white, or off-white. Suddenly, as if a curtain had been pulled away, Tracy realized what she had been looking at was Dr. Mort Itchin's lab coat. It had apparently been covering up the camera. Now, having started the recording and removed the coat, a figure was putting it on in such a way that the coat was all that could be seen clearly. When the figure finally moved away from the camera, he made sure the only part of his body visible was that just below the shoulders. The camera's position on the table in relation to the coffin had made sure of that. And since the lab coat was so long that it went below the knees, one couldn't even tell what color pants the villain was wearing.

"You can't even see his face," Tracy commented.

"Just watch and listen," Simmons said.

The next voice Tracy heard was obviously Carl Jeffries'. He was already lying in the coffin.

"What are you going to do to me?" he asked, sounding terrified. And it was at this point that a viewer could see the killer's hands — *gloved* hands. He then showed Jeffries *exactly* what he was going to do him. He removed a sharpened stake from one of the lab coat's pockets and showed it to his victim.

"DEAR GOD, RICHARD! PLEASE *DON'T*!"

Jeffries, at this point, tried to get up. The murderer quickly put the stake down inside the coffin, and from the coat's other pocket removed the mallet, which he used to deliver a blow to Jeffries head. Jeffries lay back down, grabbing his head, screaming in pain. The mystery figure quickly picked up the stake.

"NO, RICHARD!" Jeffries screamed.

And with quick hands and perfect precision, the killer positioned the stake over Jeffries' heart and brought down the mallet. There was one last cry, before the blood started spurting, as Jeffries grabbed the stake with both hands. The assailant struck two more times. Then, in a very careful series of movements, he started moving backwards toward the camera until all one could see was the bloodied coat. Once the killer removed the lab coat, he allowed it to fall over the recording device. Seconds afterward, the screen went black.

Tracy had her hand over her mouth. Detective Price had been right. What Tracy had seen was upsetting and disturbing. And for the moment, she was at a loss for words.

"George turned the camera off after the coat was on top of it. The time code stamp puts the murder at exactly 8:37 p.m. The lab assures us the video has not been tampered with."

Tracy gulped and then repeated, "You never see the killer's face. The killer went out of his way to make sure you couldn't see his face."

"He said the name Richard. Twice."

Tracy shook head and stood. "There could be an explanation for that."

Detective Price's jaw dropped. "You've got to be kidding me, Tracy."

"I am not."

Price folded her arms. "I gotta hear this."

Tracy cleared her throat. "Well…maybe Jeffries thought he was rehearsing or something. Maybe he didn't realize what was happening until it was too late."

"Tracy," Price sighed. "If Jeffries thought this was just some rehearsal, he wouldn't have used the name Richard. He would have said Doctor or Doctor Mort or something like that."

"Well…"

"Did you not hear the terror in Jeffries' voice? This *House ofFunerals* thing was a light-hearted…I mean it was a fun-type thing."

Tracy smiled. "Then maybe he thought he was rehearsing for something else. I understand Jeffries still had dreams of stardom.

Maybe he thought he was playing a scene where his killer's name was Richard. The person who gave him his lines — who wrote his script, so to speak — was using Jeffries as an accomplice to his own murder to implicate Richard George."

Price looked at Tracy, stunned. "That's incredible, even for you."

"Excuse me?"

"No way can you ever sell that."

Tracy scowled. "So, I'm stubert."

"You're *what*?"

"Never mind. Look Detective, I'll appeal to your common sense here. Why would George film the murder and then forget the camera? How could *anyone* forget they were recording a murder?"

"Maybe he heard something and panicked."

Tracy shook her head. "No. Even if you're right that the killer panicked, he still would have taken that camera. No way in hell can you believe he would have left it. Richard George was set up."

"He hated Jeffries."

"So did a lot of people. Besides, how did he get in?"

"What?"

"Neither Richard George nor Carl Jeffries was an employee of the station. Neither had keys. You checked with Corky, right? Did he let either of them inside? No, he didn't. So, someone else had to. Someone with keys; someone who works at the station."

Price snorted. "There were plenty of opportunities over the past couple of weeks for George to have made or had made a copy of the backdoor key."

"You better find that locksmith who made it," Tracy challenged. "You can't make that claim without proof."

"We'll find the locksmith."

"I doubt it."

Price cleared her throat. "Maybe it was a simple matter of leaving the back door ajar; blocking its closure with a rock or something."

"Or maybe I'm right and you're wrong."

Price had had enough of the back and forth. "Tracy, we're done here. We'll dot all those i's and whatnot over the next few weeks. For now, though, Richard George is our man."

"Fine," Tracy snorted.

"It's almost noon. You probably didn't get any sleep last night. Go home."

"I'm going," Tracy grunted. And then she did.

Tracy was pumping breast milk when her mother walked into the kitchen bearing a disapproving look.

"Why are you doing that here?" her mother asked. "What if the kids should see?"

"What does that mean, Mom? My kids have seen my breasts lots of times. So has Brian. What's the big deal?"

Violetta just looked at her daughter. "Look at your eyes. You need to sleep."

"I will. After I'm done pumping, I'm going to eat and then I'm going to bed. I'll go to mass at five."

Violetta said nothing else. She left her daughter alone in the kitchen.

Tracy never did nap, however. Her mind was too active. Immediately after dinner, she assisted with getting Nicole and Peter ready for bed, nursed the latter, and then headed toward her own bedroom. But she still was awake when Brian finally came through the door.

"How is it you're still awake?" Brian mused.

"I'm a freak of nature, I guess."

Brian changed into his pajamas and joined her. She rested her head on his chest. He started stroking her hair.

"Now you can add soothsayer to your list of skills."

"What?" she asked sleepily.

"You predicted this, remember?"

"Oh right," she sighed. "Brian, this is going to be a tough one."

"Haven't they all been?"

"Not like this. They have the murder on video; the victim calling out my client's name. I think I know how the killer could have worked that. But I don't know how I could ever prove something like that. I mean it's not like the killer would have left the script lying around. This guy or gal was *very* clever."

"You're very clever too, love."

"That's not always good enough. I might be smarter than the average bear. But I also need some luck once in a while. Sometimes, I've just been lucky."

"Fine. But for now, try and sleep. We can talk about this tomorrow."

"I have to be at Richard George's bail review tomorrow. I don't think he'll make bail though."

"Then I hope you don't blame yourself if he doesn't."

"This is going to be a tough one, Brian."

"You said that already. Now close your eyes and sleep."

"I'm sorry I missed spending most of the weekend with you guys."

"It's okay. I'm not angry with you. But I will be if you don't try and sleep."

Tracy said nothing in return. This was one time she didn't feel like being stubert.

Tracy looked at the clock and then sprang into a sitting position. It was 7:42 a.m., Monday morning. She should have been awake an hour ago. Now she was going to be late for work. She showered and dressed as quickly as she could. Then she went looking for Peter so she could nurse him before leaving. She sat down on the couch. It was 8:14. When Brian came into the living room, she glared at him.

"You turned off the alarm, didn't you?" she accused.

"You needed to sleep. I checked your calendar. No appointments until late morning."

"I need the time to get ready for the bail review," she said angrily.

"You said last night—"

"I don't care what I said last night! You had no right to do that!"

Brian gulped. "I'm sorry. I was only thinking of you."

Tracy's expression softened slightly. "Brian, I'm in a customer service-oriented occupation. I don't have the luxury of strolling in the office whenever I feel like it."

Brian nodded and apologized again. Then he looked at her sternly.

"Look, you also have a family now. You have some responsibilities to us too. And one of those responsibilities is to take care of yourself. So, if you're going to run out the door anytime a client calls here, then you've got to reciprocate. If you want *us* to be understanding, then *you* have to be understanding too." He stood up. "I have to check on Nicole."

Tracy watched Brian leave the room. She sighed. She looked down at Peter, who was looking up at her. That brought a smile to her face. He pulled back, smiled, and then squirmed, his way of saying, "Put me down, Mommy. I'm done." So, she put him down. He had already started walking a bit, using furniture and whatever else was available for support. But if he was in a hurry, he started crawling. He had mastered that art and was something of a speed demon on hands and knees. He squealed as he headed toward the playroom, where he knew the fun was happening.

Tracy stood and watched, heard Nicole shout, "Look Daddy! Petaw's here!" and then gathered her things. But she couldn't leave without giving and getting her hugs and kisses. So, she followed Peter's example.

"Bye Mommy! I love you!" Nicole gripped her mother's legs.

Brian picked up Peter and brought him over to Tracy. Peter started squirming, so Brian put him down as soon as his mother had kissed him. Brian and Tracy looked at each for a few moments before embracing firmly.

"I love you," he whispered to her. "You know that, right?"

"Yeah, I know that. I love you too."

"Good luck today. And if you're feeling down, call me. I'll cheer you up."

She squeezed him tighter, kissed his cheek, and then turned and left.

The unwelcome news was as expected. There would be no bail for Richard George. The horrific, brutal, sick, shocking, repulsive, yadda yadda yadda…The Assistant State's Attorney who attended the bail hearing must have consulted a thesaurus before arriving. Tracy couldn't offer anything — not criminal free history, not solid citizenship, not lack of evidence — to mitigate the ugliness of the murder. Besides, there *was* evidence: the video. The state didn't need anything else right now. The footage hadn't been shown; just described. That was enough.

Now back in her office, Tracy had her hands pressed against their respective sides of her head, staring down at her desk. Neal Bennett entered.

"How about I go get you some ice cream? That sometimes cheers you up."

Tracy looked up at him and forced a smile. "Thanks for the offer, Neal. But I'm really not up for it. I just want to go home and crawl into bed right now…forever."

Neal sighed. "Megan Wallace has called a couple of times. She wants to talk to you."

"What can I say to her?"

"I didn't get the impression she called to yell at you. Maybe talking to her would be helpful. You both believe in Richard George's innocence, despite…"

Tracy snorted. "Yeah, despite…" She cleared her throat. "Thanks Neal. I think you're right. I'll call her."

Neal nodded and smiled before leaving Tracy's office. She reached for her phone.

"Oh, Tracy," Megan Wallace began after the customary greetings, "how are you feeling?"

"Me?" Tracy asked sounding perplexed.

"Yes. I know you like Richard very much. We all do."

"I'm sorry I couldn't get him released, Megan."

"It's not your fault. I've heard about the video. Have you seen it?"

"Yes," Tracy sighed.

"Is it true Dad said Richard's name?"

"Yes," Tracy sighed again. "But you never see the killer's face. I don't think it was Richard in that video. I'm not sure how the killer got Carl Jeffries to say Richard's name, but there are several possibilities. I'll figure it out."

There were a few moments of silence before Megan said, "Steve's now thinking of cancelling the whole thing. We probably should."

"Probably," Tracy agreed.

"Tracy," Megan continued, "I know what you've done in the past. If I made sure you had free access to the studio, would you be able to talk to people? Steve and I would make sure everyone cooperated with you."

Megan Wallace couldn't see the wide smile that spread across Tracy's face. "Of course, I'll talk to people. I am helping Richard after all."

With obvious relief in her voice Megan said, "Thank you, Tracy. I can't thank you enough."

"Please email me a schedule of the studio's activities and when people involved in the *House of Funerals* revisit will be available. Then I'll look at my schedule and coordinate with you."

"I will! I promise you I will!" Tracy thought she heard sniffling from the other end. "I can't…Thank you."

"You're welcome, Megan. I'll be out to the studio as soon as I'm able to be. I'll let you go now so you can start putting that schedule together."

Megan thanked Tracy yet again before ending the call. Tracy, now aware that her presence at Channel 42 was beyond welcomed, stood up straight, came from behind her desk, and marched into Neal Bennett's office.

"Neal, our collective talents are needed once again. And we have a real tough nut to crack this time. So, I want you to give me a status report on everything we're working on; get Keandra working on one too. I need to see what our availability is."

Neal leaned back in his chair and folded his arms. "You're going to somehow prove Carl Jeffries made a mistake saying Richard's name during the crime?"

"No mistake. Jeffries was tricked into saying Richard's name. I just need to figure how the killer worked it."

"*Just?*"

"Look Negative Nealy, they don't have anything else. I did some inquiring while at the bail review, and so far, the police have no physical evidence against Richard. There are no bloody clothes, no prints on the stake or mallet, no nothing. I did find out that Jeffries got a call on his mobile phone a couple of hours before the murder, probably just after he had left the studio. But the call came from a phone *inside* the studio, a phone *anyone* could have used. Plus, they really don't know how Richard supposedly got back inside the studio after it had been locked up. Neither he nor Jeffries had keys, and a search of their respective belongings found nothing."

Neal nodded slightly. "Okay, I get you. But that video they have…"

"…A video that defies *any* kind of sense, common or otherwise. No way would Richard 'forget' to bring it with him."

"There could be an explanation for *that* part of it."

Tracy folded her arms. "Neal, we're defending Richard George."

"I know we are."

"All right then. I'll be calling El shortly to get him working on backgrounds."

Neal sighed. "*I* used to do that for you…"

"*Your* talents are needed elsewhere."

"Flatterer…"

Tracy chuckled. "I mean it though."

Neal smiled and nodded. Then he used his talents for creating status reports.

Elias Tanner, Sr., whom Tracy affectionately called El, was at his home reading his sports news weekly when Tracy called. The partner of Tracy's late father had retired from the Baltimore Police Department, but Tracy had talked him into getting a private investigator's license. Now, he worked periodically for one and only one client. But she always managed to find things for him to do.

"I heard about that one," Tanner told her. "They got the murder on video, right?"

"Kind of. You never see the killer's face, and he never says anything. He might not even be a 'he'."

"Mm. I remember Richard George. Your dad liked him a lot."

"He did indeed."

Tanner started chuckling.

"What's so funny?"

"Nothing."

"Don't give me that. What's so amusing?"

"It's nothing."

"The more you say things like that, the more I don't believe you."

"I don't want to hurt your feelings; you might wind up badmouthing your father."

"Huh? Why would I badmouth Dad? You know how I felt about him…*Still* feel about him."

"All right, Tracy. I warned you."

"Good grief, El…"

"You didn't take quickly to those old horror movies. You'd bury you head in your father's arm."

"That's perfectly normal I think."

"Sure, and your dad got a kick out of it. He told me he started grabbing you when he knew something scary was going to happen." Tanner chuckled again. "Had you jumping around like a crazed bunny rabbit."

Tracy scowled. "You think that's funny, huh?"

"Absolutely. We both did. We both laughed about it."

"Uh-huh. I guess he told you how Mom would yell at *him* when I started crying and went running to her."

"And that you still wanted to watch the rest of the movie with him. And then your mother was mad at *both* of you."

Tracy started laughing. "Yeah, that's true. But *she* was the one who pointed out the reunion news story to me. She obviously remembered all that fondly too."

Tanner cleared his throat. "So, I guess I should expect a list of names from you soon, huh?"

"Yes. Start with the employees — the ones who had keys. Then move on to the others. I'll distinguish the keyholders from the non-keyholders."

"Any ideas at this point?"

"No. Nobody there seemed to like Carl Jeffries. But the brutality of the murder… That goes beyond mere dislike. *That* was pure hatred. Or there's something else going here. But I have no idea what that could be." Tracy then told Tanner about Megan Wallace. "She hated her father. But she seems to love Richard George, so I don't see her as a suspect since this was clearly a frame. Plus, she wants me to figure out who did this. If she is the killer, she's got quite the chutzpah."

"What about her mother?"

"I've not met Carrie Wallace. She did welcome back Jeffries when he returned to the east coast. But she wouldn't have keys to the studio. Of course, she could have copied her daughter's, I guess."

"All right. Send me your list with as much detail as you can. I'll take things from there and let you know."

"Supreme! Thanks bunches, El!"

"Still sleep with the lights on?" Tanner teased.

"Hardy har har. Good day."

Tracy grinned as she terminated the call. Sure, she remembered her father grabbing her at intense moments, just before the Wolfman was about to jump on a passing bobby or the Mummy was about to strangle some poor archaeologist. How she'd scream. And then her mother would come running in; and then little Tracy would go running to her for a few seconds of comfort; and then she'd run right back to "mean Daddy" for more. She was smiling now. And then she stopped. How she still missed her father; wished he were playing with his grandchildren; wished the two of them could engage in their good-natured teasing rituals. Someone had now pretty much spoiled her memories of those times watching Dr. Mort Itchin. Those would never be the same again. But she'd be damned if she would allow this person to get away with it and get away with framing Richard George. Dr. Mort wouldn't kill anyone. So, who did? It would nag at her until she learned the answer. But learn the answer she would.

CHAPTER 7

It had been almost two weeks since Tracy and Brian had been intimate. That for them was a rather long stretch. But, as Tracy understood it, this was bound to happen eventually. Both were working very hard: she at the office, he at home. Both were tired by the time the kids had been tucked in. But this morning's mini fight had them both wanting to reconcile in the most physical way possible.

"We should argue more often," Brian grinned.

"I'm sorry," she sighed.

"About what?"

"About abandoning you all last weekend."

"I told you already. No apology necessary."

She smiled and kissed his chest. "Brian, what about that other thing?"

"Other thing?"

"About wanting to get out more. Is that why you've been kind of distant?"

"I've been distant?"

"It seems like it. I got the sense you were angry with me even before the Richard George thing."

"And that's why it's been two weeks."

"I guess."

He sighed. "I'm not angry with you. Things are going fine here. The kids need constant attention, of course, but it's all good. Your mother is more than helpful. We get along better each day. I guess I have a mild case of cabin fever. But I'm not mad about it."

"Are you sure? I really want you to tell me if changes need to be made."

"Changes?"

"Like if you want to go back to work or something."

"Work for you again?"

"Well, technically you still do. We have that home office after all."

"When was the last time I did research for you?"

"Whatever. To answer your question, no, I didn't necessarily mean come back to the office. Maybe you want to work at your father's company."

"Under Crystal? No thank you."

"You didn't have a problem with it before."

"True, but I wouldn't want to do it now. I'd have to start at the bottom. It wouldn't be fair to anyone else for me to waltz back in and demand a high-paying position I don't deserve. If I go back to work, I'd want to be like you — have my own company."

They were now face to face, and Tracy was smiling.

"Really? What kind of company would it be?"

"Not sure. Maybe something with computers and research; more or less what I already do."

"You mean like private detective work?"

"Nothing dangerous. Your occasional escapades are quite enough." She chuckled. "Computers, huh?"

"They're not going anywhere."

"No, they just keep getting smaller."

"They can't get *too* much smaller — you wouldn't be able to see anything."

"Mm," Tracy kissed him. "I know something that's getting bigger," she said, stroking him.

He said nothing in return. He wasn't interested in exchanging words at this point.

Tuesday morning, Tracy looked at the list of names she had compiled. Steve Dante: producer of most of the local programming of Channel 42 and driving force behind the live reunion show. Megan Wallace: a producer-director who was co-producing the *House of Funerals* program and trying to keep peace on the set. She was also the victim's daughter. Andrew Honeywell: director and Megan's main squeeze. Larry Peachtree: production designer and props — and something of a complainer. Ned Topolski: video engineer who had been recording behind the scenes footage. Mental note: see if she can get a look at all the footage Ned recorded. All the above were WMFT employees and had keys, most likely, to the station.

The next list was shorter. Tom Kramer: a makeup artist hired to create/apply the scary faces and more for the show. Carrie Wallace: Megan Wallace's mother and the victim's girlfriend.

Anyone else? Well, maybe she should add Corky the security guard to the first list. He *seemed* genuinely upset. But Tracy had been duped by people playing innocent before. Yup, better add him. She didn't even know his real name though.

Tracy leaned back and frowned. Who had known Carl Jeffries the longest? Richard George of course, and Megan's mother as well as Megan herself. Since Andy loved Megan, he must have disliked Jeffries. Peachtree? He had been with the station since 1983, Tracy had learned. He was 18 when he started, so that put him in his mid- fifties. Was there some history between Peachtree and Jeffries? El could hopefully find out. Of course, Peachtree was a hothead. Was he so far gone that borrowing his props or tools without permission could drive him to do something like this? That would make him a psycho. Tracy wasn't in the mood to deal with a psycho.

She finished typing her notes and observations, and then emailed the package to Elias Tanner, Sr. Next, she pulled together her own calendar, the schedules of Neal Bennett and Keandra Moore, and Megan Wallace's email. She buzzed her secretary. "Beck, put me down for WMFT starting Thursday at 1:00 p.m. I'll be there the rest of the day."

"Sure."

"And then block out Monday the 21st too. I may or may not need to go back, but I don't want to schedule anything for that day if I can help it."

"Righto."

"I think that's it for now. Thanks, Beck."

Next Tracy emailed Megan to relay the arrival plans. She sighed. She still had today, tomorrow, and half of Thursday to get through.

Should she call Detective Price for any updates? No, wait a few more days for that, perhaps after Thursday's interviews. She still had a few minutes before her 9:30 a.m. conference call. She dialed her husband.

"Hey honey, how are you this morning?"

"You snuck out while I was in the shower," he scolded playfully.

"Sorry. I had to get in here early and take care of some things. Besides, I didn't want to see that smokin' bod of yours. Might have put ideas in my head."

Brian gulped. Now his own head was filled with images of his wife's body. From a purely physical standpoint, Tracy was second to none in his mind.

"You could have joined me."

"I thought about it. Maybe tonight?"

Holy moly. "Jeez, Tracy, how about coming home for lunch?"

She laughed. "Sorry, darling; can't do."

"There are times when you make feel like a horny teenager," he whispered.

"But I'm *much* better than a magazine, aren't I?"

"Come home for lunch," he said again.

"I would if I could. I'll see you tonight, Brian. I love you."

"And I love you — in all sorts of ways."

She laughed again before hanging up. She smiled. She liked that Brian still made no secret of his desire for her physically. Birthing and nursing two children had rendered certain parts of her anatomy unrecognizable to her when compared to their previous forms. But Brian had made no criticisms, only compliments.

She chuckled again. She was now thinking of her mother's look when she found Tracy pumping on Sunday. Her mother was still rather old fashioned about certain things, one of them being having her daughter's breasts exposed at the kitchen table. She next started recalling times in the family living room, when her father would suddenly lean over and whisper in his wife's ear. How red Violetta Brubaker would get just before giggling. When was the last time her mother *giggled*? Tracy would just look at them, confused. She wasn't confused anymore. Was her mother nearby when Brian whispered just a few moments ago? What would she have thought? But if a loving, married couple couldn't engage in some playful double entendres now and again, who could?

Tracy and Brian exchanged grins all evening — first when Tracy arrived home, then numerous times at the dinner table, and still more times as they all sat on the couch during story time. Nicole, perhaps sensing *something*, had coaxed four Dr. Seuss books out of her parents. She tried for five but was unsuccessful.

Now up in Nicole's bedroom, Tracy was trying to tuck in her oldest.

"I wanna kiss pumcan."

Tracy looked at the glowing pink gourd. "Kiss the pumpkin?"

"She need a kiss, Mommy."

Tracy sighed, unplugged the light, and brought it over. Nicole, who was now sitting up in her toddler bed, kissed it.

"Night, night pumcan."

Tracy returned the decoration to the dresser's top.

"I wanna kiss skult too, Mommy."

Tracy looked at the skull and its bleeding eyes. How her daughter thought *this* was cute…

"All right honey. But this is it."

"Night, night skult," Nicole said gently. As her mother was returning the head to its perch, Nicole added, "She need a new makeup Mommy."

"What?"

"Skult's makeup all messy."

Tracy chuckled. So *that's* what Nicole thought the blood was: makeup gone wrong.

"We'll see about that later, Nicole. It's sleep time now."

"I want you sleep here."

"I sleep with Daddy, honey. There's not room enough in your bed for anyone else but you. They make special, big beds for mommies and daddies."

"Why?"

"Well, mommies and daddies sleep together to keep each other company."

"I want comperny too."

"You have 'Pumcan' and 'Skult' for company."

"I want you!"

"Not tonight, honey."

"Then Daddy!"

"I think Daddy wants to sleep with Mommy tonight."

"But I *love* Daddy!"

"I love Daddy too."

"I wanna marry Daddy so he keep *me* comperny."

Tracy laughed. "You can't marry Daddy, honey. He's already married to Mommy."

"But I *love* Daddy," Nicole whined.

"Listen, honey. There are all kinds of love. The way you love Mommy and Daddy is not the same as the way you love Peter or Grandma or ice cream. Mommies and daddies love each other in their own special way. So, even though you love Daddy, you can't marry Daddy. Okay?"

"Why?"

Tracy twisted her lips. "You'll want to marry somebody else someday, honey. I promise."

"And then I be a mommy too?"

"Yes, I hope."

"I get a BIG tummy!" Nicole giggled.

Tracy chuckled. "Yes."

"How it get big?"

Tracy blinked. "Um…we can talk about that later, sweetie. It's time for sleep."

"How, Mommy? What you have to eat?"

Tracy chuckled. "It's not eating that does it, sweetie."

"What, Mommy?"

Tracy snorted. "Magic," she said.

"*Majuc?*" Nicole more or less repeated.

By this time Brian, who was ready to file a missing person's report, had gone in search of his wife. He arrived outside Nicole's doorway just in time to hear Tracy struggling with questions she hadn't been prepared for.

"Yes, magic."

Tracy, thinking she had heard something, looked over her shoulder and saw Brian leaning against the entrance, grinning. She gave him a can-you-help-me-out-here look. He just gave her a who-me expression and shook his head slowly. Wrong move. When would he ever learn? She looked back at Nicole.

"Yes, Nicole. Daddies have magic wands."

Nicole's eyes widened. "They *do*?"

"Yes. Daddy gets out his magic wand, waves it around for a few minutes, says a few words sort-of, and — presto! — there's a baby in Mommy's tummy."

"Wow!" And then little Nicole asked, "Can I see it?"

Tracy took this opportunity to look over her shoulder again. Brian's smile was gone; his face was now red. This time, she smiled at him. She looked back at Nicole.

"No dear. Only Mommy can see Daddy's magic wand, or it loses its power. You don't want that to happen, do you?"

"No," Nicole said slowly while shaking her head.

"Neither does Mommy. So, you go to sleep now. Daddy's here to give you a kiss too."

Tracy gently pushed Nicole onto her back, and then kissed each cheek and her forehead. Brian came over and did the same. Then he followed Tracy into the bedroom.

"Very cute," he said as he closed and locked the door.

"Well, I had to tell her *something*. And you made it clear *you* had no intention of assisting."

"Nicole's a girl so *you* should talk to her about sex. I'll talk to Peter when he's old enough."

"Come on, Brian, she's not even three."

"I know that. But I've read stuff that says you can talk about body parts with kids at early ages. Speaking freely and openly about sex will make children feel like they can talk to you when it really matters."

"You can say that so matter-of-factly now because Nicole's not interested in boys. I bet your tune will be different after the puberty fairy visits her."

Brian started chuckling. "I'm just telling you what I've read."

Tracy put her hands on her hips. "Nicole is ahead of the curve, as you keep telling me. She's bright and curious and likes to share what she learns with others."

"All good things, right?"

"Yes. But think about this, Brian. Did you really want me to tell her how babies are made? Did you want me to say, 'Daddy put his penis in Mommy's vagina and made Baby Peter'? Is that what I should have told her?"

Brian twisted his lips. "Well…"

"I can see it now. We're all at dinner. Then Nicole says, 'Hey Grammaw: I know how Baby Peter was made. Daddy put his penis in Mommy's vagina!' I can see the smile leaving my mother's face. I can see the color draining away while the shock registers. I can see my mother collapsing: her face falling into her plate of mashed potatoes, her nostrils inhaling the hot, brown gravy. She suffocates and dies. I can see us at the funeral — all because *you* wanted me to tell Nicole about how babies are made. Do you want to *kill* my mother, Brian? Do you? I thought you said the two of you were getting along better than ever."

Brian stared at her. Then he smiled cautiously. "You're pulling a Joe Pesci, aren't you?"

"A what?"

"A Joe Pesci — from *Goodfellas*."

"What are you talking about?"

"That famous scene in *Goodfellas* where Joe Pesci pretends to be mad at Ray Liotta because Liotta said he was funny. Haven't you ever seen that?"

"What does a movie have to do with anything?"

"I'm just saying…"

"You're stalling; you're hesitating. You have to think about your answer."

He shook his head. "No, I wasn't. I was just thinking maybe we should start serving baked potatoes instead of mashed."

That got her. She couldn't keep a straight face anymore. She started laughing; he started laughing. Then they started embracing and kissing and fondling and doing other things that can sometimes lead to babies being made.

"I forgot to tell you something," Brian said as he gazed into his wife's eyes.

She smiled warmly. "What's that, lover?"

"Ben called."

"Ben?"

"Yeah. Remember you said I could invite him and Lisa to the Dr. Mort thing?"

Tracy frowned. "Way to assassinate the mood, Brian."

"Stop that. You said I could."

She sighed. "What'd he want?"

"Well, since the live show is probably off now, he said he still wanted to hang out with us soon. I invited him and Lisa over for dinner on Saturday."

"You didn't!"

"What's the problem? You would have seen him on Halloween anyway."

"…While surrounded by a crowd of people in complete safety."

"Tracy…"

"You should have checked with me first."

"You'd have said no?"

She twisted her lips. "Probably not, but still…"

"It will be fine."

"And what if he starts staring at my top-most lady parts?"

"I'll say something to him. I promise."

"Prepare your speech then."

Brian looked at his wife's top-most lady parts. "They are lovely though."

"Stop it," Tracy chuckled.

"Just how many cup sizes did you grow?"

"Are you going to miss them when Peter is weaned?"

"No, there was nothing wrong with them before."

Good answer. She lifted her head and kissed him.

"Other than the kids, who don't know any better, these are for your eyes only, Brian."

He rubbed his right check against hers and whispered, "And maybe my hands too."

"Maybe," she grinned. "Maybe even other parts."

Apparently, the mention of Ben's name hadn't killed the mood after all.

Tracy was at the WMFT studios precisely at 1:00 p.m. on Thursday. Elias Tanner, Sr. still had a few more names to investigate and facts to check, so Tracy decided to move forward with her interviews and get Tanner's report on Friday. She could come back Monday if she needed to. Megan Wallace embraced Tracy after she had closed her office doors.

"This means so much to me — getting your help."

Tracy felt mildly embarrassed. "Thanks, Megan. I promise to do what I can."

"I went to visit Richard yesterday, me and his wife actually."

"I haven't met her yet."

"Elaine's lovely. They've been married for more than 50 years. I think this the first time they ever been apart this long. It's…I just can't stand it." Megan was trying to hold back the tears.

"You love Richard very much," Tracy said quietly.

"I wish *he* were my father. He basically was for my first 14 years."

"…Until Carl showed up again."

"Yeah."

"Did Richard leave the station right after the Dr. Mort show got canceled?"

"No. He worked at Channel 42 until about 2002 or 2003. Then he retired. He's been local all his life."

"Mm. I would like to meet Elaine George at some point."

Megan smiled. "She wants to meet you too. Richard and I told her you were going to help him. You're something of a local celebrity, after all."

"Not on purpose," Tracy said sincerely. "So, do you have any ideas, Megan?"

"I'm sorry?"

"…About whom might have really killed your father."

"Maybe one of those crazy emailers."

Tracy shook her head. "I wish it could be an outsider, but it just can't."

"How can you be so positive?"

"Lots of reasons. The obvious is access: no stranger could have snuck in here. The main studio door was locked as was the back. The video indicates that the killer must have told your father to get into the coffin *before* the lab coat was put on. So, the killer had to know the stake and mallet were in the coat pockets before he picked it up and put it on. No outsider would have that knowledge. I'm sorry if I sound cold. But you need to face it, Megan. Someone working on this production killed your father."

Megan sighed loudly. "You're telling me one of my friends did this."

"I'm sorry."

"So am I."

Tracy smiled a bit. "Are all these people really your friends? If you could pick who the killer could be, whom would you pick?"

"I don't think I should say any—"

"This is between you and me. I have to start with someone."

Megan rubbed her eyes. "Well…I like everyone, really. They all have their idiosyncrasies of course. But I really do like everyone."

"I sense a 'but' here."

"Fine. Larry Peachtree."

"That's who I would have guessed."

"Larry's under a lot of stress. Everyone knows how particular he can be, and they sometimes pick on him. It's not really fair."

"I agree with that."

"So, he can fly off the handle sometimes. You haven't seen him when he's…calmer. He's a very nice…well…he's very gifted at what he does and he's a hard worker. But he can be a handful."

"I get it, Megan."

"But that doesn't mean I think he could kill someone."

"I realize that."

"I still can't believe *anyone* here could do what was done to Dad."

Tracy nodded. "That's why I'm here. I'm an outsider. I have no personal relationships here. Everyone has been more than nice to me since I first came here, so I have no feelings of ill will or suspicion directed at anyone. I'll just ask my questions and see what I can find."

"Okay," Megan nodded.

"So, whose idea was the coffin and bride and all that?"

"Andy did most of the script back when there were no concrete plans. But once Steve decided to do the show and brought me in, I assembled my team and we all just met and tossed out ideas. Because it was going to be live, we had to keep things doable. And since the show had always used a coffin to hide the skeleton, it seemed to make sense to max the use of the coffin."

"I get it. So, everybody shared their ideas and Andy pulled it all together."

"Right."

"Okay. I guess I just have one more question before I start talking to people."

"Ask me anything."

"Do the police have the footage Ned Topolski shot the day of the murder?"

"Yes. I'm not sure who told them about it, but Ned gave them the camera he used to record all of it."

"Oh," Tracy said, now scribbling in her notebook. "So, the camera that recorded the murder wasn't the camera Ned used?"

"No, but it *was* another of the studio's cameras. It's kept in the audio-visual closet, which is *supposed* to be locked at all times. But it isn't."

"Mm. I guess Ned didn't make a copy of his footage."

"What?" Megan chuckled slightly. "It's a digital camera, Tracy. Ned had already uploaded the video on his machine at home. Luckily, he hadn't deleted the recording from the camera memory."

Tracy smiled. "Supreme! I'd really like to see the footage if I might. There could be something on it."

"Sure," Megan nodded. "I'll have someone email it to you. Maybe I can even have Ned sit down with you and go through it."

"Thanks, Megan."

"Anything else?"

"Not right now. Let's go to the studio where Larry Peachtree is. I think I'll talk to him first."

CHAPTER 8

After Megan Wallace had left them, Larry Peachtree's face turned sour.

"I know why you're here."

"Of course, you do, Mr. Peachtree. Megan just told you."

"Ha! I know why you're *really* here."

"You do? Can you tell me, so *I* know?"

Peachtree sneered. "You're a wiseass, aren't you?"

"I've never had my butt tested for that. I'll have to get back to you."

Peachtree blinked. "I…What do you want?"

"I thought you said you knew."

"Of course, I do. You're looking for someone else to pin this on."

"Pin this on? I wouldn't put it like that, Mr. Peachtree. I'm looking for facts, for the truth."

Peachtree snorted. "You want to get Richard off. I get that. But I didn't kill Jeffries."

"I never said you did."

"You hope it's me though."

"I don't even know you, Mr. Peachtree. But you're not making a good first impression."

"I…that's rude!"

"…No ruder than assuming I want an innocent person to take the blame just so my client is cleared."

There were a few moments of silence as Peachtree decided what to say next. He twisted his lips. "What is it I can tell you?"

"Tell me what you remember about last Saturday, and we'll go from there."

"Remember? It's been absolute craziness around here. We did some finishing touches on the backdrop. We reinforced the coffin after that cretin broke the table leg. We had to repaint some of the lab table props because the *director* didn't like the way they looked when the lights hit them. This is what I deal with — trying to make *everyone* happy. It's impossible!"

"I can empathize, Mr. Peachtree. Imagine being a lawyer in this situation. Nobody thinks Richard George did this, but everyone thinks I'm here to pin the murder on them. Try talking to people with *that* mentality."

"I get your point," Peachtree hostilely said.

"I didn't notice any real fireworks last Saturday. Did you?"

"Fireworks?"

"Fights, arguments, threats..."

"Oh. I don't know. There've been plenty of those since this whole thing began. But I don't remember anything specific about Saturday."

"Mm. How well did you know Carl Jeffries?"

The prop master rolled his eyes. "I knew it! Here it starts!"

"Mr. Peachtree, I didn't know the victim at all. I need some background on him. Stop making assumptions, please."

He snorted. "I just worked with him, okay? He was already here when I started in my teens, and it was clear to me almost right away that he annoyed people. I wasn't sorry when he left."

"Do you remember when that would have been?"

"1988; 1989 maybe."

"That fits; Megan's 30 or 31?"

"I'm not sure."

"Never mind then. Is there any one particular person you remember Jeffries having a problem with when he worked here in the eighties, beyond just not getting along?"

Peachtree folded his arms and furrowed his brow. "Hmm...I really can't remember." He scratched the bottom of his chin. "There was some back and forth over Carrie Wallace. She had been working here a couple of years and she was very attractive. Jeffries butted heads with some of the others who wanted to...Well, I guess you know what I mean."

"A battle for her affections, you might call it."

Peachtree actually *smiled* at Tracy's summation. "Yes. Yes, that's a very good way of putting it. Bunch of drooling apes if you ask me. But it was Jeffries who she liked — she'd laugh at anything he said. Sometimes that's enough, I guess."

"Are any of the apes working here now?"

"The other suitors? No. They've moved on. I guess you could ask Richard to be sure though."

"Richard liked Carrie too?"

Peachtree cleared his throat. "What are you implying?"

"Nothing, Mr. Peachtree. But if Richard didn't like Jeffries and did like Carrie Wallace, he may have tried to — dissuade her, shall we say?"

"Oh. Yes, I see what you mean now. But I'm not really sure."

"Okay. I'll ask Richard about it then."

"Anything else?"

"Yes, please. Do you remember seeing anyone making a phone call around the time people were leaving the studio on Saturday? I'm not sure of the exact time yet, but the police tell me Carl Jeffries received a call on his cell phone from the studio."

"The telephone? There are several phones in the studio. I can't say that I was paying attention. I was trying to clean up."

"Oh, right, and Ned tried to interview you."

"Annoying man."

Tracy grinned. "Did you have a hot date waiting for you?"

"Excuse me?"

"You wanted to get out of here. I thought maybe you had some important plans Saturday night."

Peachtree sighed. "No. No plans, unless you call reading in bed a plan."

"Sure, I would, if it's something you're really looking forward to doing."

"I suppose."

"Say, did you ever find the culprit?"

"Excuse me."

"…The person who moved your tape from the table to the drawer."

"OH! No, I didn't. But I'll find out eventually."

"Why?"

"Why what?"

"Why is it so important that you find out?"

"Young lady, people around here need to learn to respect others. It's not the tape itself. It's that some people just think they can do whatever they want. You see?"

"I see. But did it ever occur to you that someone may have thought they were doing you a favor?"

"A favor?"

"Yes. They see you're trying to clean up; know how particular you are. They see your tape on the table and think that by putting it in your drawer they're helping you out. Then, you start yelling at everyone about it. How do you think that person now feels? Do you think they're going to tell you? You see my point?"

"Well…" Peachtree looked at the floor.

"Mr. Peachtree, I can appreciate how it can be for you. You like everything in its place and some people use that to get a rise out of you. You're just trying to do your job and people deliberately try to annoy you. I get it. When I was in school, I was the kid who studied hard and did well, and some of my peers gave me grief for it. I learned how to deal with it. And I'm glad I did because today I have peers who give me grief. But I don't let them get to me — most of the time, anyway. I guess what I'm saying is the next time someone tries to get your goat, either ignore it or laugh about it. It's win-win for you. If you ignore it, people won't do it as much because you're not reacting to it. If you laugh about it, people will see another side to you — will know you can take a prank. I know it won't be easy for you. But it may be worth a shot."

Peachtree twisted his lips. Then he scratched the back of his head.

"I don't know," he finally mumbled.

"Okay. Thanks for talking to me, Mr. Peachtree. I'll let you get back to work."

"All right."

Tracy turned to leave. Peachtree said nothing further. He just watched her enter the hallway. He should have felt offended by her presumption to say what she said. But he didn't. Her sincerity about the whole thing prevented that — sharing something about her youth with a stranger. He shook his head, and then started looking around.

"Now where is my Phillips head?"

Tom Kramer was painting a mask when Tracy entered his makeshift workshop. He smiled at her as she sat down.

"Don't mind me," she told him. "Go on with what you're doing."

He chuckled as he looked back at his alien in the making.

"Just what *are* you doing?" Tracy asked after a few moments.

He continued moving his airbrush about as he said, "Finishing up my masks. Megan said I could use the studio to finish what I was working on. It's doubtful they're going to do the show now."

"Yeah, that really stinks."

"It does." He put his airbrush down. "If they don't do it, I guess I can use these things somewhere down the road."

He motioned to the row of latex masks that sat on his shelf. There were about 10 of them, each more revolting than the last. Hideously deformed creatures with fangs and warts and evil grins and…Tracy shook her body in disgust. Kramer laughed.

"I'll take that as a compliment," he told her.

"How were these going to be used in the show?" she chuckled.

"Oh, Megan was going to have some people from the studio wear them and sit in the audience. It would add to the atmosphere. They were planning some camera pans, and at one point I think Dr. Mort was actually going to come out into the audience and interact with the monsters."

Tracy sighed. "That would have been *so* great."

"It would have. So, if they're not going to use them, I'll just find some other use for my virgins."

"Your *virgins?*"

Kramer laughed. "Masks that haven't been worn yet." He grinned devilishly. "I'll tell you what. I'll let you take one — pick any one you want."

Tracy shook her head. "No, thank you."

He laughed. "Maybe your kids would like one. I hear you got kids."

"They're too small to appreciate something like that. Of course, my big kid might like one."

"Your husband?"

"Mm hm."

"Take one then."

"I'm not touching those things."

Kramer started guffawing. "You're too funny, Tracy."

"Mm. Can we talk a few minutes, Tom?"

"Sure, we can," Kramer answered, wiping his eyes with his forearm. "What can I tell you?"

"Anything you can remember since you started working here, especially last Saturday."

"Of course. My first day was actually October 4. They had emailed a list of what they wanted but I couldn't get here October 2 when they were starting things."

"Why not?"

"I've been doing some work for one of the big Halloween haunted houses in the area."

"Oh, those things. Yuck."

Kramer laughed again. "Don't like those either, huh?"

"A bunch of sweaty people running around making loud noises…I get that for free at home."

Kramer's whole body was shaking. "That's great…"

"Seriously though, Tom, I do *love* Halloween. I love the atmosphere and the decorations and seeing little kids dressed up. They look so cute. And I love the candy too — especially the candy. And I can watch an old black and white horror movie with little problem. But I don't like the gory stuff and I don't like being sandwiched between a bunch screaming ninnies who cry out at slightest sound."

Kramer was nodding. "I hear you. Me, I love all of it. It's my favorite time of year. But it's also my busiest. Thankfully, it's work I love doing."

"I can appreciate that. I'm not one of those people who judges others for liking what they don't. And I have to admit I liked seeing how you paint those things."

"Thanks."

"How did you get along with Carl? Was he rude to you too?"

"Truth be told I didn't really deal with him. I had to work with Richard George on *his* makeup. I spruced up the prop skeleton that Jeffries was going use. But he was supposed to be hidden behind the coffin. So, there was little for me to do for him."

Tracy nodded. "I heard he *wanted* to have a bigger part of the show."

Kramer grunted. "That's true. He thought Mr. George couldn't pull it off. You know at one point he did ask if I would make him up to look like Dr. Mort. I think he wanted to show Megan and them how he would look. I told him I didn't have the time. He may have called me a name. I don't really remember."

"You didn't let him get to you."

"No. He was a jerk. I deal with people like him all the time. And I didn't even think he was that funny."

"His jokes were intentionally bad."

Kramer nodded. "Then he succeeded."

Tracy made some notes in her notebook. "Other than the jibes and occasional heated exchange, did you witness anything that was on the verge of turning violent? Did you see any physical exchanges?"

"No, nothing like that. He was a little guy with a big mouth. As I said I've met his type before. If someone had raised a fist to him, he'd have turned and ran. He acted like he was really something; he flirted with the ladies around here, making reference to his…well…"

Tracy chuckled. "His magic wand?"

Kramer started shaking with laughter again. "Yeah," he said finally. "He thought he was quite the magician. Guys like that…" Kramer shook his head.

"Tom, I just don't understand this. Everyone seemed to know what everybody else thought of Carl Jeffries. He was a harmless big mouth whom no one seemed to take seriously. I just can't believe though that someone would kill him over that, not even the hyper-sensitive Larry Peachtree."

Kramer was no longer smiling. "I heard how he died. Sick."

"It was. I guess my point is that I think there was something else going on with him. There must have been. Did you see him maybe off in some corner having a private conversation on the phone or with someone here?"

He shook his head. "I'm sorry, Tracy. I can't think of anything."

"They didn't give him keys to the building, did they?"

"No."

"So, when you come here, you have to sign in at the front desk or something?"

"Yes."

"Are there any electronic entrances around here, something you'd use a card key for?"

"No, I don't think so. It's an old building and they haven't modernized it."

"Are the studio doors locked during the day?"

"No. They get locked after everyone has left for the day — well, the day staff anyway. There aren't too many people here at night."

"So, anyone can come and go prior to when the security guard comes on duty."

"I guess."

"Did you ever notice anyone kind of just wandering around, not looking like they belonged here?"

"Hard to say. Megan might be seeing how things are going and then someone unfamiliar to me would come and get her. But I can't think of anyone like you're asking about."

No surprises there. "One more question."

"Sure."

"Did you notice if anyone used one of the studio telephones around quitting time on Saturday?"

Kramer paused before saying, "Sorry. I can't say one way or the other."

Tracy smiled. "No problem. It's one of those long shot questions."

"I wish I could have been of more help."

"You *were* helpful. If Carl Jeffries flirted with the wrong lady, he may have ticked somebody off."

"A jealous boyfriend or something?"

"Possibly." Tracy hopped off the stool on which she'd been sitting. "I'll let you get back to your…to your babies."

Kramer grinned. "Thanks. And let me know if you want one of my *babies* to take home."

Tracy shuddered. "Don't hold your breath."

She twisted her lips just before exiting Tom Kramer's studio. He started laughing again as he picked up his airbrush. Time to resume birthing a new baby.

"I'm afraid that's it for right now, Tracy," Megan Wallace told her. "Ned's not here and Steve's in a meeting for at least another hour."

"Is Andy here?"

"He's attending a casting meeting."

"Can I ask for what?"

Megan sighed. "For a new Dr. Mort."

"What?"

"Tracy, please don't repeat what I'm going to tell you."

"I won't if it doesn't factor into my defense of Richard."

"Fair enough. This whole Dr. Mort thing is actually a pilot of sorts."

"A pilot?"

"Steve Dante wants to bring back a horror host show to the WMFT. There's no competition for a Saturday night fright flick. If the Dr. Mort live show is a hit, he's probably going to get the green light."

"*Is* a hit? You mean the show is going on after all."

"That's the plan. But Richard was never going to be the host of the new show. The station owns the rights to the character, not Richard. The intent always was to find a new Dr. Mort."

"And that's what Andy is doing."

Megan sighed. "They want to try and find someone. There's been so much invested in this — and I'm not just talking about money. There was always the fear that Richard might not be able to do it because of his age. But he seemed to be doing fine and Andy was never happy with anyone else."

"Oh, they've been looking for the new Dr. Mort for a while already."

"Yes, since early September. The field has been narrowed and it's quite possible that, after Andy's meeting, we'll be bringing on a new Dr. Mort."

Tracy sighed. "I see."

"Don't feel so bad," Megan smiled. "Richard knows all about it. He was fine with it. He wouldn't have wanted to host a new weekly program. But by having him host this live show — and sort of pass the baton — it would appeal to nostalgic fans and possibly a new generation. But that last part was kind of secret."

"Did Carl know?"

"No. It was bad enough that he was trying to steal the spotlight with the Halloween show. If he knew about…Well, he'd have been more impossible than he already was. And he would have spoiled it."

"Spoiled it?"

"He didn't understand that the station owns the rights to the characters. The former owners made sure of that in case Richard or Dad were thinking of jumping ship. From what I heard, that was Dad's fault, actually. Apparently, he hinted about going somewhere where he was appreciated. Anyway, when our lawyers were negotiating the contract for Dad coming back, he of course wanted more money than we could offer. They told him if he wouldn't do it that we would find someone else. He in turn said they couldn't use his Nagging Skeleton character. They told him he was wrong. He threatened a lawsuit. Eventually Mom calmed him down. But you can see what I mean, right?"

"Oh, sure. He would have sued you guys once a new person was brought in to play Nagging."

"Right."

"Well, that explains why he asked me about copyright infringement the day I met him."

"He did?"

"Yes. I had almost forgotten about it. He certainly was *thinking* lawsuit."

"He would have lost. But you know how the rabid fans are and what the internet can be used to do. Richard would have given us his blessing but not Dad. Dad would have drummed up support for himself and just turned the whole thing sour. You know how people are when a new actor plays a favorite character. We're just a local station, after all. The owners wouldn't have wanted to spend a dime to defend a frivolous suit and to deal with the fan boys."

"And the whole project would have gone kaput."

"Exactly."

"And you're sure your father didn't know what was going on?"

"I'm pretty sure he didn't. He never said anything. And I'm sure he would have if he had known."

"So, Richard, Andy, you, and Steve knew what the big plan was. Anyone else?"

"The station manager Jerry Debusey knew of course; he gave us the preliminary okay. But no one else working on the live show knew."

"Mm. Is Jerry Debusey around?"

"Yes."

"Maybe I can talk to him too."

"Sure, I don't see why not." Megan sighed. "I don't honestly know what's going to happen now. Steve thinks the publicity will have people tuning in. You know how people are."

"I sure do."

"And then there's you."

"Me?"

"Tracy, the hope is you'll figure this thing out before the show."

Tracy blinked. "I can't promise that, Megan."

"Oh, I know that; Steve knows that. I never would have said anything but…Well, I guess I figured since you now know about the plans and all…"

Tracy sighed. "I'm glad you told me. And, I have to tell you, Megan, this could be what I've been looking for."

"Looking for?"

"Motive. If Carl Jeffries were deemed a threat to the station's plans, *this* could be the reason he was killed."

"No…"

"It's a better motive than someone killing him because he was annoying. A new Dr. Mort show means new employees, more advertising dollars, and some promotion of the station if things work out well. If your father was seen as threat to all of that…"

"I can't believe that. Only a few people even knew—" Megan blinked. "Andy would *never* hurt anybody. Neither would Steve."

"I'm not saying it has to be Andy or Steve. Somebody else could have found out. Isn't *that* possible?"

Megan looked at her folded hands. "I guess so. I guess someone could have overheard us talking about it or seen an internal memo. It's not like we're Fort Knox or anything."

Tracy, seeing how she'd upset Megan Wallace, stood. "I think I'll go now, Megan. I can come back Monday and talk to the others."

"Okay."

"Can I ask you a favor?"

Megan looked back up at the attorney. "Yes."

"I'd like to talk to your mother. I know she hasn't been involved directly in the show. But she knew the victim better than anyone probably. I need to get a better understanding of what made your father tick. Understanding the victim can lead to the truth sometimes."

Megan nodded. "I guess that'd be fine. She's talked to the police a few times already. And she loves Richard too. I'll talk to her."

"Thanks. Maybe I could meet her for lunch at some point over the next few days — if she's up to going out, that is. But I don't mind visiting her at her home if she'd rather not go out."

"She should go out though. It would be good for her."

"Whatever she wants to do…"

"All right. I'll call you after I talk to her."

"Okay, thanks. And I'm sorry if I upset you."

Megan shook her head. "You don't owe me an apology. You're trying to help Richard and I understand that means looking at everyone. I guess I really didn't think about the flipside of this."

"Flipside?"

"Yeah. If Richard didn't do it, then someone else obviously did. You're telling me it could be someone else I like — that I care about. I think that part of it is finally starting to sink in."

Tracy nodded. She completely understood. Megan Wallace was consumed with worry over what Tracy might find. The truth *was* sinking in, and Megan was drowning in it.

Jerry Debusey had been the station manager for WMFT for the past 20 years. He had taken the job after working, like Steve Dante, in New York for many years. At 42 he had entered the offices of Channel 42 and helped the station seemingly function as both a network affiliate and an independent. He had no problem preempting network programming if he felt something of local interest was a better option. He also wasn't averse to running older films during the late night/ early morning hours, as well as weekend afternoons. Under his watch, WMFT sponsored local film festivals and supported the Baltimore arts. Now, at 62 years old, he was just as committed to Channel 42's success as he had been when he started.

"So, you're the young lady I keep hearing about?" Debusey said as he offered Tracy a seat.

"Depends on what you're hearing," Tracy smiled.

"Your father was Peter Brubaker, right?" Debusey asked next.

"Yes."

"I remember us covering that story. I prefer to cover the stories where the cops are heroes instead of villains."

"I prefer that be the case too."

"Your grandfather was with the force too, right?"

"Yes, he was."

"Mm. Why didn't you join? We've all heard about your abilities; seems you're just as suited for the job as your father and grandfather."

"Personal reasons, Mr. Debusey."

"Call me Jerry."

"Personal reasons, Jerry. I think it would have been very tough on my mother."

"Ah, I think understand." Debusey sighed. "Quite a mess we have here, isn't it?"

"Yes."

"Megan thinks you can get us out of it."

"I will certainly try."

"I didn't really know Carl Jeffries very well. But Richard was here when I started. Good man, I think."

"As do I."

Debusey leaned forward. "This live show idea: I really was looking forward to seeing how it would work out. Now…"

"The show was Steve Dante's idea?"

"Yes, it was. He thinks we should bring back horror movies to Saturday nights, maybe even Friday nights too."

"But you weren't sure."

He leaned back in his chair. "It might work. There aren't too many old horror movies that aren't available from other sources. Why watch 'em interrupted and maybe edited? But the horror host thing…I was willing to give it a shot."

"Maybe you still can."

"Maybe."

"Have you been following what's been going on during the rehearsals?"

"Steve gives me a status report. Other than the unexpected clashing of egos he thought things were going quite well."

"I guess they weren't," Tracy mused.

"You so sure this was an inside thing?"

"Yes, as do the police. You don't have any threatening emails or letters to suggest otherwise, do you?"

Debusey shook his head. "No, at least nothing that suggested violence. Most threats, if you can call them that, were more along the lines of, 'I'll never watch your station again' and that sort of thing."

"What brought that on?"

"Jeffries. He posted somewhere in cyberspace that he might not be back as his skeleton character. That brought out the diehards. But we worked that all out and I thought things would be fine."

"You know what I find interesting, Jerry?"

"What?"

"Steve Dante was the one who really seemed to want this. But he lets Megan Wallace pretty much run things and he stays out."

"Megan is very capable."

"Oh, I didn't mean to imply she isn't up to the task. And I can understand that Steve may have felt that Megan would be able to deal with her father very directly. I just meant that for a passion project that could lead to the revival of the Saturday night creature feature, Steve didn't seem that involved."

Debusey looked at her curiously. "Just what are you suggesting?"

"I'm not really suggesting anything. I just think it's odd. But what do I know about television producers, right?"

A grin crept across Debusey's face. "When someone starts playing the self-deprecation game, I know they think they have something."

Tracy did her own grinning. "I don't know if there's anything to *have*, Jerry."

He chuckled. "Okay. You have Megan's confidence, and you now have my mine. You can talk to the staff as long as you understand they all have work to do."

"I understand. I'll try not to take up too much of their time. I don't want to be a bother."

"Of course, you don't." Debusey rose and extended his hand.

"Good luck to you," he said as they shook.

"Thank you. I'm sure we'll see each other again over the next couple of weeks or so."

"I'm sure we will too."

Bonkers was the first one to greet Tracy when she came through the mudroom door. He was followed by Nicole, and then by Peter, who was curious to where his sister was suddenly headed. The children soon returned to the playroom, with Bonkers in tow. Tracy kissed her mother, who was predictably hovering over a hot stove, and then started heading towards the bedroom to change. Brian followed his wife.

"Interesting day?" he started after a quick embrace.

"Oh, my yes."

"Do tell."

She turned and grinned. "Virgins and magic wands and monsters...oh my!" She resumed changing.

Brian blinked. "This is another one of your weird jokes, right?"

"No. It's the honest-to-goodness truth."

"You need to explain things then."

She turned around again as she pulled a sweatshirt over her head. "The victim bragged about his magic wand." She sat on the edge of the bed. "I guess he was well endowed or thought he was." Tracy grinned. "How do you stack up?"

"What?"

"Are you above average?"

"Am I what?"

"Is your wand bigger than the average man part?"

"Good Lord, Tracy..."

"Well guys are always bragging about their size, aren't they? How do they know? Who did the research and who volunteered to be part of the group?"

"The group?"

"Brian, if you're going to determine an average you have to get a group and take some measurements."

"You're nuts."

"Where are the results published? I've never really given it that much thought until now. Maybe we can look it up."

"Knock it off already."

"Have you measured yours, Brian?" Tracy started chuckling.

Brian shook his head. "You said something about virgins..."

"There's a guy at the studio creating some masks for the show. He refers to unworn masks as virgins."

Brian sat down next to her. "I see. Monster masks."

"Yup." She kissed him quickly on the lips. "Tom — that's the mask maker — said I could have one."

"Really?"

"Yes, but I turned him down."

"Why? That would have been cool."

"Well, I'm glad I did because it's very likely there will still be a Dr. Mort Itchin show."

"No kidding."

"Nope. But that's all I can say about that. Some of this is hush-hush."

"Ah." They grinned at each other.

"The kids are by themselves, Brian. I need to get downstairs and either watch them or help Mom."

"You're right."

"We can talk more after everyone else is in bed; do some research."

She continued smiling as she unlocked the bedroom door and headed down the steps. *Talking* wasn't exactly what Brian had on his mind, but the research part sounded interesting.

It happened. Tracy had been joking about it — at least she thought she had been joking. And then it happened.

"Grammaw!" Nicole said happily.

"What, dear child?" Violetta asked.

"Guess what!"

"What?"

"Daddy has a majuk wand!"

Brian looked up from his plate in horror. Tracy covered her mouth, trying not to laugh, her recent conversation with Brian still very much on her mind.

"He does?" Violetta asked.

"Yeah! He made baby Petah with it!"

Brian had stopped breathing. Tracy felt tears in her eyes, her body on the verge of a conniption. She was watching her mother. She was watching the realization of what Nicole was referring to spread across her mother's face. And then Tracy's mind started a play-by-play.

As the smile started leaving Violetta's face, announcer one said, *"Looks like Grandma here has realized what her granddaughter is talking about."*

Announcer two asked, *"What do you think she'll do in this situation?"*

"Hard to say really. Let's just watch and find out."

Violetta cleared her throat, picked the napkin up from her lap and wiped her mouth.

"What do you think she'll do now?"

"She's trying to figure that out, I'll bet."

"That's a bet I won't *take."*

They chuckled in unison.

"But you can't see it, Grammaw, or it won't be majuk anymore. Can I have more corn, pwease?"

"OH MY GOD LADIES AND GENTLEMEN! Nicole Shane wasn't finished!"

"I thought it couldn't GET any better. It just did!"

"Eat your dinner Nicole," Brian said sternly. "You can have more corn when you eat everything else."

"Uh-oh, we have some interference from the sidelines here."

"Dad sure does look uncomfortable, doesn't he?"

Nicole, confused, looked at her father. "Why you mad, Daddy?"

"I'm not mad, sweetheart. It's just that your dinner is getting cold."

"NICE recovery, Dad."

Violetta looked at her daughter, glared at her really. Perhaps instinctually Violetta had realized who supplied Nicole with her information. Tracy had the top of her red face covered with one hand. She finally dragged it down to reveal her teary eyes. Her mother was still glaring at her. And that just started Tracy laughing again.

"We have some *kind of standoff here, don't we?"*

"I don't think the Shane house has EVER been this quiet."

Violetta stood and threw her napkin on the chair. She headed towards the kitchen.

"I tell you folks. It's a good thing Violetta Brubaker didn't serve mashed potatoes this evening."

The last thought made Tracy lose all composure. She started laughing loudly as she stood.

Her children looked at her, and, as children sometimes do, they followed their mother's example. Soon Tracy, Nicole, and Peter were all laughing. Seeing his children laugh made Brian laugh too. Finally, Tracy headed towards the kitchen.

"Looks like we have a time out situation here folks. A strategic meeting is no doubt needed here."

Tracy found her mother standing by the kitchen table. "What's wrong Mom?" she asked, just before she started laughing again.

"This is NOT funny, young lady!"

"Keep your voice down, Mom."

"Look what you've done!"

"What are you talking about?"

Violetta started pointing at Tracy's chest. "You show them all over the house and look what's happened."

"Show what, my elbows?"

"OOH! Tracy instantly goes into her smartass routine."

"NO!"

"Well say what you mean then."

"Stop that!"

"They're called breasts, Mom. You have them too."

"OH, YOU DIFFICULT CHILD!"

"And Violetta goes for the old chestnut, folks!"

"Mom, easy. What Nicole said has nothing to do with my nursing. She had some questions about love, and mommies and daddies, and babies. I answered her as best as I could."

"You shouldn't have said *anything*. You should have told her you'd talk about it later."

"It's important Nicole learns *now* we can talk about these kinds of things. Unlike you, I want my daughter to feel comfortable talking to me about sex."

"OH!"

"You see! That's *exactly* what I'm talking about. That attitude makes sex sound like something evil."

Violetta folded her arms. "There's a time and place to talk about such things."

"And when is the time and where is the place, Mom?"

"You're being disrespectful."

"No, I'm trying to have an open conversation about a topic that makes parents uncomfortable. Just look how *you're* reacting here."

"She brought it up at the *dinner* table!"

"Don't say it, Tracy!'

"Resist the temptation, Tracy; it will only make things worse."

"Better brace yourself folks. This is about to get even uglier."

"…IF that's possible."

"You're confused, Mom. It gets brought *up* in the bedroom."

"AND SHE GOES FOR IT!"

"WHATA WOMAN!"

"OH!" Violetta cried out.

"Look, I'll tell Nicole not to talk about it anymore, okay? I'll say she should only talk about it with Mommy, Daddy, and Grandma, and no one else, or something like that."

Violetta shook her head. "If she's like you were, she won't listen."

"OH! Violetta now goes on the offensive!"

Tracy sighed. "Mom, I love you. You know that. But you were never the easiest person to talk to, especially about stuff like this. And the more you try to avoid talking about something, the more curious a child will become about it. I don't want Nicole to think sex is some nasty thing that she can't talk to me about. I want her to understand what it is, what it isn't, and under what circumstances it's appropriate. And to do that, I need to start now."

Violetta had her arms folded. "And what does Brian think about this? The way your father worried…"

"Worried?"

"That you'd…"

"…Sleep with a boy before I got married?"

"You wouldn't talk this way to him!"

"Actually Mom, I did. I was scared to death, but I asked him about what I had heard. He was nervous, but he was honest and open. And guess what? I didn't sleep around. Brian's the only man I've had sex with. I hope Nicole and Peter will save themselves for marriage. But I know with the way things are today that it's an uphill battle. And I have also decided that I won't lie to them. If they ask me if I had sex before I got married, I will tell them the truth. I won't be a hypocrite. Your grandchildren will be entering adulthood before you know it; before

I'm ready for them to. That's why this openness has to start now, not later when the secrecy seeds have already been planted and taken root. Am I getting through to you at all?"

Violetta sighed. She threw up her arms. "They're *your* kids, Tracy. *You'll* be the one who has to deal with them."

"I know that. I'm doing the best I can. I couldn't go to school for motherhood. You set a great example in most things. But I wish I could have talked to you about certain feelings I had, certain curiosities and desires. But that's all in the past now. I want Nicole to know she can talk to me about *anything*. I can't see how that can be a bad thing."

Violetta sighed. "We should finish dinner. The food's all cold now."

Tracy smiled, went over to her mother, and hugged her. "I love you Mom. It will be okay. I'll talk to Nicole."

"That's what started this whole thing in the first place."

Tracy chuckled. "Good one, Mom. My announcers approve."

"Your what?"

"Never mind. Let's go eat."

"I think that's it, ladies and gentlemen for the first of what promises to be many *discussions about that subject that keeps everyone talking and shutting up at the same time!"*

"Goodnight, everyone and thanks for joining us for another episode of THE TRACY GAMES*!"*

"I hope you're happy," Brian grumbled as he closed the bedroom door.

"Ecstatic." Tracy looked around the room. "Do we have a ruler in here? I have a research project in mind."

Brian either didn't hear her or chose to ignore her comment.

"What if Nicole starts talking to someone else about that?" Once again, a look of horror came over his face. He sat on his bed. "What if she wants to tell her Aunt Crystal about…? My sister would never let me hear the end of it."

"Relax, Brian. I told Nicole before tucking her in that she can talk only to certain people about your magic wand."

"Will you stop already?"

"I think that's first time I heard you tell me *that*."

"Very funny."

She sat down next to him. "It will be fine. Did you hear me and Mom in the kitchen?"

"No. I was too busy trying to keep Nicole's mind on other things."

"Nicole's still innocent. I didn't corrupt her."

"I know that."

Tracy took Brian's hand and placed it on a not so innocent part of her body. "But as for me…" She kissed his cheek.

"You are such a troublemaker sometimes."

"I know," she whispered. "I make other things too. Some things are better made when two people are involved."

He turned to look at her. "It's not fair you're so damned smart and beautiful."

"Life's not fair, honey. Why fight it? I want a magic show."

Why fight it indeed? But for the show to go on, certain things first had to come off. So, they both got to work on that right away.

CHAPTER 9

"Good *morning*, El!" Tracy said cheerfully as Elias Tanner, Sr. came into her office. She rose to embrace him.

"My, you're in a good mood," he told her.

She sighed. "Not really. This case is a challenge. But I'm very happy to see you."

"And I you. How's your mother?" When Tracy stared laughing, Tanner asked, "What is it?"

"I'll probably embarrass you."

"When has that ever stopped you before?"

She grinned at him. "You're absolutely right. El, when did you give El-J *the* talk?"

"The talk?"

"Yeah. Mommies and daddies and babies."

"Oh," Tanner nodded. "I guess when he was 10 or 11. Why? Your kids are nowhere near puberty."

"I know. But Nicole is already asking questions. She's very bright and curious."

"Just like her mother."

"Shucks. Anyway, she asked about babies, and I didn't want to brush her off. So, I kind of gave her an innocuous answer. And last night, the mommy eggs roosted."

Tanner started chuckling. "And your mother was there."

"Yes."

"Oh boy."

"I know for a fact that my dad was something of a...well, my mother's very beautiful herself."

"She is. You don't have to say any more."

Tracy grinned. "Starting to feel a smidge uncomfortable there, El?"

"Tracy, you will someday understand why discussions between parents and children about sex can be uncomfortable. Once your kids are capable of having kids, your relationship with them changes. And I imagine it's even more stressful with daughters."

Tracy looked at Tanner. "Did Dad ever talk about me with respect to this subject?"

"Of course, he did. He'd be so happy with how things worked out for you."

"Huh. That's funny."

"Why's that?"

"He scared away my boyfriends."

"Come on, Tracy."

"He did. He'd meet them, offer them a drink, and then tell them how many people he'd killed over the years."

Tanner laughed. "Now I know you're full of it."

Tracy chuckled. "Okay, so, I'm exaggerating. But he did look them over with those eyes of his; study them. Those eyes would suck all the enthusiasm from my date and leave him bereft of joy."

Tanner was shaking his head. "Look. You know how your father felt about you. So, of course, he wanted to make sure the man you were dating was a decent sort. But I'll tell you something. Your father believed that things shouldn't be easy all the time, especially in important areas. His thought was that when a man did fall in love with you, he would be willing to fight for you. He wouldn't run away because your father asked some uncomfortable questions. So, maybe he did try, as you say, to intimidate your date. But his intention was to make it clear he was still your father and your protector. If someone were going to try to take his place — as your protector anyway — he'd have to prove he could do it. You understand me?"

She sighed. "Sure, I understand. But jeez, El, Just because a guy wanted to go on a date with me didn't mean he was ready to marry me. I think Dad could have saved his scrutiny for the boy that dated me more than once."

Tanner nodded. "Perhaps you're right. But…Well, your father knew of the dangers that young women face. You understand me?"

"Of course. That's why he paid for Judo lessons and signed me up for the mace-of-the-month club."

Tanner laughed. "I hope you'll do the same for Nicole."

"You bet I will. She'll be so good that she'll be in tournaments."

"I'll just say one more thing on the subject then. Regardless of the issues you had with your parents, look at the kind of daughter they raised."

Tracy bowed her head. "You're going to make me cry, El."

"But I mean it, Tracy. You're one of the finest people I've ever known. I know we've had our differences sometimes, but I've always had the highest opinion of you. Lots of people do. So don't be too hard on your father and mother. They deserve *some* of the credit after all."

Tracy covered her eyes.

Tanner looked at her sympathetically. "Should I give you a few minutes?"

She shook her head, sniffed, and said, "I'm fine. I just wish Dad were still here."

"I do too."

After few additional moments of quiet Tracy said, "Let's talk about the Jeffries murder. What have you heard?"

"Nothing new. Cause of death was massive blood loss due to the stake. There were no signs of drugs or alcohol in his system from what I understand. So, he was stone cold sober during the whole ordeal."

"I saw the video."

"Right. He didn't leave a will, so his estate is supposed to go to his daughter since he wasn't married and had no other relatives. Now, here's the first interesting item."

"Oh?"

"No father was listed on the birth certificate. Carrie Wallace left that blank."

"That's understandable. Jeffries had taken off already, I think. I guess she didn't think he'd ever be back."

"Possibly. To establish paternity, they'll need to do a DNA test."

"Easy enough, although I don't see what the big deal about paternity is. Jeffries was supposedly a leech taking advantage of Carrie Wallace. What estate could he have?"

"How about $90,000?"

Tracy blinked. "What?"

"Interesting point number two. No one can tell right now where Jeffries got the $90K — in cash — they found in his safe deposit box."

Tracy was leaning forward. "Are you sure about this, El?"

"Yes."

Tracy pressed a fist against her lips. "I knew it."

"Knew what?"

"Knew there was something going on with that guy."

"Could be gambling winnings; could be money he brought with him when he came back east."

"Money he earned in Hollywood, huh?"

Tanner chuckled. "Hollywood. Right."

"Now what's so funny?" Tracy asked, mildly annoyed.

"Interesting point number three. Carl Jeffries *did* have a career of sorts."

"What kind of career?"

"He used the name George Carlsbad. Ever heard of him?"

"No. Should I have?"

He smiled. "You? No."

"Will you stop that? What's so funny?"

"Pornography."

"*What?*"

"For six years — from 1991 to 1997 — Carl Jeffries worked in the porn industry."

Tracy stared at him. "My God," she mumbled. "Maybe his wand was magic after all."

"What?"

"Nothing. So why did his, um, star fall?"

"Company he worked for closed its doors."

"Its zippers you mean," Tracy grinned.

"Cute. I'm not sure why he didn't just go to work for another company. But I suspect it's because he shacked up with one of his costars, a woman named Amber Hardshoe."

"Oh, good grief."

Tanner laughed. "Okay, her real name is Wendy Rakowski. She still lives in Los Angeles and she's still in the industry, as a producer-director."

"Hooray for her."

"Mm. I think he lived with her until he moved back here in 2002."

"And then became Carrie Wallace's roommate."

"Yes. I don't think he's had a job since he's been back."

Tracy did some quick math. "Okay, so, Jeffries is about 45 or so when he moves back. And Carrie supports him in all kinds of ways."

"That's how it looks."

"I don't see why he'd want to move in with Carrie if he had all that money. He must have gotten that after he moved back."

"It's possible, of course, he had some under-the-table thing going on. That could be where he got the money."

"I know you said he was sober when he was killed. But did Jeffries have a history with drugs maybe?"

"Not that I found. He had no criminal record, neither in Maryland nor California. Of course, maybe he just never got caught. But if you're thinking he was dealing drugs or something, there've been no indications of that."

Tracy shook her head. "This is weird. I really do need to have a sit-down with Carrie Wallace now."

"I know the police have talked to her. Not sure what she told them though."

"I'll ask her when I see her."

"I can do interviews, too, remember."

Tracy smiled. "I've already asked Megan to set something up for me."

"All right."

"I wonder who at WMFT knows about Jeffries career. I wonder if Carrie knows."

"Would you like to look over his filmography?"

Tracy cleared her throat. "No, thank you. I am still innocent in *some* things. I'd like to keep it that way if I can help it."

"Want me to hop on a plane and go see Amber Hardshoe?"

Tracy frowned. "We'll postpone any working vacations for now, El."

Tanner chuckled. "You're the boss."

"Mm. Do you know if Jeffries had AIDS or something; tested positive for HIV maybe?"

"I don't think so."

"I know that people in that business get tested regularly, especially if they're not wearing protection."

"Not so innocent after all, it would seem."

"Oh, you're cute. I know that Jeffries was flirting with some of the female staff at the station. If he were infected and someone found out, that could be a reason to kill him. I mean if he was sick, he didn't have so much a magic wand as he had a lethal weapon."

Tanner snorted. "I guess you or I should talk to those female staff members then."

"Possibly. Okay, anything else about Jeffries?"

"No, not right now."

"How about the others on your list?"

"Megan Wallace was born December 28, 1988. She went to work for WMFT in September 2010; started as a production assistant and is now one of the station's producers of local programming; single with no criminal record. Andrew Honeywell moved from North Carolina in 2014 and started at the station in October of 2014. He's 36 and divorced. No criminal record. Lawrence Peachtree has been with the station since 1983; widower with no criminal record."

"Widower? What happened to his wife?"

Tanner sighed. "Suicide."

Tracy covered her mouth. "Oh no…"

"She became severely depressed after losing her baby — a son — who died when she was seven months along."

"Oh, El…"

"I know. She had an emergency C-section but…Anyway, she overdosed on sleeping pills a few months later. Peachtree never remarried."

"He has no one?"

"A younger sister who lives in Chicago, where he's originally from."

"When did this all happen?"

"1986. They'd been married just over a year."

Tracy shook her head. "I feel like such a jerk."

"Huh?"

"I had the presumption to give him advice. I had no idea what he was dealing with. I should have kept my big mouth shut."

Tanner sighed. "Not something he'd bring up in casual conversation."

"Yeah. I wonder if Carl Jeffries was an ass to him about the whole thing. I wonder if Jeffries insulted Larry or made wisecracks."

"And all these years later Peachtree killed him over it?"

"I don't know. Peachtree is wound pretty tight. If Jeffries came back and started in on him again, maybe Larry lost it. Everyone else there — except for Megan — just kind of laughed Jeffries off. Larry Peachtree doesn't laugh *anything* off."

"I know the type, sure."

"Not sure why he'd frame Richard though. Can you find out if Larry went to any counseling after his wife died? Maybe he saw a psychiatrist or something."

"I can try. But that kind of thing is confidential and even if I couldn't find anything it wouldn't mean he didn't seek help."

"I understand. Okay, El, who's next?"

"Next we have Edmund Topolski. 25; been with the station for three years; won a short-film award while in college."

"That's cool."

"In fact, he and Jeffries share the same alma mater."

"They attended the same college?"

"Yes. But obviously not during the same time."

"Of course not."

Tanner nodded. "Like the others, no criminal record."

"Does *anybody* in this case have a criminal record?"

"Thomas Kramer does."

"He does?"

"DUI conviction; lost his license for a while. But that all happened years ago. Last five years he's kept clean. He has his own firm — Kramer's Kreeps and Kreatures. It's really just him though. He actually worked in the movies for a while."

"Really?"

"Some low-budget outfit. The company is no longer in business; that folded in 2014. In 2015 he went to work for Stickler Amusements — they own several theme parks. I guess somebody really liked the work he did on the Halloween attractions because in 2017 he went to work for a local film company that shot low-budget digital movies that they then sold to streaming services. In 2018 *that* company closed and he started his own company. Does pretty well for himself it seems."

"He worked in Hollywood?"

"I know what you're thinking. But Kramer didn't start his Hollywood gig until 2005; that's *after* Jeffries had moved back east."

"Is he a bachelor too?"

"Has a live-in girlfriend. She's lead singer in a local rock band called Shame Machine."

"No kidding. I wonder if and where they were playing last Saturday."

Tanner smiled. "Eight o'clock stage time at *April May's Tunes*. That's a medium-sized bar in Essex."

Tracy sighed. "You know, except for Larry Peachtree, I didn't ask anyone I talked to yesterday where they went after they left Saturday. I was afraid how that would come across. I wanted to save such a question for someone who seemed a likely candidate. I'm not sure I have one though."

"Sorry."

"I really would like to know if Tom went to see his girlfriend sing on Saturday."

"You can find a way to ask him, I bet."

"Mm. Who else you got there, El?"

"Corey Firth aka Corky. He's 41 and married with a five-year-old son; been nighttime and Saturday security at Channel 42 since 2015. No criminal record."

"Gun owner?"

"Yes. But Jeffries wasn't shot."

"I realize that. But how do you think the killer convinced Jeffries to get into the coffin? Asked him to? He either tricked Jeffries or threatened him."

"Pointed a gun at him, maybe."

"That's what I'm thinking."

Tanner looked back at his notes. "Carrie Wallace is now working for the Baltimore County school system as a system coordinator."

"That can't pay much."

"It doesn't; less than $20 an hour."

"Mm."

"She had Megan when she was 23. She's 54 now. Has a one-bedroom apartment in the county."

"…Which she until recently shared with Carl Jeffries."

"Yes."

"Do you know if he was on the lease?"

"I don't, but I'd be surprised if he were."

"Then that was a no-no having him there, right?"

"Most leases would forbid such an arrangement, yes."

Tracy shook her head. "Something weird about that relationship, El."

"I think you said that already."

She sighed. "That $90,000…did your source say if it consisted of tens and twenties, or anything else?"

"No. And it could be more than 90. It was just a ballpark figure."

"I doubt he was getting it from Carrie Wallace. He must have had some side business that he was using to build a nest egg. Maybe his ultimate goal was to leave Carrie's nest."

"Hard to say."

Tracy folded her arms and leaned back in her chair. Then she grinned. "El, if Carrie was at work during the day, her apartment would be empty."

"Except for Jeffries."

"Exactly. He'd have the place to himself."

Tanner narrowed his eyes. "What are you thinking?"

"Impure thoughts."

"Come again."

"He had a gift to share with the women of the world, El. What if that's exactly what he was doing."

Tanner snorted. "A male prostitute?"

"Why not?"

"How do you come up with this stuff?"

Tracy frowned. "The guy was an over-confident cad and former porn star who shacked up with at least two women that we know of. Each time he seemingly had no source of income. But what if he did? Maybe he was paying his share of the rent and food and all of that."

"Just because he was a porn star doesn't mean he…Oh never mind."

"I'm just saying that it's possible, okay. I happen to know that the porn industry has been suffering for years now and that some stars have started escorting on the side."

Tanner blinked. "How could you possibly know something like that?"

Tracy looked at her lap. "Not all my clients are angels. I had a client who was assaulted by one of her dates and she needed help. I may not personally condone such a career choice, but no one has the right to assault another person. And that's all I'm going to say on that matter."

Tanner twisted his lips. "All right. I'll see if any of my friends in vice can help me."

"Supreme!"

He smiled. He started looking through his notes. "I guess that's it. I'll pull all of this together into something more formal and email it to you."

"Oh, what about Steve Dante the producer? I know he's been with the station for six years and won some awards. But that's about it."

"Sorry. I must have skipped over him. Let me see here…"

"No problem."

"All right: here he is. Steven Dante: 56 years old; married to his wife Bethany for 23 years; two grown sons who live in New York."

"New York?"

"Yeah. Dante was born in Maryland but moved to New York in 1991. He took a job with a station there as an assistant producer and moved his way up to station manager. He moved back here in 2013 where he took the job with WMFT — retook actually."

"Retook?"

"He worked at WMFT from 1986 to 1991."

Tracy leaned forward. "Wait a minute. Something's off."

"Sorry?"

"When I talked to Steve, he made it seem like he had been working there only six years. He even said something about changes to the station happening long before he got there. But he was actually there very soon after the changes in ownership. He misled me."

"Why would he do that?"

"I don't know. But since I have no doubt that *your* facts are correct, I have to think he had a reason. Plus, that means he was there while both Richard George and Carl Jeffries were employees. And it was *Dante's* idea for this reunion. He wanted Jeffries here even though he must have witnessed first-hand how he was."

Tanner started nodding. "He wanted to make it seem like he didn't know Jeffries at all."

"It appears that way, doesn't it?"

"But if you're suggesting that Steve Dante was planning a murder, then he certainly would have foreseen his own resume being reviewed. He would have known his working there in the eighties would be found out. So, what purpose would it serve to lie? Are you sure you just didn't mishear him or misunderstand him maybe?" Tanner saw Tracy glaring at him. "Okay. You're sure. Forget what I asked."

"I have a pretty good memory, El. I'm sure."

"I got it."

Tracy stood up. "I told Brian that place was like a soap opera. I even predicted a murder, although I was only being melodramatic. But it turned out I was right."

"Obviously."

"I suddenly have the feeling that this reunion may have been motivated by more than just nostalgia and potential ratings."

Tanner stood up. "Somebody got Jeffries involved knowing how things would go."

She looked at him. "Yes. Richard George hated him. Megan hated him, and so then too did Andy Honeywell probably. Peachtree didn't care for him, and it wouldn't surprise me if Jeffries were insensitive to Peachtree's personal tragedies. And maybe there's more to find."

"Lots of hatred, I'll give you that."

Tracy sighed. "I think there was a secret director here, El. I think somebody wrote, cast, and directed a murder."

"But Jeffries called out *Richard's* name, Tracy."

"Yes, El. I haven't forgotten that. Some kind of movie magic, I think. Or rather, TV magic. Maybe our killer also handled the special effects."

"Any ideas as to who this creative genius might be?"

She shook her head. "Not yet. But I'm going to make my own sequel. And in Tracy Brubaker Shane stories, the good guys and gals *always* win."

CHAPTER 10

"You look great," Brian smiled. Tracy was wearing a sleeveless black evening gown and matching heels — although the shoes were hard to see since the dress mostly covered them.

"It was this or sweats," Tracy mumbled as she continued putting on her earrings.

"Don't be like that," Brian said as he placed his hands on her bare shoulders.

She turned. "Look Brian, if Ben starts in with his usual crap, I want you to pull him aside and say something. If you don't, I'm going to suddenly have gastrointestinal issues and excuse myself for the evening."

He sighed. "I think you're being too sensitive. He's just…Ben."

Her husband's dismissal of her feelings infuriated her, and she unleashed.

"Listen Brian! I am your *wife*! I am the mother of your children! What *should* matter to you here is how *I* feel, *not* Ben. I am doing this for you because I love you and I know you're feeling a little lonely — missing your buddies. But that doesn't mean you can just blow off how *I* feel about this. Do you understand that, Brian?"

Brian sighed. "I'm sorry; I am. I promise you if he says or does something that you don't like, I'll say something to him right away. You just let me know somehow."

"Believe me, you'll know."

She stormed out of the bedroom, still angry that she had to explain something to her husband that should have been obvious.

"You so pretty Mommy," Nicole said as Tracy entered her bedroom.

Tracy smiled. "Thank you, sweetheart. Now, you need to be a good girl for me and stay in bed. Mommy and Daddy will be downstairs with some grownups. Can you stay in bed for me, please?"

"What if I thirsty?"

"I filled your water cup for you. And you have Bonkers to keep you company."

Hearing his name, the pooch raised his head from his carpet and started wagging his tail. Nicole smiled at the sight.

"Poor Baby Petah," Nicole said. "He alone."

"Peter's okay, honey."

"He need his own Bonkahs."

"One Bonkers is enough."

Hearing his name again, the hound got on all fours and came over to Tracy. She grinned and petted his head gently.

"Good night, boy." Tracy stood up. "You two behave in here. No Broadway shows."

Tracy started moving towards the door. Human and canine eyes watched her.

"I love you," Tracy told Nicole as she closed the door.

The smile immediately left Tracy's face. Now she had to send someone else to bed — or at least upstairs.

Tracy found her mother in the kitchen. "Mom, I've got this."

"I can help."

"I know that; I appreciate everything you've done. But you can go relax. It's almost 9:00 p.m. and Brian's friends will be here soon."

"It's not good to eat this late."

"Brian made it this late so the kids would be in bed. This won't become a habit. I can promise you that."

"I'll help serve."

"Mom! It's fine. I can handle it."

"You'll get that nice dress messy."

Tracy rolled her eyes. "*Goodnight*, Mom. I love you."

Tracy put an arm around her mother's shoulders and started leading her out of the kitchen. Violetta resisted at first, but eventually started moving.

"You better not destroy my kitchen," Violetta said with total seriousness.

"I wouldn't *dream* of it," her daughter responded, both now having reached the stairway.

Tracy kissed her mother quickly on the cheek and watched as the elder Brubaker started ascending. Tracy waited until she heard her mother's door close. She chuckled as she shook her head. Next, she moved towards the formal dining area of the home. Brian looked up as his wife entered.

"The table is all set. I have carafes of water and tea here."

Tracy smiled. "It all looks great, honey."

She had called him "honey." He breathed a sigh of relief and came over to her.

"You're not mad at me anymore?"

She smirked. "No. But I *am* serious about what I said."

"I know. I'll keep my promise to you."

"Okay." She kissed him gently.

"You look incredible," he whispered.

She said nothing in return. Instead, she turned and exited the room, shaking her hips as she did so. She wanted to turn her head to see his reaction. But she decided instead to start setting out the appetizers.

The doorbell rang at 9:08 p.m. Tracy's stomach started crocheting a knot sweater. Brian moved towards the doorway. Tracy stood up from the sofa and moved towards her husband as he opened the door.

"Hey buddy!" Ben Falcone said as the friends hugged. Lisa Falcone and Tracy did the same thing.

"Hey amigo!" Tracy said. Lisa started chuckling.

"Tracy!" Ben said.

Tracy forced a smile as he embraced her. She tried to position her back so her breasts wouldn't make contact with her visitor's chest. But he just pulled her closer.

She pulled away. "Hi Ben," she said. "I have to go check on the food." Tracy turned and hurried towards the kitchen.

"Let me take your coats," Brian offered, and then quickly hanged in the hallway closet what had been turned over to him.

"Real nice-looking place," Ben said.

"Find it okay?"

"Oh yeah; no problem."

"Where are those adorable children of yours?" Lisa asked.

"Upstairs, presumably asleep, as is my mother-in-law."

"Oh," Lisa said, sounding disappointed. "I was hoping to see them in person. I've only seen pictures."

"We can arrange that another day," Brian said.

"Great!"

"Can I get you something to drink?"

"What do you got?" Ben asked.

"Water, tea, and all kinds of soda. We can also make some coffee if you want."

"Give me something with sugar and caffeine," Ben answered.

Brian nodded. "How about you Lisa?"

"Water is fine for now. Maybe some coffee after dinner would be nice."

"You got it; be right back. Have a seat on the sofa. Tracy made some spinach-artichoke dip, and it should still be warm."

"Oh!" Lisa exclaimed. "I *have* to try some."

She moved towards the living room. Brian, to the kitchen.

"Are you okay?" Brian said as he entered.

"As long as he doesn't touch me the rest of the night."

Brian frowned. "He just gave you a hug. You're always hugging people."

"Never mind. Did you ask what they wanted to drink?"

"That's the other reason I'm here."

Brian opened the refrigerator door, grabbed a can of Coke and bottle of water, and then moved towards his wife.

"Come join us; Lisa's sampling your dip."

She smiled. "Okay, but you sit next to me on the couch."

"Of course."

They kissed quickly and went to join their guests.

"This is *so* good, Tracy," Lisa Falcone enthused.

"Thank you," Tracy acknowledged as she and Brian sat on the loveseat. It ran perpendicular to where the Falcones were sitting. "Do you guys want glasses for your drinks?"

"No," Ben told her. "I prefer drinking from the can."

"Your house is so pretty," Lisa told Tracy. "And I just LOVE what you did with the front lawn."

Tracy looked at Brian. "Hear that, Brian?"

"Yeah, I heard."

Tracy looked back at Lisa and said, "You'll have to come over during the day sometime and I'll give you the tour."

"We can see the downstairs though, right?" Ben asked. "Brian was telling me about his home theater setup; sounds incredible."

Tracy grinned. "That's one word for it." Everyone chuckled.

"How are your kids doing?" Ben continued.

"They're great," Brian smiled.

"I'm so jealous," Lisa said.

Tracy looked at her. The smile Lisa was donning seemed artificial.

"You don't have time for kids, Lisa," Ben opined. "You're way too busy with everything else you got going on."

"I could *make* the time, Ben."

Tracy gulped. "Are you still traveling a lot for your job?" she asked Lisa.

"Yes. But it's not as much as it used to be. More and more people are becoming comfortable with video meetings and that kind of thing. But with sales, face-to-face is pretty important."

"And the more clients she gets the more work they give her!" Ben said proudly. "Soon, I can quit *my* job and stay at home like you, Brian." Ben started laughing. "I'd love that."

"Brian takes care of the kids," Tracy said. "His job is more important than mine."

"Hey, I didn't mean nothing," Ben responded.

Brian twisted his lips. "Tracy's mother makes my life a lot easier than it would be without her here."

Ben started laughing again. "You're a saint, Brian. I don't know how you can live with your mother-in-law."

"HEY!" Lisa shouted. "My parents are nothing but kind to you."

"I didn't mean nothing," Ben said.

He took swig from his soda can, and then shoved a cracker piled with dip into his mouth. Lisa handed him a cocktail napkin.

"Thanks, babe," he told her.

"I love your dress," Lisa said.

"Thanks."

"You look so good; I can't believe you've had two babies. I bet I'd blow up like a balloon."

Tracy chuckled. "People are different. You just never know."

Tracy turned to see Ben looking at her, or rather, just above her mid-section. She gulped.

Ben looked at Brian. "I bet you're really going to miss it when she stops nursing, 'ey buddy?"

Brian looked at his friend, confused. "Huh?"

"Things will go back down to normal."

Brian pursed his lips. "Ben, I don't think—"

"Hey, I didn't mean nothing. Tracy always filled out a dress nicely."

That didn't take long. Tracy looked at Brian and he looked back at her. Ben helped himself to another appetizer.

"Ben," Brian said while standing up. "Can you help me with something in the kitchen?"

"Sure, pal. No problem."

Brian quickly exited the living room. Ben Falcone shoved another dip-topped cracker into his mouth before following.

Tracy looked at the remaining guest. "Are you okay, Lisa?"

"What? Oh, sure." Lisa sighed. "I'm sorry about Ben. He just speaks his mind sometimes."

"I can tell."

"He really doesn't mean anything though."

"So, he keeps saying. You don't mind if he makes comments about another woman's body?"

"Don't all men?"

"Not out loud like that. A person can't help if they have a certain reaction to something, but they *can* control how they handle it."

Lisa snorted. "Not everyone; some people have medical conditions that cause them to blurt stuff out."

"Are you saying Ben has a medical condition?"

"Well…No."

"Mm. Does he make comments about all of your friends?"

"Let's not talk about this anymore, okay?"

"Okay; I'm sorry."

"Me too."

"Ben, I need to talk to you about something and I need you to listen to me," Brian began.

"Sure, buddy. Anything you need."

"Good. I need you to stop making comments about Tracy's body."

"What?"

"Don't make any comments or innuendos about my wife's body."

Ben blinked. "What are you talking about?"

"Jesus, Ben. Her breasts."

"Oh! That! I didn't mean nothing by it."

"I understand that. But Tracy's conservative about some things and she doesn't like anyone to make the kinds of comments you're making. It makes her uncomfortable and Tracy's not one to hold back."

"Hey, I'm just a guy, Brian. No one told her to wear that dress she's wearing."

Brian narrowed his eyes slightly. "Wait, you just didn't suggest what I think you did, did you?"

"Relax. I just meant that she looks really great in that dress."

"Then just say, 'You look nice, Tracy' and leave it at that."

Falcone shook his head. "I don't know what the big deal is. We're all friends."

"The big deal, Ben, is that it makes Tracy uncomfortable. So, I'm asking you, as my friend, to please not make those kinds of comments anymore. Okay?"

Ben Falcone folded his arms. "What? I'm supposed to change who I am anytime I'm around that wife of yours? Maybe she should lighten up a little, or at least stop wearing clothes like that."

Brian couldn't believe it. Why was this so difficult for Ben to understand?

"Just please respect my wife and her wishes. That's all I'm asking. Would you want me making comments about Lisa? Your wife is a very attractive woman."

"I know that."

"Would you want someone saying something about her body?"

Falcone smiled. "They can look and say all they want buddy. She ain't going home with *them*."

Brian sighed. "Maybe you should ask Lisa if she feels the same way about it."

"Man," Ben said, shaking his head. "You used to be so much fun."

"What the hell are you talking about?"

"You, man. What happened to you?"

"Nothing."

"You were so much fun to hang out with."

"We had some good times, sure."

"Then you hooked up with Tracy again…"

"Don't go there, Ben. She's made me very happy."

"Yeah, I can tell how freakin' *happy* you are," Falcone said sarcastically.

"You're the cause of my demeanor right now, *not* Tracy."

"Yeah. Little miss perfect."

"What the hell is wrong with you, man?"

"You. You marry that high and mighty Tracy and suddenly you're a stuck-up douche. I wonder what that wife of yours would say if I told her some of the things *you* used to call out. You didn't hold back what *you* were thinking."

Brian felt the anger taking hold of him. "You're talking about when I was out with you and the guys drinking, right? I shouldn't have said those things; I was drunk."

"YEAH, you were! Man, we had some great times though, didn't we? And if some gorgeous hottie came in, we'd *all* let her know it. Remember that?"

"I guess."

"Tracy knows all about that?"

"Some of it."

"Uh-huh. So, you get why I find you asking me this favor so damned funny, don't you?"

"Favor?"

"Whatever."

"My drinking days are behind me. Tracy knows that."

"Well, that's too bad for you. I'm sorry you ended up with such an ice princess. I thought Tracy was always fun to hang out with."

"She *is* fun to hang out with, and she's *not* an 'ice princess.' But all of that is none of you damned business."

"You didn't used to be like this, man. You used to know how to have a good time and kid around. All I'm doing is kidding around."

Brian stared nodding. He had by now taken a good look at Ben Falcone's eyes.

"How much have you had?"

"What?"

"How many did you have before coming here?"

"Screw *you*, man! That's none of *your* damned business!"

Brian shook his head. "So, I take it you refuse to honor my request."

"I am who I am, buddy. It's not fair you want me to be someone I'm not."

"I can't believe you won't do this for me. You say you're my friend, but you won't do this for me."

"Your wife loves you. It's not like she'd leave you or anything over some comments *I* make. She should just suck it up."

At this point Brian Shane wanted to hit Ben Falcone; hit him hard. This should have been such a simple thing and now it had turned into something ugly. Brian breathed in deeply.

"I didn't want to have to put it this way. But here it is. If you can't do what I'm asking you to do, then you have to leave."

"You're shitting me!"

"No. You've turned this into a 'me or her' situation. Guess who's going to lose 100 percent of the time?"

Ben Falcone stared at Brian in disbelief. He shook his head.

"I feel really sorry for you, man."

"Don't," Brian assured him. "I don't need anyone's sympathy."

Falcone glared at Brian, and then abruptly turned and exited the kitchen.

"COME ON, LISA!" Ben shouted as he rejoined the women. Lisa and Tracy stood up.

"Ben, what's wrong?"

"*We're* not wanted here!"

"Actually, Ben," Brian said while taking his place next to Tracy, "Lisa's welcome to stay."

Lisa looked at Brian. "Brian, what's going on?"

"I'm sure Ben will give you his version on the way home."

Lisa looked at Ben and then at Tracy. Brian had by now started towards the closet to retrieve coats.

"Lisa," Tracy said, "you call me later if you need to. I'll talk to Brian." Tracy touched Lisa's shoulder.

"COME ON, LISA!" Ben shouted. He was now standing in the open doorway.

Lisa, tearfully, looked at Tracy. And then she left. Her husband didn't even give her time to put on her coat.

After Brian closed and locked the door, he remained standing. He looked out the door's side window, watching the couple move towards their car.

"I thought so."

Tracy, who was still standing by the loveseat, asked, "Thought what?"

"Lisa's driving." He put his hands on his hips and turned.

"Oh..." was all Tracy said in response.

"I just can't believe it."

"I'm sorry, Brian. I didn't mean for things to turn out like this. I really didn't."

She wasn't sure if he was mad at her, so she remained where she was.

Brian shook his head. "It's not your fault." He started chuckling. "I *am* getting tired of you being right all the damned time, though."

"Sorry."

"Uh-huh. Did you realize he was drunk too?"

"Um...I guess. I smelled it when he hugged me."

"Great."

Tracy started moving towards Brian. "I'm sure it will be okay."

"Well, if you say it will be I guess it will be."

They were grinning at each other, and soon were embracing.

She said, "We still have all this food to eat."

"Then let's eat."

And so, they ate.

Later in the bedroom as they changed into much more comfortable attire, Brian sat on the bed, looking dejected.

"Now I know a little how you felt."

"What?"

"Come on, Tracy. Don't play dumb. You know what I mean."

She sat down next to him. "I don't, really."

"Can't you see the parallel here? You made a simple request of me once, and I stormed out of your life for 10 years. And tonight..."

Tracy shook her head. "You're not being fair to yourself, Brian — unless you asked him to stop drinking when you two were in the kitchen."

"No, I didn't go *that* far."

"Then, it's not the same. I wouldn't describe what I asked you as simple."

"I did say 'a little;' I know it's not exactly the same."

Tracy embraced him and kissed his cheek. "Don't do this, Brian."

"10 years, Tracy…10 years we didn't have because of me." "Don't, baby. Don't…"

He stood up. "I can't help it sometimes. I will NEVER understand why I did what I did."

She rose and stood in front of him, placing her hands on his cheeks. "You weren't yourself. Just like Ben, you had been drinking before you came over."

"Stop making excuses for me."

"Not excuses, baby. Explanations."

"Whatever."

"Brian, please stop. We're together now and we should just be happy about that. We don't know what may have happened in those 10 years. We really don't. We never will. We could have been out one night together and got run over by elephants or something. Maybe our separation saved our lives."

"Funny."

"I'm not trying to be funny. My point is you should try to stop thinking about it."

"…Easier said than done sometimes."

"Brian, I love you." She kissed him. "And I am sorry this all happened."

Brian grinned. "Don't be sorry."

"But I am."

"And I say don't be. Tracy, thanks to tonight, whatever nostalgia I felt about the good old drinking days is gone; vanished. I suddenly am quite content to be where I am."

She couldn't help but smile. "Vanished huh?"

"Completely."

"Mm. You're quite the magician, Brian."

She sat down on the bed. Then she covered her mouth, giggling.

"What's so funny?" he asked as he sat next to her.

"Well, if we never lost those 10 years, Nicole would be almost thirteen now."

"Not necessarily."

She was still grinning. "I realize that. But that's the thought I had. And then I was thinking how much more interested she might be in… magic wands."

"Hey!" Brian said, which only made Tracy laugh out loud. "Don't be saying stuff like that. I'm in no hurry for that to happen, especially since she's probably going to be as beautiful as her mother." He sat down next to her.

When she stopped laughing, she kissed him again. "You're a good man, Brian Shane."

"I'm not."

"You are. You had some problems, but you faced them. I couldn't love any other man the way I love you and I couldn't imagine not having you in my life. And I'm so glad you're the father of my babies. So, you're just going to have to take my word for it when I say you're a good man. You did say earlier that I'm right all the time, didn't you?"

He looked at her. "I did."

"Then there's no disagreement."

He kissed her. Yes, she was right. If she thought of him as a good man — worthy of her and her love — then it must be so. What *she* thought was what mattered to him most, given the high opinion he had of her. Maybe he *was* good, if flawed.

The couple was now in their usual post coital position. Tracy had her head on Brian's bare chest, and he was looking up at the ceiling while running the fingers of his right hand through her hair. She kissed him a few times before she asked, "Brian, if Ben were to call tomorrow to apologize, what would you do?"

He sighed. "I know what the *right* answer is."

"Uh-huh. Would you give the right answer?"

"I'd have to; I'd be a hypocrite if I didn't."

"For what it's worth, I'd be willing to give him another chance too."

He kissed the top of her head. "Thanks, love. But I doubt he'll call."

"I think he will."

"Why?"

"Lisa. Lisa will understand what happened and want to apologize even though she's not the one who should be apologizing. She'll try and get Ben to call you. If he refuses, she will."

"I like Lisa."

"Me too."

Brian gulped. "You think that could have been you."

"What?"

"You think if you never gave me the ultimatum and just kept quiet, you could be just like Lisa. I could see what was going on."

"Oh."

"Ignoring his behavior or making excuses for him."

"Yes; I've been there."

"I'm sorry."

"I didn't mean it like that. I just meant I understood what was going on with her. It can't be easy for her."

"I know."

"It was obvious she wants a family."

"Yes, that *was* obvious."

"Not to Ben apparently; he just dismissed it."

"And we both know why."

"That makes me so mad, Brian, when I see a person being dismissive of what is obviously important to someone else. I see it a lot at negotiation and settlement conferences. Somebody wants something and somebody else starts telling them they shouldn't. I have to bite my tongue."

"You had to do a bit of that tonight, I bet."

"Once I bit my lip too hard and I really started bleeding. I'm not making that up."

"I can see that happening."

Tracy grinned as she repositioned herself, so she was on top of her husband. She looked into his eyes.

"You might be right, Brian. I may look at Lisa as version of me if I made different decisions. Maybe…maybe we can help."

"What?"

"I want to reach out to Lisa. I want to help her."

"I don't know about that. Besides, would she really want her kid to have Ben as a father?"

"We're proof of how things can change for the better. We should try to help other people who are in the position we once were in. At least we should offer. If we get turned down, then okay. But I like Lisa; and Ben is your friend — at least he used to be. You see good things in him, right?"

"I guess."

"Well, if your friend needs help, you should offer to help him. If he refuses, then at least you tried. Right?"

Brian sighed. "My 'friend' might not like any meddling. He kind of threatened me."

"Threatened you? You mean he said he'd kick your butt or something?"

"No, more like he'd tell you how I used to be at the bars sometimes."

"What does that mean?"

"Making comments like Ben did, only to total strangers — and probably more offensive ones."

"Oh."

"It was just talk of course. But it was still wrong, and I wish I could change it."

Tracy smiled. "You've put all that behind you. Ben hasn't yet. Did you guys say the things you said at the bar when you were sober?"

"No."

"See?"

Brian chuckled. "I see."

"Ben can say what he wants to say to me if you think that will help."

"What are you talking about?"

"I'm saying I can take it, Brian. The only reason a person would want to tell a man's wife what that man used to say to women at a bar is to hurt her; to create a problem. And I'm saying there is no problem. The past is the past and we have a life together now. Maybe if he saw how his hurtful words *weren't* having their desired effect, he'd wise up a bit."

"He'd never say that stuff sober. And I don't want him coming over here drunk trying to pick a fight. There is no good that will come of it."

"Mm. You're right, honey. I wouldn't want the kids to hear or see any of that."

Brian sighed. "The kids…"

"What does *that* mean?"

"I'm suddenly thinking of Nicole and what she'll have to deal with — the jerks like me, I mean."

"*Former* jerk, you mean."

"Right," Brian chuckled.

"Maybe together we can help reform another jerk."

He smiled. "Isn't being a lawyer enough for you? Why do you have to play fairy godmother sometimes?"

"Oh, you're cute." She kissed his nose. "I just want people I like to be happy. And if I can help, I want to help. I want to help Lisa."

"I wish you had a wand of your own. You could just wave it and take care of things from a distance."

Tracy grinned. "Where's the fun in *that*? Being close is much more rewarding. Wouldn't you agree?" She stared kissing him.

He would agree. He'd be a fool not to, given that his wife was always right.

CHAPTER 11

While Brian Shane thought his wife to be seldom, if ever, in the wrong, Tracy Brubaker Shane thought her secretary Rebecca Dietz was a much wiser woman. Tracy had known Rebecca for almost 10 years now. The assistant's one and only child had finished school and now had her own apartment, and Tracy planned to ask Rebecca any and all questions about raising a daughter. Rebecca knew every aspect of the firm, every client. She also knew Tracy better than anyone outside Tracy's immediate family. They had had many personal talks throughout the years. Monday morning, they had another one.

"So, did Lisa or Ben call yesterday?" Rebecca asked.

"Lisa did. Early. Ben was still asleep. Basically, he got trashed when they got home Saturday night. He was still sleeping it off."

Rebecca shook her head. "How did Lisa seem?"

"Apologetic, of course, and then she made excuses for him: job stress, financial stress, life stress…"

"*Life stress?*"

"Okay, that was my embellishment. But you see what I mean."

"Sure. Classic behavior on your friend's part."

"Lisa said Ben doesn't drink each and every night. It's usually just the weekends. The thing is his weekends are from Thursday to Sunday."

"In theory I would support such a weekend."

Tracy chuckled. "Anyway, I did finally get Lisa to admit she knows Ben has a problem. But every time she brings it up to him, he just dismisses it. And she does want a family but is scared to get pregnant

144

with the way things are. I asked what I could do to help, and she didn't really answer me. So, I just kind of let her vent and told her she could call me anytime."

Rebecca nodded. "Do you know if this Ben is abusive?"

"Lisa insists he isn't. I didn't notice any bruising or anything like that on her. He may tell her to leave him alone or to go away, but she swears he's never hurt her or even threatened to hurt her. And he wasn't mean to her on Saturday."

"That's a relief."

"She really loves him, Beck. I can tell. But their situation is no good. If Lisa *were* to get pregnant…" Tracy shook her head.

"I hear you. Where did you leave things?"

"I was hoping Ben would call. She said she wanted him to and apologize to me and Brian. I don't know if they had a conversation or not."

"Mm. Are you thinking of calling her again maybe?"

"I am. Brian thinks I should give it a few days. If I start calling too often Lisa may get annoyed with me. That's what Brian thinks anyway. He might be right. I guess there's a fine line between trying to be helpful and actually being bothersome."

"I guess since he's not hitting her, you could wait a few days. On the other hand, if too much time passes, she may lose that fire you've probably lit by reaching out to her. By keeping in touch with her you can keep the fire burning, so to speak."

"Mm. I see your point."

"But I don't know these people; you don't either, really. It's hard to really predict how something like this will turn out. You have wonderful intentions, Tracy. But you need to be careful."

"Ben might get nasty, you mean."

"He could. Or, in a few days, he may call Brian and ask for his help. He certainly knows how things worked out for Brian." Rebecca smiled.

"Shucks," Tracy grinned. "I debated telling Lisa to give Ben an ultimatum. I didn't though. An ultimatum from a wife to a husband is a completely different animal compared to one from a girlfriend to a boyfriend."

"Yeah, I wouldn't suggest an ultimatum unless things have gotten really bad. It sounds like things could get worse though."

"They've been married for six years; together for eight. I think he's been like this for most of those years. Lisa's just learned to live with it. But I can tell she's not happy about it."

Rebecca stood. "I hope it works out for your friend. Maybe knowing she has a friend she can turn to will help her turn a corner. Let me know how things work out."

"Time to pay your fee," Tracy grinned, just before embracing Rebecca firmly. "Thanks, Beck."

"Sure, Tracy."

Tracy watched Rebecca leave the office. The personal business now out of the way, it was time to focus on the other business at hand. Tracy had left today open in case a return visit to WMFT was needed. And due to Friday's meeting with Elias Tanner, Sr., one most certainly was.

"I really didn't mean to mislead you, Tracy," Steve Dante told her. "I did spend a few years here in the eighties. But it's really just a footnote to my career. Besides, all of the people I worked with directly aren't even here anymore."

"But Richard George and Carl Jeffries were here. And Larry Peachtree was here too."

"I had no direct contact with any of them. I knew who they were and saw them regularly. But I was just a production assistant, which means I was mostly an errand boy. I watched and learned, though — a lot. When the New York position opened up I took it."

"I see. So, why did you come back to Maryland and WMFT?"

"Same reason I went to New York: opportunity. The station owners and I were getting into arguments about programming. They wanted more tabloid type stuff; I wanted more *real* news. I wanted to do some investigative journalism — do *real* stories. People don't think much of the news anymore. Do *you*?"

"I see what you're saying, Steve."

"Yeah, well, I was looking into changing jobs, and then the producer position opened up here. It was a no-brainer."

Tracy nodded. "I like what you said about watching and learning."

"Oh?"

"Sure. You kept your eyes and ears open. Maybe you saw or heard or otherwise learned something about Carl Jeffries."

Dante sighed. "I see what you mean. I wish I could help you."

"You can. Tell me about Carrie Wallace and Carl Jeffries."

Dante looked at her a moment. "I guess I have to. Megan and I were the ones who wanted you asking questions after all."

"Yes, you did."

"But I don't feel comfortable talking about Megan's mother behind her back."

"Whose back: Megan's or Carrie's?"

"Both, actually."

"Sounds like there's something to tell. Please tell me."

"There really isn't. Carrie was a perky, pleasant, lovely young woman. She had — still has — this great laugh. So, guys would try to get her to laugh; thought that might get them somewhere with her, you know?"

"Yup."

"I was married so Carrie was off limits."

"Good man."

Dante chuckled. "Jeffries flirted with all the single ladies in the office. Well, somehow, he seemed to tickle Carrie's fancy best. And he was something of a celebrity where a lot of the guys hitting on her were crew. So, she hooked up with Carl."

"Mm. And what happened?"

"An affair, I guess you'd call it. She may have even fallen for Carl. But he left, as you know. I don't think he asked Carrie to join him."

"Ah."

"I found out later that she had gone to Richard George because, as I also later found out, he had warned Carrie about Carl. She told him she was pregnant. He helped her — he and his wife. They're such good people."

"I believe it."

"I left, of course, so I really can't give you any more specifics. I do think it's great that Megan is working here now though."

Tracy nodded. "I have to be honest with you, Steve. There's something about this I still find troubling, outside of the murder of course."

"What's that?"

"Why you insisted that Carl Jeffries be asked to be part of this. You had to know how Megan felt."

"Well…"

"And I know about your plans, if that makes your answering me any easier."

"You do?"

"Yes."

"Well, then you can figure out the answer."

"I don't want to make guesses, Steve."

"Look. Jeffries was going to find out about the show at some point. If I didn't offer him a part, he'd have badmouthed the whole thing, and *that* would have been the main story. I thought by making this goodwill gesture, it might make things easier when we told him about plans for a new Dr. Mort show."

"…Which he would have no part of."

"Not true."

"Really?"

"Really. I would have offered him a job as co-writer or consultant; something along those lines. He wouldn't be in front of the camera. But then he never really was."

"That's probably not as he would have seen it."

"You may be right. But it's all moot now."

"Yes, it is, isn't it?"

Dante pursed his lips. "Just for the record, I didn't kill Carl."

"Okay, Steve. I guess I got a little overzealous with my questioning. Sorry."

"Forget it. I know you're trying to help Richard. But if I were the killer, why would I want someone with your reputation poking around?"

Tracy smiled. "Because you're a very clever killer, maybe? But I'm kidding of course."

They looked at each other. Both knew she wasn't really kidding; she wasn't kidding at all.

"Ned has the video set up," Megan Wallace told Tracy. "I'll take you to his private editing room."

"Private?"

"He'd like to think so," Megan grinned. Tracy grinned in return. When the women reached Topolski's office, Megan called out, "Knock, knock. Tracy's here to see you, Ned."

Ned turned and smiled. "Sure. Follow me, Tracy. I have all the footage I shot the day Carl was…Well, it's all ready to go."

"Thanks, Ned."

The two sat down on adjacent stools. Tracy looked at the monitor and said, "Ready when you are, Ned."

"Okay."

Ned started the show. Tracy watched intently. She remembered the brief talks with Tom Kramer and Larry Peachtree. But she was more interested in what was going on in the background, especially towards the end of that Saturday. She looked for an unfamiliar face. She paid close attention to the lab table where the camera had been found. She tried to spot someone using a studio phone. She watched things through twice, almost 50 minutes of footage times two. Nothing stood out.

"Can you enlarge certain areas of the frame, Ned?"

"Sure."

"I want to focus on the areas around the lab table."

"Okay. I guess we can start from the beginning."

"No, around lunchtime would be fine."

"Lunchtime?"

"Just before lunch, Andy Honeywell showed me the stake and mallet. At that point, they were under the lab coat. That's not where they were during the murder. But I really can't get into that."

"Okay."

"So, let's find the first time the lab table was filmed during or after lunch."

"Got it."

"I understand you and Carl actually attended the same college," Tracy said as Topolski scanned through the video.

"I'd heard that."

"But you two didn't know each other before he came here for the live show."

"No."

"I thought maybe you guys met at some alma mater function."

"No."

"How about at your awards presentation?"

"Huh?"

"You won a short film award, didn't you?"

"Oh. I don't think Carl was at that little reception they had. Why would he be?"

"He was a graduate and something of a local celebrity. I just thought he may have attended."

"Sorry."

"How did you end up here?"

Topolski looked at her. "Steve Dante saw my work and contacted me."

"Was Steve at that awards banquet?"

"Yes, he was. So were some other local TV people."

"I see. Like it here?"

"Sure."

Tracy smiled. "I guess I should get back to the video, huh?"

"I guess."

The next time the lab table was visible was 1:32 p.m. The lab coat seemed to be in the exact same place where Honeywell had left it. But Tracy was going off her memory. It could have been moved with enough subtlety that she didn't notice. Plenty of people moved passed it; at one point the coat was put on by Richard George.

"Look at that," Tracy said. With the area enlarged, she could clearly see George put the stake and mallet in the pockets.

Topolski nodded. "Yeah, I saw that."

"Can you replay that with the volume turned up? I heard a voice."

"Sure."

Tracy re-watched the scene, as well as re-listened.

"That was Andy Honeywell's voice telling Mr. George to put those items in the pockets, right?"

"Yeah. He is the director after all."

"He is at that."

"Megan tells me you're meeting her mother tonight," Andrew Honeywell began.

"Yes, for dinner at a place near where she lives."

"Why? Why bother her?"

Tracy sighed. "She knew Carl Jeffries better than anyone, Andy."

"Oh right; sure."

"How did Thursday go?"

"What?"

"The casting meeting."

Honeywell nodded. "Yeah, Megan told me she told you about the big plan."

"I haven't said anything to anyone else, Andy; promise."

He smiled. "I guess it doesn't matter. Tomorrow the rumors will start flying."

"Oh?"

"We're bringing someone in tomorrow. We're going to dress him up and rehearse him and see how it all goes. We'll say it's just an understudy or something like that. But that story won't hold for long."

"Who is he?"

"Local actor named Victor Steinman. He's pretty good actually. I've seen some local theater that he's done."

"I'd like to meet him if I could."

"He'll be here 9:00 a.m. sharp tomorrow."

"And what about the skeleton?"

"Not sure yet. We're thinking of using some old audio recordings of Carl and just play them. But that means no new material. So, I'm not sure."

"Gotcha."

"I'm really busy, Tracy. Why did you want to see me?"

"Some questions about the day of the murder."

"Of course. Go ahead."

"Notice any big fights that day?"

"No."

"Did you notice anyone using a studio phone close to the time you had sent everyone home?"

"I don't think so."

"I was watching some video footage Ned Topolski shot. He happened to be recording when you told Mr. George to put the stake and mallet in the pockets of the lab coat."

"Okay, what of it? We had the coat made with the deep pockets for that very reason."

"So, lots of people knew where those things would be?"

"I guess. It wasn't any secret."

"When you and Mr. George were done with the scene, do you remember if he left those things in the coat or took them out? The video coverage stopped before I could tell."

Honeywell thought over Tracy's question. "I think they were still in there. I can't recall him putting them anywhere else. I wish I could I be more certain."

"I guess people are bothering you with all kinds of questions during the breaks, huh?"

"Yes, that's true."

"Somebody managed to slip one of the station's cameras under the lab coat. It could have been done after the studio was supposedly empty of course. But do you remember anyone hovering around the lab table?"

"Hovering? No. Most people would have reason to pass by it though, use it to put something on."

"Yeah. I did see in Ned's video a lot of people pass it; nobody put anything on it though. Of course, there's only about five minutes of total coverage. So, there were plenty of opportunities to do what needed to be done unobserved."

"I guess so."

Tracy sighed heavily. "Andy, I'm so frustrated. I can't find anything to help Mr. George. The police have Carl Jeffries calling out Richard's name and I have nothing to explain that. Nobody seems to have seen anything or heard anything. I've talked to several people and the answers are all the same. I'm stumped."

Honeywell looked at her sympathetically. "I wish I could help."

"Maybe you can."

"Just tell me how."

"Well: you both write and direct, right?"

"Sure."

"You're a creative person, right?"

"I'd like to think so."

"Okay. Then tell me how you would do it."

"Do what? Kill Jeffries?"

"Not just that. I mean how would you have gotten Carl to say Richard's name?"

Honeywell blinked. "You're not very subtle, are you?"

"I'm sorry, Andy. I know how what I just asked may have sounded. But I really am curious if you have any ideas. I could think of only one."

"And what would that be?"

"The killer made Carl believe he was rehearsing a scene, maybe for some low budget horror movie or something. And the stake driver's character name was Richard."

"And Carl was given dialogue to say the name Richard. Is that it?"

"Yes, exactly. Then, after Carl said his line, the killer finished him off. What do you think of that of idea?"

Honeywell started nodding. "I guess I can see that as a possibility. But what if Carl had figured out what was really happening, and called out the true killer's name?"

"Then this killer would not have left the camera behind. He would have tried to frame Richard in some other way, such as planting evidence."

Honeywell grinned. "You sound like a creative person yourself."

"I have to be sometimes. But what do you think of my theory? As one creative person to another, is there some other way he could have worked this?"

The two continued staring at each other. Finally, Honeywell said, "I love Megan and I hated what her father was doing to her. But I didn't kill him."

"I never said you did. But I need help finding out who did. Or do you think Richard *did* do this and you just don't want to admit it?"

"Of course, I don't."

"Well, won't you help me work through this frame then?"

Honeywell nodded. "All right. I'll try and think of something. But I do like your script idea."

Tracy smiled. "Thanks."

"You're welcome."

"So, you love Megan huh?"

"Yes, I do."

"She said you two had a spat that night."

Honeywell sighed. "Yes. It was all my fault. I took things out on her, and I shouldn't have. Given what happened later…I just wish we'd been together when Megan got that call."

"Where did you go after the fight?"

"Excuse me?"

"Megan told me she tried reaching you after she learned what happened but couldn't."

Honeywell studied her a moment. "I didn't come back here and kill Carl Jeffries, if that's what you're implying."

"Of course, I'm not. You already made that clear. Besides, how would you know you would have that fight with Megan, right? How would you have known in advance to call Carl and have him meet you at the studio later?"

He again studied her. "Creatively speaking, I guess one of us could have staged it. Or maybe we're covering for each other."

"No, Andy. If you were covering for each other, you'd be each other's alibi."

He shook his head. "I'm sorry for sounding so standoffish. I guess it can't be easy for you. You have to find another suspect to take Richard's place."

Tracy frowned. "I wouldn't put it *quite* like that. But yeah, if Richard didn't kill Jeffries, who did? That's the uncomfortable part of this whole thing."

"Look, I really need to get back to work."

"Just one more question, please."

"Okay."

"Who wrote the scenario for the reunion show?"

"You mean the script?"

"Yeah."

"I did most of it. But Richard and Carl made some changes, which were all fine."

"What about during the original show? You told me earlier you saw some of the scripts. Do you remember who wrote *those* scripts?"

"Richard and his director mostly. Carl did a little uncredited work on them but not much, from what I've heard."

"Okay. Thanks, Andy. Maybe I'll stop by tomorrow to see Victor Steinman in action."

"Sure. No problem."

"See you."

Tracy left the director sitting in the studio editing room. She had another stop to make before leaving the studio.

Tracy found Larry Peachtree sitting down in the cafeteria. He was flipping through location photographs while eating a sandwich. She approached him.

"Hi, Larry."

He turned. "Oh: it's you again."

"It is. But I'm here for a different reason this time. I wanted to say how sorry I am about your family. I found out what happened to them."

Peachtree gulped and put his lunch down. "Thank you," he said softly.

"I have two children of my own. I feel so bad for you. I know that's something you'll never get over."

"No."

"What was your wife's name?"

"Janice."

"I like that name. Did she work here at the studio?"

"No. She was kindergarten teacher."

Tracy sighed. "I'm so, so sorry, Larry."

Peachtree was staring at the table. "She couldn't stand it anymore. Day in and day out she was surrounded by other people's children. After we lost Joshua, she thought going back to work would actually help her. It just depressed her more."

"I guess the people here were very understanding. Is that why you've been here so long?"

"Excuse me?"

"I guess the people here were supportive and comforting; helped you through those very painful times. Is that why you've been here so long?"

"Oh, yes, they were. It was different back then. The environment, I mean. Those comforting people you refer to aren't here anymore, except for Richard, I guess."

"Richard was kind to you."

"Of course. So was his wife. They had kids."

"Yes." Tracy took a deep breath. "Was Carl cruel to you?"

"No. As a matter of fact he left me alone for the most part—" Peachtree stood up. "SO THAT'S IT!" he shouted. "You think I killed Carl because he taunted me!"

Tracy shook her head. "No, Larry."

"I don't believe you! You're not here to express sympathy! You're here to pin this murder on me!"

"*NO*, Larry. We've been through this before. I came here to say how sorry I was and to also apologize for presuming to give you advice last time."

Peachtree looked at her skeptically. "I'd like you to just leave me alone, please. Just go."

Tracy nodded. "I'm going."

Tracy turned and left the fuming Peachtree to finish his late lunch. She wanted to call on one other person before her early dinner with Carrie Wallace.

Richard George sat across from Tracy at the Baltimore Central Booking and Intake Center. She forced a smile.

"Hi Richard. How are you holding up?"

"It's not so bad. Met some fans, actually."

Tracy chuckled. "No kidding? I guess that can only help."

"I guess."

There was an awkward silence. "I'm meeting with Carrie Wallace in a couple of hours."

George's eyebrows leapt upwards. "Why?"

"…To learn more about Carl Jeffries."

George shook his head. "There's nothing to learn."

"There is, Richard. Much to learn, in fact."

"What are you talking about?"

"$90,000, for starters."

"*What?*"

"Found in his safety deposit box."

"What safety deposit box?"

"The one he had and, apparently, kept quiet about. Then there was his stint in the adult entertainment industry."

George leaned back slightly. He looked to his side. "I should have figured that would come out."

"You knew?"

"Of course, I knew. Someone at the station had found out about it while Carl was still…active."

"But you kept quiet about it. I'm guessing for Megan's sake."

He shook his head. "Have you told her yet?"

"No. But it's going to come out."

"Why?"

"It may have something to do with his death."

"How?"

"I'm not sure yet."

"Well, if you're not sure you shouldn't say anything."

"Look, Richard. I won't be telling Megan if that's what you're worried about. But you should be worrying about yourself, not Megan."

"I don't want to see her hurt."

"I'm not trying to hurt anybody. Do you think she'd care though?"

George sighed. "I don't know, and I don't want to find out."

"Okay, Richard. I hear you."

"Good. Have you found anything else?"

"No. I know Carl Jeffries was a creep and that people didn't like him. But I haven't come across a strong motive."

"So, you don't really have anything yet, do you?"

Tracy frowned. "I'm sorry, Richard."

"Me too."

"I take it Carrie knows about Carl's past also."

"Sure."

"But she still loved him."

"Love? Carrie was…Never mind."

"Never mind what, Richard?"

"Tracy, Carrie was an innocent and Carl took all that away. She sleeps with a guy and calls it love. She had no idea what she was doing. It messed her all up and she got pregnant." George twisted his lips. Then he sighed. "Of course, Megan is a lovely woman. I've known her all her life. She…"

"She what, Richard?"

"I'm glad I know her is all. Carrie did a wonderful job with her. So…"

"I'm not trying to hurt Megan."

"I know that. But just how long will it take until the headlines read: 'Horror Sidekick Former Porn Star'?"

Tracy sighed. "I hear you. But to be honest, I'm not sure how many people really care at this point. People are more interested in you."

"You were the one who said somebody will find out eventually."

"I know. What was the name of the person who told you about what Carl was doing?"

George rubbed his forehead. "Good Lord. That was so many years ago."

"I understand. But I'd like to talk to him; see if he knew any other things about Carl."

"You better get a plane ticket then."

"Why?"

"Guy's name is Oliver Culp. He moved to Los Angeles…can't remember when, exactly."

"He got a job there?"

"I think he went looking for one. He wasn't a very good cameraman and he finally screwed up one too many times. He got fired and took off."

"Okay, Richard, thanks. I'll have my PI track him down."

"Sure."

"Can I get you anything?"

"No. Elaine visits me and that will get me through things for now."

"All right. I just wanted to see how you were doing and to assure you I haven't given up."

George smiled. "I appreciate everything. But I don't want people getting unnecessarily hurt on my account. I want to be absolutely clear on this point."

"You have been. I don't want to hurt anyone either."

"Nature of the beast, I guess."

"Sometimes," Tracy agreed. "Goodbye for now."

Tracy stood and then left George. He was already counting the hours until his wife's visit tomorrow.

"El," Tracy said into her smartphone. "I have a new name for you: Oliver Culp."

"Who's he?"

"Used to be a cameraman for WMFT until he got fired. I think he and Carl Jeffries were pals. At one point, Culp went to L.A. I'd like you to track him down for me."

"Sure."

"Who knows, El? Maybe you'll get a trip to the west coast after all."

"Uh-huh. How are things going otherwise?"

"Not very well. I've got no clear motive and no clear suspects. So, I'll keep learning all I can about Carl Jefferies. Eventually I'll find a very good reason why someone wanted him dead. Anything else running on the rumor mill?"

"No. The money is still a question, but the SA is prepping their case against George for the preliminary hearing."

"Joy. Okay, El. I need to make my dinner date with Carrie Wallace."

"Good luck. I'll be in touch."

Megan Wallace didn't look anything like her mother. And Carrie Wallace, from a distance anyway, did not look 54 years old either. Early forties, tops. Her hair seemed devoid of tell-tale gray. As Tracy approached the woman who was seated in the waiting area, however, some of Tracy's initial impressions were proved wrong. There *was* gray in her hair, and her face showed signs of tiredness and stress. When Carrie Wallace stood and smiled, Tracy imagined the woman had used every ounce of strength she could muster to do so.

"Thank you so much for meeting me, Ms. Wallace," Tracy said after the introductions.

"Carrie, please," was the response.

The two women were then shown a table in the center of the diner.

"Anything here that you'd recommend?" Tracy asked.

Carrie smiled. "I usually just get a chef's salad with chicken."

"Ah." Tracy's eyes were scanning the menu. "All day breakfast, I see. Have you tried any of their omelets?"

"No."

"Well, I think a Western Omelet is a safe choice."

Carrie smiled and laughed softly. "I imagine it would be."

As it was just after 5:00 p.m., the service was speedy. The women had their drinks in front of them and their food orders put in within five minutes.

"How are you doing, Carrie?" Tracy asked sincerely.

"I'm doing all right. I'm more concerned about Richard."

"I saw him earlier today. All things considered he's doing well. Elaine visits him every day."

Carrie nodded. "I want to visit him myself, but I can't make it during the week. And I feel so guilty."

"You shouldn't feel guilty. I know Richard is worried about you. I bet he'd love to see you."

Carrie sipped her iced tea. "Megan told me you wanted to know all about Carl."

"Yes, whatever you're willing and able to tell me."

"There's not too much to tell. I met him while I was working at the studio. I started there right out of college. I was 21, almost 22. Carl was there making commercials at that point. His show had been canceled."

"The Dr. Mort show."

"Yes. Richard had always been part of the news department, so he just continued doing that. Carl had been hired expressly for the horror thing, so they found something else for him to do after the show ended."

"I see."

Carrie smiled. "He was always playing some goofy character and clowning around."

"He was pretty funny, huh?"

"Yes. He told the worst jokes, the worst puns. But he'd still make you laugh. I think it was his sincerity."

"He believed he was funny, so you did too."

"I guess that was it."

Tracy cleared her throat. Now came the hard part. "Can you tell me about your relationship with him?"

"I'm sure you heard by now. We started going out. We dated maybe a year. One day he told me he was leaving the station to go to Hollywood." Carrie studied Tracy. "You're too young to remember this, of course. But stand-up comedy really started coming into its own toward the end of the eighties. Cable networks had all those specials and a couple of comedy clubs opened in the Baltimore area."

"And Carl wanted to do that?"

Carrie nodded. "Yes. I told him he should try some open-mike nights or something like that here first. He didn't have the patience though."

"One chef's salad with chicken and one Western with hash browns," the server announced as she placed the plates in their correct locations. The women thanked her.

Carrie Wallace stared into the center of her plate. "He never asked if I wanted to come with him. He said he wanted to start things over and make a clean break from his past." She looked up at Tracy, who bore a sympathetic expression. "About a week later he was gone."

Tracy sighed. "Were you two living together?"

"No. I would stay at his place a lot. But I never moved in. I had my own place. It wasn't long after he left that I found out I was pregnant."

"And you didn't know how to contact him?"

"No. He didn't leave anyone his forwarding address. I'm not sure he even had one."

The women paused their conversing to begin their meals. "The omelet is very good," Tracy said with little enthusiasm.

"I knew it would be," Carrie responded in kind. "My parents… they had this real small apartment they moved into after I moved out. They were also pretty upset. One night while at work, I just completely broke down. It was Richard who pulled me aside, held my hand, and listened. He said he would help in any way he could. He said they — he and Elaine — had a free room in their house I could stay in if money became a problem. The Georges were just so wonderful."

Tracy felt teary-eyed. And she felt a sudden loathing for Carl Jeffries she hadn't felt until now.

"I guess there's no mystery why Megan cares so much about him."

Carrie sighed and then forced a cherry tomato into her mouth. "At one point she was calling him Grandpa. I had to stop that. I didn't want to presume anything."

"When did she learn about her father?"

Carrie shook her head. "When he showed up again. This friend of his he saw in L.A. told him about Megan."

"Was this friend named Oliver Culp?"

Carrie nodded. "Yes, I think that was him. This Oliver went to Los Angeles and looked Carl up."

"Carl didn't know?"

"No. As I told you, he left no forwarding address. He wanted to start all over. I never tried tracking him down. I figured I'd never seen him again." Carrie smiled. "I kept looking for him on all those comedy shows and stand-up shows. I never saw him. And then, out of the blue, he shows up at my apartment."

Tracy didn't have much of an appetite at this point. She knew the reason Carl Jeffries came back *wasn't* to play Daddy. She looked at Carrie.

"But you took him back, anyway."

"Yes. He begged forgiveness. Said had he known he would have been back sooner. He blamed *me* for not trying harder to find him."

"Manipulative prick," Tracy thought.

"I knew he was probably saying whatever he had to so I'd let him move in with us. But Megan was at that age. Part of me thought it might be good to have a man around the house."

"What did Megan think?"

Carrie shook her head. "She hated him; hated him right from the start. He begged her to give him a chance and tried blaming me for him not being around. Megan wasn't having any of it. Megan and I were very close. I'm happy to say we still are. But it didn't take long for Carl to change his tone."

"What do you mean?"

"He went from apologetic and conciliatory to being defiant. He was her father, and he was living with us now and that was that. I begged Megan to try and get along with him. She obliged by just not talking to him. Sometimes there'd be a standoff between them. But we survived until Megan moved out, right after graduating from college. I'd hoped she'd stay for a little while after she graduated. But I could understand why didn't want to. She was a woman now — her own woman with her own plans."

Tracy was mindlessly forcing egg, ham, cheese, and vegetables into her mouth. "I have to ask this Carrie. Did you really love Carl Jeffries?"

It took a while before she answered. "I don't really know what love is to be able to answer that."

Tracy covered her mouth. Carrie Wallace was just looking at her uneaten salad.

"There's never been anyone else, Carrie? You're so lovely and you seem so kind and you raised this wonderful daughter…I just can't…" Tracy looked at her lap.

"You're very kind. But I really didn't have any time when I was younger. I worked to take care of Megan, make sure I could provide for her. I loved her so much and wanted to spend all the time with her I could. And suddenly she was more interested in her friends and boys. And then Carl showed up again. I guess I was lonely and desperate enough to believe what he told me, even though I should have known better."

Tracy sighed and nodded. "For what it's worth, Carrie, Megan is a great person. I know she loves you very much."

"She is a fine woman." Carrie looked at Tracy. "I couldn't completely hate Carl, you see. He's Megan's father, after all. Does that make sense?"

"I think so."

"But, if I'm honest, I don't feel as upset about his death as I probably should. I'm more worried about Richard than anything. He'd never do something like this." Carrie Wallace's tone changed. Angrily she said, "Do you hear the lies they're spreading in the press?"

"What lies?"

"That Carl called out Richard's name when he was attacked."

Tracy blinked. "I've heard that."

"Disgraceful!"

Tracy bit her tongue. "Carrie, did Carl ever help out with the finances? Did he help pay for rent, or food, or anything?"

"Once in a while he'd give me some money. But that was usually after I was starting to reconsider his living with us."

"Do you know where he got it?"

Carrie shook her head. "No. He worked odd jobs, he told me. He'd be out of work for a while and then find something else. That's how things went."

"Mm. Did the police mention his safety deposit box?"

Carrie's eyes grew wide. "Yes! They did! I couldn't believe it."

"Did they tell you how much they found?"

"Almost $100,000 — all cash. I didn't know what to tell them."

"You didn't even know he had a box, right?"

"Right. He never told me."

"Have they done any follow-up with you? Maybe they learned something?"

"No. I haven't talked to them for a while."

"Mm."

"Can I get you ladies anything else?" the server asked as she refilled glasses.

"Just some to-go boxes," Tracy said.

"Sure."

Tracy watched the server leave. "I have one more question, Carrie."

"I know. You want to know about Carl's Hollywood career."

Tracy blinked. "When did he tell you?"

"Not too long after he showed back up. He was…He expected… Well, he was a good lover. And he had learned some things he wanted to share with me."

"Okay," Tracy said, clearing her throat. "You don't have to share the details."

Carrie chuckled. "I wasn't planning to."

"And Megan doesn't know."

"No! You won't tell her, will you?" Carrie Wallace's back was stiff, her face alarmed.

"Not unless it becomes absolutely necessary. If it has nothing to do with his murder, I'll have no cause to. I don't want Megan hurt any more than you and Richard do."

Carrie relaxed. "Thank you. I'm not sure if it would really matter to her, at this point. But I don't want my daughter to be the butt of jokes. She has such a great future."

Tracy grinned. "Have you met Andy Honeywell?"

"Andy…Megan's in love with him."

"So, I gathered. Do you like him?"

"I think so. He can be aloof sometimes. But I know he's under a lot of pressure — both he and Megan. I'm just so thankful she *did* fall in love with someone. I was so worried about that. She had no father figure; no role model."

"She had Richard, didn't she?"

As Carrie pondered the question, the server placed to-go boxes and the check on their table.

"Yes, I guess she did for many years. I guess she kept those years in her heart and was able to shut out Carl."

Tracy reached for the check. When Carrie started to protest Tracy shook her head.

"This is the least I can do for dredging up painful memories. I wish there'd been an easier way to handle this."

Carrie Wallace decided not to argue. She didn't have the strength for it. Soon the women were parting. They hugged before getting into their respective autos and heading to their respective homes.

Tracy was sitting at the dining room table, her right hand covering the bottom half of her face. Her children had been tucked in, her mother had retired, and Brian was outside with Bonkers. The fingers of her left hand started drumming on the table. They continued to do so until she heard the noise from outside. Tracy turned in the direction of the sliding-glass door and smiled as Bonkers quickly moved towards her.

"Goodnight boy," she said as she leaned over and embraced him.

The pooch then proceeded up the stairway where his carpet awaited him.

As Tracy resumed her sitting position, she continued to look towards the back. Brian was sliding the door along its track. She then watched him latch it, position the security bar, and then pull the blinds. Brian noted the sour look on her face.

"What's wrong?" he asked as he joined her at the dining table.

"I was just remembering the door."

"The door?"

"The studio door."

"Oh."

She smiled. "Sorry, honey. I just meant that the only way the killer could have gotten in without the security guard seeing him was through a back door. He needed keys."

"Okay."

"But Richard George didn't have a set of keys. So, how do the police think he got in there?"

"Had a copy made maybe?"

"They better find that locksmith. But since I don't think he did it, they never will."

"Do the backdoors automatically lock?"

"Yes."

"Maybe he propped it open."

"Maybe. But that's risky since someone could have come along and noticed that."

"And Jeffries didn't have a key either, right?"

"Right."

Tracy stood up and went towards the door. She pulled the blinds back, lifted the security bar, and unlocked the door. She pulled the door back, bent down at the knees, and stared at the locking mechanism. Brian watched her. He grinned.

"Maybe the killer mon*keyed* around with the lock."

Tracy looked at him and chuckled. "Oh, you're cute." She stood up. "But the police would need evidence he did so."

"Well, isn't this good news for you then? You can bring this up in court."

"I suppose. But no matter how much noise I make about the door, they still have that video. That's the—"

Brian saw the color drain from his wife's face. "What is it?" he asked. "What's wrong?"

"I'm an idiot."

"What?"

"I should have realized this right away. I'm a complete idiot."

"Tracy, you're *not* an idiot. Now what's going on?"

"The missing tape that wasn't really missing."

"Huh?"

"Somebody moved Larry Peachtree's electrical tape from the table where he left it. He said he left it on the lab table, and I did see it there when I was watching some video."

"So?"

"Somebody returned it to Larry's drawer, after they used it. Don't you see?"

"No."

"Brian, someone used the tape to make sure the door wouldn't latch."

Brian stared at Tracy for a few moments. "Okay, I get it. And you think that's how the police are going to say George got back in?"

Tracy nodded. "This is *not* good news. I just don't see how things could get any worse for Richard George."

But Tracy was mistaken. Things *were* about to get worse for her client. Much, much worse.

CHAPTER 12

"Detective Deborah Price is on line one, Tracy," Rebecca Dietz announced.

"Thanks, Beck." After Tracy pushed the required buttons, she greeted her caller. "Good morning, Detective."

"Good morning, Tracy. You and I need to talk."

"Sure."

"Can you stop by my office today?"

Tracy gulped. "We can't talk on the phone?"

"I don't think you want to hear this over the phone."

"That bad, huh?"

"That bad."

"All right. I'll be over around noon. Is that okay?"

"Yes. I'll see you then."

Tracy almost broke the receiver when she slammed it down. Based on Detective Price's tone, Tracy's planned visit sounded more like she'd be attending a wake.

Detective Price folded her hands and rested them on her desk. She looked at the apprehensive attorney.

"You need to listen to me, Tracy."

"Okay," Tracy said nervously.

"I like you; you know that. I respect you. I know your history. But it was only a matter of time."

"Time?"

"…Before you went to bat for the wrong person."

"Richard George didn't—"

"Tracy," Price interrupted, "you need to listen to me."

Tracy took a deep breath. "Okay."

"You know about the money found in the safe deposit box yet?"

"I heard some things."

"I figured you did." Price looked down at the file on her desk as she said, "Jeffries had $98,560 dollars in his safe deposit box."

"Okay."

"You know Jeffries moved back to Baltimore in 2002?"

"Yes."

"Between 2003 and 2019, your client withdrew $350,000 from his bank account; cash withdrawals, not checks or auto-debits."

"Maybe he—"

"And before you start coming up with possible reasons for the withdrawals, we already have your client's prints on some of the money we found in the box."

"He could have loaned Jeffries some money. They were old friends."

Price sighed. "Tracy, listen. We know how he got back into the studio."

Tracy's heart sank. "You do?"

"Yes. We had the crime lab check all the back doors. On the one leading directly into the studio where they're filming, they found a small piece of black electrical tape. You see where I'm going with this?"

"20/20 vision, Detective."

Price sighed again. "Carl Jeffries was extorting your client, Tracy. There's no doubt about it. It's only a matter of time before we find out why. We know your client reentered the studio by taping the latch so it wouldn't lock. We have the victim on video saying your client's name. Do you understand what I'm telling you?"

"I have 20/20 hearing too."

"Look, I know Carl Jeffries was a pretty lousy human being. And he was a blackmailer. Plus, your client is 77 or something like that. You might be able to work something out with the SA."

"Even with that video?"

"If this doesn't go to trial, the public will never see that video. If your client insists on letting this go to trial, he'll spend the rest of his life in jail. Are you hearing me?"

Tracy just nodded.

"Okay. Go see your client. Tell him what I told you. Arthur Pankow wants to hear from you by the end of the week."

"Okay."

Price sighed. "I'm really sorry. You know that, right?"

"Sure." Tracy forced a smile as she stood. "I'll see Richard today."

The detective rose and the women shook hands. Then Tracy made a hasty retreat to her car. After she seated herself, she stared at the steering wheel. Then she threw her keys at the windshield. And then she started crying.

Richard George listened to the evidence against him. Tracy managed to present the State's case without getting overly emotional. After she was finished, she awaited her client's response.

"I didn't kill Carl Jeffries," was all he said.

"Then someone's done a real number on you, Richard."

"I guess they did."

"Why were you paying Jeffries money?"

"They can't prove that. They can't prove it was blackmail, I mean."

"Are you telling me you've been loaning Jeffries money?"

"What could he be blackmailing me over?"

"I don't know. You tell me."

George stared at her. "I didn't kill him."

Tracy shook her head. "Richard, you know what? I still believe you. Despite everything they have, I still believe you. But I don't know if I can help you. I'm not Wonder Woman; I'm not a magician."

George looked down at the table. "Be honest with me. Do you think I have any chance here?"

Tracy gulped. "If it weren't for that video…It was just such a brutal murder. Even if I could get the jury to dislike Carl Jeffries and like you, Arthur Pankow — the State's Attorney for Baltimore City — will keep reminding the jury of how horribly Jeffries died. It will negate any sympathy I could generate for you. So, to answer your question, I wouldn't want this to go to trial."

"You think I should let you work out some plea deal, then?"

"I guess so," Tracy said sheepishly.

George smiled. "You said earlier we have until the end of the week."

"That's what Detective Price told me."

George nodded. "Okay, Tracy. If you can't find anything by the end of the week, you have my permission to plead out." He smiled.

It was too much for her. Tears started running down her cheeks.

"I'm so sorry, Richard. I'm so, so sorry."

"Tracy…" He leaned towards her. "Don't cry over me. I've made some mistakes in my life and now I'm going to pay for them. I didn't kill Carl, but maybe I deserve to be punished for it just the same."

Tracy shook her head. "Don't say that."

"Tracy, you can only do so much. Like you said, you're not Wonder Woman. You're not a magician. I don't know how or why all this happened. I guess someone hates me almost as much as they hated Carl. But who that person is, I have no idea."

Tracy wiped her eyes. "I still have time. I still have a few days."

"Okay. Don't bother wasting time coming to see me. Just do what you can do. But if you can't find anything, try not to be too hard on yourself. I'm not blaming you for any of this. I've grown very fond of you."

She couldn't bear to be in George's presence any longer. She stood, said a tearful goodbye, and exited the interview room. But as she walked hurriedly and intently towards her vehicle, anger slowly took over. By the time she slammed her car door shut, she was full of rage. She dialed Elias Tanner, Sr.

"El, I want you to go to Los Angeles," she said as soon as Tanner answered. "Find Oliver Culp and find that Amber Hardshoe or whatever she's calling herself these days and—"

"Culp is dead, Tracy. Drug overdose seven years ago."

"GOD DAMNIT!" she screamed.

Tanner knew this mood. He wasn't going to try and calm her down. He knew that would only make things worse.

"I do know where to find Wendy Rakowski, aka Amber, though."

"You do?"

"She has her own production company. I thought I'd try calling her first. Then, if she won't talk to me over the phone, I can hop on a plane."

"I need you to call her today. I don't have any time left."

"I gathered that. I'll call her right away."

Tracy let out a loud sigh. "This is bad El; this is *so* bad."

"Yeah; I can tell."

"It's somebody who works at the studio. They set this whole thing up."

"You're sure?"

"Damn right, I'm sure. They knew the schedules of everyone and their way around the studio. They knew that pissant Peachtree would start whining and accusing everyone when his tape got moved, and that that would give the police the answer as to how Richard got back into the studio. They even made sure to leave a piece of tape on the door so the police would find it. And I bet they knew that Jeffries was blackmailing Richard too."

"Wait. Blackmail?"

"Yes, El, blackmail. Richard wouldn't admit to it. But he's willing to go to jail rather than letting whatever it is come out."

"Jesus, Tracy…"

"I know, El; I know. But enough of this. Call that Amber and if you can't get a hold of her then get on a plane. I'll reimburse you."

"I'm not worried about the money. I'll call her now."

"Thanks, El."

"Tracy, try and take it easy. I understand how bad this looks. But letting your emotions take over won't help matters. You have to use that brain of yours — and maybe that imagination too."

Tracy couldn't help but smile. "Imagination, huh?"

"Sure. You have to imagine how the killer worked this all out, don't you?"

"True, El, very true. Thanks for everything. Call me as soon as you talk to Amber."

"Will do."

She sighed. She looked at her reflection in the rearview mirror. She said to it, "No more Mr. Nice Gal." Then she started her engine. Her destination was the WMFT studio.

Megan Wallace hadn't known Tracy very long. But she knew her well-enough to know that something was wrong. Megan closed her office door.

"What's wrong, Tracy?" she asked worriedly.

"Richard's in real trouble. Obviously, I can't go into all the details. But we're desperate."

Megan gulped. "What can I do?"

"Be honest with me."

Megan blinked. "What does that mean?"

"I'm sorry for being offensive. But the time for niceties is over. There's something going on here that I think people aren't telling me."

"Something like what?"

"…Something that put almost a hundred thousand in your father's safety deposit box."

"I don't know anything about that. Mom told me about the money, but she doesn't know about it either."

"Somebody does."

"I swear if I knew something Tracy, I'd tell you."

"Your father came back to Maryland and started collecting money. I want to know why; I *need* to know why."

"Tracy, I swear—"

"Then your mother knows. She has to."

Megan twisted her lips. "She said that your meeting went well. She said you were very kind."

"I thought it went well too. And I'd like to think that, generally speaking, I'm a kind person. But somebody is either lying to me or hiding something. And if I don't find out what that is, Richard is going to prison. Do you understand that, Megan?"

Megan covered her mouth; tears came to her eyes. "Are you telling me my mother knows what's going on here?"

"She let Carl move back in with her after he abandoned her."

"She said she still loved—"

"Bullshit!" The profanity was unleashed before Tracy realized it. She covered her mouth. "Oh, Megan, I'm so sorry."

Megan Wallace stared at Tracy in shock. "Wow…okay."

"I'm sorry, Megan. I really am."

Megan surprised Tracy when she said, "Don't be. I had that very same reaction when Mom told she still loved him. I guess I came to believe her since Dad stayed with us for so long." Megan smiled. "I heard you could be a tough cookie when you wanted to be."

Tracy laughed embarrassedly. "I don't like when I get like this though."

"Tracy, I swear to you I don't know what is going on. But if you think Mom is hiding something, then I will help you find out what that is. Would tonight be soon enough?"

Tracy smiled. "Yes. It can't be any later, actually."

"All right. She should be home by 6:30 p.m. I'll call her now and let her know we're coming. Can I do anything else for you?"

"Yes. Is there anyone else at the studio who was here when your father and Richard were, besides Larry Peachtree? I need to find someone who's not a suspect in this case."

"Well, Steve was here when—"

"Not him either."

"Oh, of course. I can't think of anyone."

"Figures."

"I'll ask around. Maybe I'm forgetting somebody."

"You don't strike me as the forgetful type."

Megan smiled. "Not normally."

"Hey, is that new guy here? I think his name is Victor Steinman."

The smile left Megan's lips. "Oh, Lord."

"What happened? What's wrong?"

"Andy is having problems with Victor."

"What kind of problems?"

"Victor has his own ideas — about *everything*."

"Oh no…"

"Yes. The spirit of my father still haunts the studio."

"And remember, keep your labs tidy!"

"CLEAN, Victor!" Andy Honeywell shouted. "The line is: keep your labs clean! How many times do I have to tell you that?"

"But I like 'tidy'," Steinman insisted.

"But you're not playing *you*; you're playing Dr. Mort Itchin. And Dr. Mort's closing line has always ended with clean, not tidy."

Tracy was standing next to Megan, who was shaking her head.

"I don't simply want to do an imitation, Andrew. I told you that."

"I understand, Victor."

"I am an *actor*!"

"An out-of-work actor," Megan mumbled. Tracy giggled.

"And I have theater experience. I need to be able to *create*!"

"We do not have time to indulge your ego. We have barely a week to get this right. So, you must stick to the script and do as I tell you. When this is all over with, we can talk about your creativity."

Steinman snorted. "I give you freshness and you want stale. I give you originality and you want imitation!"

"JESUS CHRIST!" Megan shouted finally. She marched towards the stage. "Victor, do what your director tells you to do or get the hell out of here!"

Steinman stared at his potential sparring partner. Then he narrowed his eyes.

"And who are you again?" he challenged.

"*I'm* the producer, something of a creative force myself. You *did* meet me, Victor."

"Oh," Steinman snorted. "I don't know how you treat others, young lady, but—"

"You're fired! Get out!"

And then Megan Wallace turned and stormed out of the studio.

Steinman watched her.

"Come back here!" he shouted.

"Do I need to call security?" Honeywell asked. "You heard the lady. You're fired. Go." Then Honeywell turned, almost knocking Tracy over. "Oh, sorry. Didn't know you were here."

"Are you a producer?" Steinman, now watching Tracy's exchange with Honeywell, asked the attorney.

"Who, me?" Tracy asked innocently. "Oh my, no. I'm just a vampire bride."

Victor Steinman looked around for someone else he may talk to. He saw no one. Then the studio doors re-opened. Megan had returned with an intimidating fellow with forearms thicker than most people's necks.

"This is Jack, Victor. He's here to help you find your car."

It was the final indignity. Steinman turned abruptly, grabbed some items from the back of the stage, and marched towards Megan and her friend Jack.

"You haven't heard the last of this!" he shouted as he passed through the doorway. Megan did not respond.

"Follow him Jack," she said quietly. Jack obeyed. Megan looked at Tracy. "One Carl Jeffries in a lifetime is enough."

Tracy started laughing. Then so too did Megan Wallace. And then it finally occurred to Tracy why she felt such a fondness for Megan. She reminded Tracy of herself.

Carrie Wallace welcomed her daughter and Tracy into her apartment. She offered her guests something to drink; they both declined.

"Mom, Richard's in serious trouble and we need your help," Megan said as the women sat down on the leather couch.

"Of course," Carrie agreed.

"You need to tell us the truth, Mom."

Carrie furrowed her brow. "I don't like your tone. I am your mother, remember."

"Why did you let Dad move back in here?"

"What?"

"When he showed up out of nowhere, why did you let him live with us?"

Carrie looked at her lap. "I still loved him."

"I don't believe you. Tracy doesn't believe you either."

Carrie jerked her head up and looked at each accuser. "You have no right, Megan," was all she said.

"That's not a denial, Mom."

"Ms. Wallace," Tracy began. "Richard needs your help. I really can't go into all the details, so you'll just have to trust me on that point."

"Trust *you*? You're practically a stranger and yet you tell my daughter I'm a liar. And now you want me to trust you?"

Tracy tilted her head slightly. "If I had any doubt of it, I don't anymore."

Both Wallaces looked at her. "And what does that mean exactly?" Carrie asked.

"After hearing about you and meeting you yesterday, I thought you were a meek person; the kind of person someone like Carl Jeffries could push around. But you're not meek, are you Carrie? You're a very strong person. I saw your daughter in action just a little while ago. She got her strength from you, not her father. *He* was a loud- mouthed bully."

Megan looked at her mother and then at Tracy. "Of course," she said. "I see what Tracy's getting at. I should have realized it myself."

"You both are being presumptuous," Carrie said defensively.

"No, Carrie. When Carl Jeffries showed up at your door, you'd have told him to kiss your ass and leave. Maybe once upon a time you were naïve and trusting. But after how Carl treated you and what you have been through, you weren't that person anymore. So, Carl must have had something else up his sleeve; some other reason you'd let him stay here."

Carrie Wallace stood up. "I'd like you to leave, Mrs. Shane."

"Mom!" Megan shouted.

"Stay out of this, Megan." She looked at Tracy who was now standing also. "Richard and I have spoken recently. I know he's in trouble. But I can't help you. Now please leave."

"Mother!" Megan shouted angrily.

Tracy put a hand on Megan's shoulder. "It's all right, Megan. I'll go. But I will say one more thing to your mother." Tracy stood tall, confident. "Ms. Wallace, the private detective I use is contacting someone who knew Carl when he lived in Los Angeles. He's going to find out why Carl Jeffries came back here and then he's going to tell me. I *will* find out what's going on here."

"GET OUT!" Carrie shouted.

Then she left the living room area. Megan's eyes were wide. She looked at Tracy.

"Tracy, what's going on? Please tell me."

"I will when I find out Megan."

Tracy said goodnight and then left Megan standing alone and frightened in her mother's apartment.

Tracy was disappointed when her usual welcoming committee did not greet her. But when she stepped into the living room, she understood why.

"There you are finally!" Crystal Shane shouted.

Tracy covered her mouth as the tears formed. One would think she hadn't seen her sister-in-law for years.

"None of that now," Crystal ordered. Soon the women were embracing tightly.

"It's so good to see you, Crys."

"Brian called and said you needed cheering up. So, here I am."

Tracy released her best female friend and wiped her eyes. "Brian called you?"

"Yup. I knew it was serious when he practically *begged* me to come over."

"He didn't."

"Maybe a little."

Tracy laughed. "Where are El-J and Kenneth?"

"In the playroom with your brood."

"I didn't even notice your car."

"Tisk, tisk. Distracted driving is not a good thing, sis."

And then Tracy grabbed Crystal again. "Thanks for coming, Crys."

"Are things that bad, Tracy?"

"For my client, yes."

"Everything's okay with you, Brian, and the kids, right?"

"Yes."

"Good. I was worried something might be wrong at home."

"Home is perfect."

"Of course, it is since I'm here now."

"That's what I've always loved about you, Crys: your modesty."

"I've told you before, modesty is for wimps."

The two friends sat down. "How's *your* family, Crys?"

"Just great."

"Any news?"

"News?"

"Yeah, you know."

Crystal rolled her eyes. "I'm not here to talk about future offspring with you, sis. I want to know how I can help you."

"You just being here is enough."

"You should have called me."

"I'm sorry."

"Okay. So, you want to go out and knock back a few?"

"A few what?"

"For you, I guess it'd be ginger ales."

"Maybe a glass of wine."

Crystal smiled broadly. "Now, you're talking! Let's go!"

"I can't, Crys. Not tonight."

Crystal frowned. "Then you owe me one. I want to share some conversation over some wine with you."

"Okay, Crys. I promise we will."

"Soon," Crystal said firmly. "Soon."

It was a bad idea to sit nearly two-year-old Kenneth Tanner next to practically three-year-old Nicole Shane. The two were too busy entertaining each other to eat their macaroni and cheese. It was even more frustrating because Violetta Brubaker had balked at the idea of serving something not made from scratch. Tracy went ahead and prepared the boxed meal anyway. And now neither Nicole nor Kenneth was enjoying it. As for Peter Brubaker, he was watching his sister and cousin and giggling appropriately.

"Kenneth," Elias Tanner, Jr. said sternly. "Eat your dinner or we'll go home."

"NO!" Kenneth protested.

"Then eat."

"You eat too, Nicole," her father ordered. "Or I'll put you to bed."

"NO BED!"

"Then eat."

Tracy and Crystal exchanged grins. They both seemed to know each other's husband wasn't like this normally. Brian rarely raised his voice at Nicole; Elias, Jr. was frequently his son's partner in crime. After dinner, Tracy and Crystal returned to the living room while everyone else busied themselves elsewhere.

"Look Tracy, you can't go on getting so wrapped up in your clients like this."

"I know, I know."

"You have to keep your emotions in check. Even if you're scared, you can't let that show. I speak from experience."

"I know."

"You know, huh?"

"You're not telling me things I haven't told myself."

"I guess not. The friend in me wants to keep on hugging you, but the practical me wants to shake some sense into you."

"Many have tried, Crys. All have failed."

Crystal started laughing. "Oh, Tracy…you're a wingnut."

Tracy chuckled. "Auntie Wingnut, that's me."

Crystal, smiling, shook her head. "Brian also told me there was some bad scene here Saturday."

"Yeah. Ben Falcone."

"The drooler."

Tracy laughed. "The what?"

"Brian's known Ben since college. He's been to lots of our parties. And he always showed up thinking my friends were popsicles in the desert."

"Good grief."

"I swear to you, the guy had a hard-on before he said his first hello."

"Stop already!"

Crystal laughed. "Sorry, but it's all true. Pop-eye was also something we used to call him."

"I get it. You can stop now."

"Well, to be honest though, he was never anything more than a window shopper. Maybe all guys are like that but a lot more subtle about it."

"He makes me uncomfortable."

"Of course, he does! He should act like a grownup now. His wife is pretty and she's very nice. I met her at Ben's wedding. I was Brian's date."

"Oh."

"Brian was one of the groomsmen."

Tracy sighed. "I like Lisa, too. I guess she's more or less accepted that's how Ben is and just deals with it. But Ben showed up Saturday either buzzed or outright drunk. That's why there was a scene."

"Déjà vu."

"Tell me about it."

"I don't have to."

Tracy sighed. "I was hoping Lisa would call me back after we spoke Sunday, or that Ben would call Brian. But neither of us has heard anything. I hope Lisa's okay. I've been meaning to call her."

Crystal looked at Tracy skeptically. "Stay out of it, sis."

"What?"

"Don't 'what' me. This is your pal Crys, remember?"

Tracy chuckled. "I like helping people."

"We all get that. But *they* haven't asked for your help. Helping someone who asks for your help is one thing. Trying to offer it unsolicited makes you a Butt-In Betty."

"Did you just call me a butt?"

Crystal started laughing. "If the diaper fits, baby…"

Tracy shook her head. "You're supposed to cheer me up and here you are calling me names." But the attorney was laughing just the same.

"Hey, doesn't it make you all warm inside knowing that all these people care about you so much? I had to rearrange my schedule to be here."

"Did you really?"

Crystal grinned. "No, not really."

Another headshake. "You're so awful and wonderful at the same time."

"That's the secret to my success, Tracy dear."

"I'll bet. Hey, did Brian tell you I wanted to see pictures of him from Halloween?"

"Oh, he did ask me about old photo albums. But I really haven't had time to find them and go through them."

"Rats. I was hoping to see you guys as Bert and Ernie."

Crystal laughed. "How humiliating…"

"Come on, Crys. I bet you two look adorable."

"There's a reason those albums are buried somewhere."

The mood turned serious again. "Is it because seeing old photos would remind you of your parents?"

"Something like that, I guess. But I've never been the kind of person who likes to look back. I'm always about the here and the now and the future. I have so much going on."

"I can understand that."

It was Crystal that heard the buzzing and asked, "Is that my phone or yours?"

Tracy leapt from the sofa. "Mine! I'm waiting for a call from your father-in-law."

"Tell Dad I said 'hi'." Crystal watched Tracy grab her phone and disappear into the kitchen.

"Talk to me, El," Tracy said immediately.

"Hello to you too."

"This is the part where I tell you your son and his family are here. But before I let you talk to *them*, *you* have to talk to *me*."

"Why are they there?"

"Never mind that now. Did you talk to Amber?"

"I did finally get a hold of her."

"And?"

"Are you sitting down?"

"YOU GOT SOMETHING!"

"You bet I do."

Tracy sat down. "I'm sitting. Tell me."

"Because Carl Jeffries was in adult entertainment, he was getting medical tests all the time."

"Yes, I knew that already."

"Tracy, Carl Jeffries was sterile."

"Wait. As in no babies?"

"As in no babies."

"Then that means…"

"Yes, it does."

"Then who is Megan Wallace's father?"

"That, Tracy, is the next thing we should find out."

"Oh, we'll find out all right, El. We may even have the answer by this time tomorrow."

CHAPTER 13

When Tracy Brubaker Shane had told her reflection, "No more Mr. Nice Gal," she hadn't been kidding. Carrie Wallace learned that fact as she approached her automobile Wednesday morning.

"Hello, Carrie," a voice said from behind.

Carrie's eyes widened after she turned. "What the hell are you doing here?"

"On your way to work, are you?"

"Yes. Now please leave."

"I will. But I want you to know something before I do. You'll need to decide today. I don't have time to wait."

"What are you talking about?"

"I'm talking about the fact that Megan is not Carl Jeffries' daughter."

Carrie Wallace stared at the attorney. She wasn't sure if Tracy was taking a wild guess, or if she had discovered the truth.

Tracy removed all doubt when she said, "I'll subpoena the medical records from Los Angeles if I have too. I'll fly Amber Hardshoe out here to testify how shocked Carl was when his pal Oliver Culp showed up one day and told him about the daughter he had back in Maryland. You get me, Carrie?"

Carrie started shaking her head. "Please don't."

"Why? I'd think Megan would be thrilled to learn Carl wasn't her father."

"You…you can't. Please!"

"I gave you a chance to come clean. I guess I understand now why you couldn't say anything with Megan there. So, I'll give you a chance to make it up to me. Find a way to take a couple hours off and come visit me today at my office. If this matters that much to you then you can find a way." Tracy removed a business card from her pocket. "Take it. You'll need it."

Carrie took it. Her hand was shaking. Tracy remained stoic.

"If I don't hear from you by 1:00 p.m., I start making calls."

"You don't know what you're doing," Carrie whispered while shaking her head.

"On the contrary, Carrie, I know *exactly* what I'm doing." Tracy turned abruptly and headed towards his car.

"I have no idea what I'm doing anymore," Tracy told Neal. She was seated at her desk with her hands covering her face, elbows on the desktop. "I totally lost it yesterday. I teared-up in front of Richard; I basically accused Megan of lying; and this morning, I screwed up my would-be intimidation of Carrie Wallace by talking about a trial that will never happen. I'm done."

Neal sighed. "Everybody has a bad day now and again, Tracy. I'm sorry you had one."

"How can any of them have any confidence in me? I'm a total spaz."

"Stop that. You're a good attorney and a good person."

"I suck."

"You don't. Now, stop feeling sorry yourself and let's talk things through. That usually helps."

Tracy revealed her tear-streaked face. "There's nothing to talk through."

"Just stop it. You want me to quit?"

"You should. You should find a firm worthy of your talents."

"I already did. So, tell me what you have."

She sighed. "I know Megan Wallace is not Carl Jeffries daughter. I know Carl Jeffries was blackmailing Carrie Wallace and Richard George. I know someone somehow got Carl to cry out Richard's name during the murder. I know the killer used electrical tape to make sure the back door wouldn't lock. I know everyone disliked Carl Jeffries and that Megan probably hated him. But Megan wouldn't frame Richard for the murder. Unless, of course, she's lying about her feelings for him. But then, why ask for my help?"

"Who else you got, then?"

"I have Larry Peachtree. He's a 'place for everything and everything in its place' type person."

"Obsessive-compulsive?"

"I'm sure of it. Maybe Carl Jeffries borrowed his screwdriver one time too many. Or maybe Jeffries mocked Peachtree's pain. I don't know." Tracy twisted her lips. "You know, Neal, Larry could have staged that scene."

"Come again?"

"The tape scene. It would be consistent with his personality to go nutzoid over his missing property. But now that the significance of the tape has been made clear, he could have done that to make himself look innocent."

"And his motive?"

"I don't know. El couldn't find anything on him with respect to getting professional help or anything like that. The killer could have taken advantage of Larry's temperament by swiping his tape. Or, perhaps, the killer meant to return the tape to the table. But after he got back from fixing the back door there could have been people on stage or too close to the table. When Andy called it quits for the day, the killer panicked and just put the tape back in the drawer."

"I guess that's possible."

"I just don't know. I don't know if the killer meant for the tape's use to be discovered or not. If he didn't work full time for the studio then he wouldn't want the tape discovered. If he did work for the studio then he would, because he'd have to show how someone without keys could get back in. You see why this is driving me nuts?"

"Sure."

"So, Peachtree's outcry could have been legit, or it could have been a way to make himself look innocent, another part of the plan. We're dealing with a very clever killer here, Neal. I'm suspicious of every last one of them at this point."

"Who else we got?"

"Megan's boyfriend. He's the director of the show. Maybe he didn't relish Carl being his father-in-law someday. Maybe he got tired of seeing Megan upset. And there's Steve Dante whose idea this whole reunion was. He misled me about his history with the station. I don't care how he tries to spin things."

"Mm."

"There's makeup artist Tom Kramer and videographer Ned Topolski. But they hardly knew Jeffries. What motive could either of them have? And let's not forget the not-so-meek-and-mild Carrie Wallace. She must have loathed Carl more than any of them. She admitted she was sleeping with him. But I didn't ask her if he was forcing her to."

"Jeez."

"I know. It's all so ugly. I'm just not sure who knew the truth about what. I'm hoping Carrie calls me and agrees to tell me everything she can. If Jeffries' source of income was blackmail, what did he do with his free time?"

"Quite a list there, Tracy."

"And I have less than three days to work through it all. Art told Debbie that Richard has to cop to this by Friday."

"Why?"

"Some BS about not being able to give Richard a break once the true nature of the video is out there. Maybe Art wants to show it at the preliminary hearing. But with all the truths that have come out, Richard wants to shut this down. So, if I can't find something to help him by Friday, he'll take a plea."

"Okay. I can certainly understand why you're so upset about this. It's very upsetting stuff."

"Thanks, Neal."

"I'll put my gray cells to work on this. Maybe I'll come up with something."

Tracy smiled appreciatively. "You're the best."

"Really? How about a raise?"

"Did I say best? I meant to say, you're pretty good, Neal."

He chuckled. "Very well then. I'll just put *some* of my gray cells to work then."

"Use the good ones," Tracy grinned.

It wasn't long after Neal had left her that Rebecca Dietz announced a caller on line two.

"It's Richard George, Tracy."

Soon Tracy said, "Hello, Richard. Is everything okay?"

"Apparently not. Carrie just left here."

Tracy gulped. "I see."

George sighed. "I'm going to take the plea, Tracy."

"Richard, there isn't any plea offer yet."

"I'm going to call the State's Attorney and confess."

"Richard! NO! You can't!"

"I can and I will."

"Richard—"

"I'm sorry it's come to this; I really am. But I can't have Carrie hurt anymore."

"I never wanted to hurt her, Richard."

"I believe you. But Megan must never find out. I need to do what I can to make sure of it."

"I understand but—"

"No, you can't truly understand. You just can't. And I can't let this go on. Since you learned everything you learned as my attorney, I know you can't tell Megan what you found. I know you're an ethical person. So, I know if I plead guilty and be done with this, everything will stay as it is."

"Look Richard, the truth is going to come out anyway."

"Why?"

"Because Carrie didn't list a father on the birth certificate. To establish Megan is Carl's heir they'll do a paternity test. Otherwise, she won't get all that money."

"She doesn't want the money; she doesn't want *anything* from Carl. She's already told the police this. So, you see, there will be no test."

Tracy breathed deeply. "Richard, you said you'd give me until Friday."

"That's before you confronted Carrie."

"I'm doing what I'm doing for *you*."

"I know that, Tracy. And I appreciate your commitment to me. But—"

"*Please*, Richard."

There was silence on the other end. Finally, George said, "All right, Tracy. Friday it is."

"*Thank you*, Richard."

"But you have to leave Carrie alone."

"But I still need to talk to her; find out what Carl was doing all those years he lived with her."

"NO Tracy! That's my only condition."

"You're cutting my legs off, Richard."

"So, you don't agree then?"

Tracy sighed. "What choice do I have?"

"All right. Come see me Friday after you've exhausted everything."

"You don't sound hopeful."

"Goodbye, Tracy. And good luck."

Tracy slammed the receiver down. She was as angry as she'd ever been — at both her client and herself. Why didn't she just cut him loose? If *he* didn't care, why should she? Tracy suddenly loathed Carrie Wallace. She was the one pulling George's strings. She was the one who really wanted this thing shut down. She wasn't the timid creature she pretended to be. And Tracy believed that Carrie was playing Richard like a fiddle. Suddenly Tracy felt that maybe Carrie and Jeffries were perfect for each other. Maybe Carrie…maybe Carrie wanted Carl Jeffries out of her life and used George to help her. Or maybe she used somebody else. Regardless, she was perfectly willing to let a killer go free and let an innocent man take the fall. To Tracy, such a person was contemptible.

All right. So, Carrie Wallace wanted to play games, huh? Tracy Brubaker Shane could play games too. She still had friends at WMFT, Megan Wallace being one of them. Megan now was suspicious of her mother. And Tracy could use that to find out about Carrie Wallace. And Tracy very much wanted to learn as much about Carrie Wallace as she could.

A voice in Tracy's head said, "*Carrie Wallace, Welcome to* THE TRACY GAMES!"

Megan Wallace stared at her unannounced guest. "I'm not sure I understand your question."

"I think you understand it. I just think you're wondering why I'm asking it."

Megan sighed. "My mother was too busy for lovers when she was raising me, and I certainly can't help for the time after I moved out."

Tracy sighed. "Look, Megan. I need your help. Your mother isn't going to help me, and she can't know you and I are having this conversation."

"Dear God, Tracy, what's going on?"

"That's what I'm trying to find out. So, again, I ask you. Did your mother have any boyfriends prior to Carl showing up again?"

Megan folded her arms as she leaned back in her desk chair. "I'm sure she did. But there's no way I'll be able to remember any of them. There was no one that stuck around too long. My mom had me. Not many men want an instant family."

"Maybe somebody from WMFT?"

"What? No."

"How can you be so sure of that?"

"She hates this place."

"She does?"

"Sure. After she had me, she didn't want to come back here — ever."

"How do you know that?"

"I just remember asking her once why she didn't come back here after she had me. She told me she'd never come back."

"But she let you go work here."

"*Let* me?"

"Sorry. I didn't mean it like that."

"Forget it. I didn't mean to snap at you. But you're right. She wasn't too crazy about me coming to work here."

"Why not?"

"Bad memories; what Carl did."

"But she let Carl back into her life."

"But I don't know why; she refuses to tell me. I know she didn't love him. I'm sure of that now."

"Then that brings me back to the second part of my initial question. Since both of us believe your mother didn't love Carl, could there have been someone else in her life?"

"I don't know. She never mentioned anyone, and I didn't visit often."

"Okay. Did you notice any changes in her mood recently? Before the murder of course."

"Huh?" Alarm spread across Megan's face. "Wait a minute here. Are you suggesting my mother is involved in the murder?"

"Not directly. But if someone who cared about your mother knew what Carl was doing, and knew how Richard felt about Carl, he could have thought he was doing your mother a favor — getting rid of Carl I mean. I know your mother would never want to hurt Richard, of course. Someone else though might not care."

Megan started nodding. "Okay. I see what you mean. But that would mean this person works at the studio. And Mom wouldn't hook up with anyone here."

"You so sure?"

"Well…I guess I can't say. I mean if she were seeing someone, she wouldn't tell me because then I would have known the thing with my father was a farce. And she certainly wouldn't have told my father."

"Exactly."

Then Megan shook her head. "No, that doesn't make any sense either."

"What doesn't?"

"That Mom would set out to date someone from the station. She never came here — not even to visit. Why would she suddenly decide…?" Megan looked at Tracy angrily. "Oh…you are a smart one, aren't you Tracy?"

"What?"

"You *do* think my mother's involved in this. You think she seduced someone to help her murder my father."

"I didn't say that, Megan. Curious that you did though."

"Meaning what?"

"Meaning that you have some suspicions of your own. You know she lied to you all these years about loving Carl. What else did she lie to you about? That's what you're wondering, right?"

"I can't believe she'd do something like *that*."

"She may not have. There's no evidence to suggest that she did. But her actions have been strange."

"Yeah; they have."

"Your mother has shut me down even though I'm trying to help Richard. That doesn't make sense, does it?"

"Shut you down?"

"She refuses to see me anymore."

"Oh."

"I can't really get into all of that."

Megan sighed. "I don't know how I can help."

"Keep after her without letting her know I talked to you about her."

"She'll stop taking my calls if I get pushy."

"She's done that before?"

"A few times; like when I told her to kick Dad out."

"Ah."

Megan started chuckling. "Maybe I could invite myself over and ask to borrow her phone; scroll through the numbers she's been calling."

Tracy smiled. "That's an interesting thought."

"I shouldn't though."

"I don't want you to do anything that could hurt your relationship with your mother."

Megan rose to her feet. "I just can't believe my mother could be involved in this. She'd never let Richard take the fall for it."

"All right, Megan." Tracy stood. "But somebody set Richard up. I can't figure out why since everybody likes him. Maybe they did it because they like someone else more."

Tracy, now having put several bees in Megan's bonnet, turned to leave. Megan said nothing as Tracy closed the door behind her. But a buzz was in the air.

"Hi, Corky," Tracy said as she approached the security desk.

"Oh, hi."

"You doing okay?"

"Just great."

"Supreme! I'm glad to see you still have your job here."

"Thanks."

"How have things been around here? Are people looking over their shoulders all the time?"

"It's been nuts, Tracy; completely nuts."

"How so?"

"Just like you said: everybody's paranoid. There's so much tension. You want some coffee? I just made some."

"No, thank you. What kinds of things are going on?"

"Lots of whispers in the hallways; people not being as friendly as they used to be; people talking about leaving the station; that kind of stuff."

"Are *you* going to leave?"

"No. I like my job."

"That's good."

"Good news is I hear they're going set up cameras for the parking lot now. I may soon have a video console to monitor."

"Too bad they didn't have one of those already in place."

"Very true."

Tracy leaned towards the seated guard and lowered her voice. "Heard any rumors you can share? Sometimes there's a kernel of truth in those."

"Not really. I don't really mingle if you know what I mean. People pretty much just say 'hi' or 'bye' to me and that's it."

"Oh. Even Megan and Steve?"

"Well, *they* talk to me. Ms. Wallace is nice."

"I like Megan too."

"You know she came to my defense when the police started giving me a hard time."

"Why did they do that?"

"Just a misunderstanding. One of the cleaning people said they thought they saw me out back sneaking a cigarette or something."

"When?"

"That Saturday of the murder. But I never left my desk."

"I guess they made a mistake."

"That's what Ms. Wallace told them. I think it all worked out. I haven't heard anything since."

"Corky, do you know which member of the cleaning crew thought they saw you?"

"No."

"I remember the crew coming in when I was leaving that Saturday. Do you check each and every one of them in?"

"No, not really."

"What if one of the regular crew is sick and they have to send a replacement? Would you notice?"

"I guess not. But the other crew people would."

"Meaning what?"

"Well, they wouldn't just let someone tag along with them."

"But someone could, in theory, just show up and say they've been assigned to the team."

"I'm sorry. I wouldn't know anything about that." Corky's eyes widened. "Hey, maybe someone snuck in pretending to be part of the cleaning crew."

Tracy nodded. "That's what I was wondering about. But I guess if that had been the case, the police would have found out about a stranger joining the team when they interviewed the cleaning people."

Corky sighed. "I guess so."

"Besides, the police probably lost all interest in you and the cleaners when they arrested Richard George."

Corky shook his head. "Poor Mr. George. I hope he'll be okay."

"Me too, Corky. Me too." Tracy looked around. "Who *does* smoke around here, Corky?"

"Smoke? Not anyone that I can tell. Well, Mr. Debusey used to. But he quit almost a year ago."

"Really."

"Yes, ma'am. He has a pretty stressful job."

"I'll bet."

Corky sighed. "And I know this live show was stressing him out even before the murder."

"Really? How do you know that?"

Corky looked around. "Well, there was some big argument between him and Mr. Dante. I think Ms. Wallace was there too."

"Was it about Carl Jeffries?"

"Yes, I think so. Mr. Debusey had heard about all the trouble Mr. Jeffries was causing. He wanted him gone but both Mr. Dante and Ms. Wallace wanted him to stay. Something about him suing the station, I think."

"How'd you find this out?"

Corky's cheeks reddened. "Well, I didn't mean to eavesdrop or anything. I was just refilling my coffee, you know? I only heard bits and pieces."

"I guess Mr. Debusey raises his voice when he argues, and that's why you couldn't help but hear him."

"Yes, ma'am. He's a really nice guy but he can lose it occasionally."

"And did his quitting smoking make him lose it more than usual?"

"In the beginning, I guess. But not so much now."

"Mm. So there's nobody else you can think of who might sneak out for a smoke break?"

"No, sorry."

"That's okay. Did you ever see Carl Jeffries fight with anyone? Or maybe heard him arguing over the phone as he was leaving?"

Corky shook his head. "Sorry, no."

"And you're not aware of Mr. Debusey confronting Carl Jeffries over that argument you overheard."

"No."

"The Saturday night of the murder, you didn't notice Carl leaving with anyone, did you?"

Corky looked thoughtful. "No. No, I can't really remember."

"Do you remember seeing him leave though?"

"I think so; pretty sure I did."

"Is there anyone you *don't* remember seeing leave?"

He shook his head. "Since everyone arrived early in the day they didn't have to sign out. So, I can't really be sure if someone left by a back exit or something."

"Right. Most people would park in the front lot and come through the main entrance. It wouldn't make sense for them to park in the back unless they wanted to come and go by the back entrance."

"I guess."

"You don't monitor any of the cars, do you?"

"Nah, nothing like that."

"Mm. Well, good night, Corky. Thanks again for talking to me."

"Any time, Tracy. Any time."

"El, have you been able to find out anything further about Carl Jeffries?"

"No. There's nothing in vice's records about Carl Jeffries or his alias, George Carlsbad."

"So, Jeffries just lazed around the apartment all day?"

"It would seem so."

Tracy snorted. "What about the Baltimore porn industry?"

"What about it?"

"Could Jeffries have been working for one of them?"

"Tracy, the guy was in his sixties."

"Not when he initially moved back to Baltimore, he wasn't."

Tanner sighed. "Let's just say he was for the moment. Let's say he worked as a producer or a director or in some other capacity. How is that relevant? The person who killed him had to have been at the studio that Saturday."

Tracy thought a moment. "Moonlighting," she said finally.

"Moonlighting?"

"What if someone at the station has a side job?"

"Making adult films, you mean."

"Exactly. They need directors, cinematographers, makeup people, and all that."

"Again, let's assume you're right. What would that mean in this case? If Carl and someone else there were making dirty movies on the side, they would both be in the same position, right? Neither would want that fact coming out and neither could threaten the other without exposing, no pun intended, himself."

"Or herself."

"How's that?"

"Never mind; stupid thing to say." Tracy sighed loudly. "But to go back to your earlier point, Carl Jeffries' career was pretty much over. And he probably didn't really care who knew about him. People were *paying* him to keep quiet. Once it became clear he would not be the star of the live show, maybe he just didn't care who knew about him anymore. This other person though may not have wanted their second job known."

"But murder, Tracy?"

"Look, El. If Carl Jeffries was blackmailing Richard George, then he could have been blackmailing somebody else. $350,000 over sixteen years is not even $25,000 a year. Plus, he had almost a hundred thousand in his box. You see what I'm getting at?"

"Sure. He was blackmailing somebody else."

"I think we should consider it. He shows up in Maryland again in 2002 and shacks up with Carrie. He's successful at blackmailing her and Richard. Something else he gets involved in after he's back presents him with another opportunity, and he seizes it."

"I think you're letting your imagination run away with you here."

"That's a chuckle and a half coming from you, El. You were the one who told me to use it."

"There are limits."

"There are no limits to one's imagination. That's what makes imagination so wonderful."

Tanner sighed. "All right. But the fact is there's nothing to suggest Jeffries was involved in anything in Maryland. Nothing."

"Fine. I guess that's it then."

"I'm sorry. I wish I had found something."

"I'll be in touch."

Tracy placed her phone on her desk. She remained seated for a few more moments, and then she stood up. There was one person she hadn't talked to yet. And now she felt this was the time to take care of that oversight.

It was a very risky move, but Tracy was out of ideas and almost out of time. Richard George had told her to stay away from Carrie Wallace. Okay, she would keep her promise and stay away. But he hadn't said anything about his own wife, Elaine. Tracy had wanted to meet her more for social reasons up until now. But the reason Tracy was now pulling her auto into the Georges' driveway was much more serious. Maybe Richard George didn't care if he went to prison for a crime he didn't commit. Elaine George would most likely have a different feeling on the matter.

The woman who answered the door was in her early seventies, thin, and dressed in a white blouse and blue jeans. Her hair was a mix of black and gray and was cut short. Tracy felt a great sense of relief when Elaine George smiled at her unannounced visitor.

"Tracy, right?" Elaine greeted.

"Yes." The attorney offered her hand, and the women shook briefly. "Please forgive the intrusion, Mrs. George. But I really need your help."

Elaine nodded. "Of course. Please come in."

Tracy declined the offer of coffee and was soon seated on a sofa with flower-patterned cushions.

"I'm not sure what your husband has told you, Mrs. George," Tracy began. "And as his lawyer I can't really get into too many details. But I'm hoping you will talk to me about Carl Jeffries."

Elaine George sighed. "Richard's in real trouble, isn't he?" she asked somberly.

"It's not looking too good," Tracy answered quietly.

"I see. And what exactly can I tell you about Carl that you don't think Richard has already?"

"Right now, I just know Jeffries was arrogant and ornery to people. I also understand he fancied himself a ladies' man. I was hoping you could tell me about your own experiences with him. Did you see him be nasty to people, maybe one person in particular? Just how much of a flirt was he? Did that ever get him into trouble?"

Elaine looked at her folded hands. Then she returned her focus to the attorney. "Carl liked to get a rise out of people. He thought he was funny, and he didn't mind being cruel to someone to get a laugh."

"Cruel how?"

"Oh, if someone made a mistake with a line or forgot their dialogue, he would berate them. If he wasn't happy with his lines, he'd insult whoever wrote them. That kind of thing."

"You witnessed this yourself or your husband told you about it?"

"Both. I'd sometimes come to the studio to meet Richard for lunch or some other reason. I'd see Carl in action."

"Mm. How about seeing him in action putting the moves on someone?"

Elaine smiled. "The moves? Well, I'm not really sure about that."

"My next question is a touchy one, Mrs. George," Tracy gulped. "Do you know if Carl hit on married women?"

Elaine George blinked. "He flirted with me sometimes."

"I don't mean mere flirting. Do you know if actually asked a married woman out?"

"Look," Elaine sighed. "I don't really know. Is there someone's wife you have in mind?"

"I know Larry Peachtree and Steve Dante were married men. Did their wives visit like you did?"

"I don't believe so. I met them at holiday parties and things like that. I don't recall ever seeing them in the studio."

"You know about Larry Peachtree's wife, right?"

Elaine shook her head. "Yes. Extremely sad."

"These parties, did Carl maybe have a little too much to drink and go too far maybe?"

"I never heard anything."

"I suppose Larry would certainly have said something if Carl came on to his wife."

Elaine shook her head.

"Why did you just do that, Mrs. George? Why did you shake your head?"

"Carl wouldn't have hit on Janice, Larry's wife."

"Why not?"

"Janice Peachtree, from what I remember, was a very sweet young woman. She had to be to put up with Larry's…idiosyncrasies, let's call them. But she wasn't…We used to call women like Janice homely."

"Oh. Carl liked his women physically beautiful."

"Yes."

"And Janice wasn't."

"No."

"You said Carl would go for an easy laugh at someone else's expense. Did he ever insult Janice Peachtree in front of her husband?"

Elaine George furrowed her brow. "I don't recall anything like that. I'm sure if something like that had ever happened Richard would have said something."

"How about after Janice Peachtree died? Did Carl make fun of that in Larry's presence?"

Elaine shook her head. "I think even Carl wouldn't have crossed *that* line. I never heard that he made cruel remarks about Larry's loss."

"Okay, how about Steve Dante's wife? Was she easy on the eyes?"

Elaine chuckled. "I'll answer that by saying she was a finalist in the Miss Maryland contest one year. Steve would make sure you knew that the first time he met you."

"Lucky man."

"But I never heard that Carl hit on her. Steve, from what I recall, was new and Carl probably had little to do with him."

"I see."

Elaine George shifted in her seat. "May I ask why this focus on Larry and Steve and their wives?"

"Honestly, desperation."

"Desperation?"

"Larry and Steve knew Carl and Richard going back to the eighties. Everyone else involved in the reunion only knew Carl for a few weeks, except Megan, of course. It's the motive that I'm having trouble with."

"And you think Carl had an affair with Larry or Steve's wife?"

"It would be a strong motive if true."

"But why frame my husband for it?"

"That's a very good question, Mrs. George."

"Yes. But I never heard anything like what you're suggesting. Carl was just a big talker, you know? And the more he talked, the more people seemed turned off by him."

"Except for Carrie Wallace."

Again, Elaine George sighed. "True. Carrie was the exception. But she was new and young and probably more than a little naïve when she started. Carl turned on the charm."

"I believe Richard warned her about him."

"You're probably right. But you'd have to ask him."

"He didn't talk about Carrie with you?"

"Not really. Why would he?"

"But you let her stay in your home after she had Megan. That was an extremely kind thing to do. I thought you knew her well, or at least Richard did."

"Richard said she needed help and we were in a position to help her. I think he felt that he didn't do enough to dissuade her from seeing Carl. I guess he felt responsible. And the truth is I liked the thought of having a baby in the house. My three weren't living with us year-round. My youngest had just started college and was living on campus."

Tracy smiled. "All grown up, huh?"

"Yes. Do you have children?"

"Two."

"Oh, that's right. Richard did tell me you had a daughter and son. You may not believe it, but you'll miss those early years."

"I believe it. Other than the diapers, I pretty much like all of it."

"I guess…I guess that's maybe why I let Carrie stay here. I knew she'd need help with the baby."

"You're very fond of Megan, I take it."

"Oh yes; a beautiful child. Part of me…" Elaine sighed.

"What is it, Mrs. George?"

"Part me wished Carrie would let Richard and I adopt Megan."

"Oh. Did you actually ask her?"

"No. I could tell she wanted to be a mother to Megan. I never saw anything to suggest she'd be open to such a thing. I'm not even sure why I told you what I just did. It's been so long."

"I won't be repeating any of this to anybody, Mrs. George. I'm just trying to find some possible reason why someone would do what they did to Carl Jeffries."

"I'm sorry I can't help you. I wish I could remember something."

"That's okay. I appreciate you talking to me." Tracy stood. "I think I've taken enough of your time."

"Not at all," Elaine said rising. "I take it you didn't tell Richard you intended to see me today."

"No, I didn't."

"Well, I won't be repeating things then too."

The women exchanged smiles and then Tracy was on her way home.

"Sorry to bother you again, Megan," Tracy said. She had reached her homestead but was still sitting in her car.

"No problem. What is it?"

"Some people overheard the argument among you, Steve, and Jerry over Carl."

Megan had to visit her memory bank. "Oh, that wasn't anything. I told you about the desire to do a new show."

"I remember."

"Well, Steve and I had to convince Jerry that Dad wouldn't be a problem. But, of course, Jerry was hearing that Dad was causing nothing *but* problems. He wanted Dad gone."

"Even at the risk of the bad publicity?"

"That's what Steve and I were trying to tell him. But Jerry at first didn't really care about that. He thought all the potential controversy would be good for the show."

"It doesn't always work that way."

"I know. But Jerry isn't the kind of the person who'd let a Carl Jeffries get the better of him. He said we had a week to calm Dad down or he was out."

Tracy frowned. "Now, I'm confused. I thought you wanted your dad out. Why didn't you side with Jerry Debusey on this?"

There was a sigh. "I did. But this was so important to Steve, and Andy had gotten pretty excited about the thing. Being able to direct a live television show would be a great thing for Andy."

"I can see that."

"So, honestly, most of my threats were just that. I don't know that I ever would have had Dad fired. But *he* didn't know that. He knew what I thought of him. I used that."

"So, keeping your father on was because of Andy and Steve."

"Yes. I don't know what I would have done if Dad called my bluff. But with Jerry Debusey now making threats too, I'm not sure Dad would have made it to show time."

"I hear you. Did Jerry and Carl have any personal run-ins?"

"No."

"How can you be so sure?"

"Believe me. If Jerry had yelled at Dad, Dad would have come whining to me. You know, how could I have sent the station manager after my own father? That kind of thing."

"I gotcha. Did Carl ever accuse you of siccing someone on him?"

Megan laughed. "No. I tended to get in Dad's face myself. I never intentionally allowed someone else to do *my* dirty work. That's not me."

"You deal with things directly."

"If I have to. You have to know when to delegate and when to take care of things yourself."

"I hear you, Sister Megan."

Megan chuckled. "Is there anything else I can help you with?"

"Not right now. Sorry for bothering so late in the day."

"No problem, Sister Tracy. I'll talk to you later."

Tracy laughed softly as she opened her car door. She liked Megan Wallace very much. And with an unidentified killer still out there, that might not be such a good thing right now.

"I want to kiss my pumcan, Mommy."

"Okay, Nicole."

"And my skult."

Tracy stood up and brought the props to her daughter. Looking at the skull and its bloody eyes made Tracy especially uneasy on this particular occasion. Two days until Richard George would accept a plea offer, and there was no escape from being reminded of this, even in her daughter's bedroom. She let Nicole kiss the decorations and then Tracy kissed the child goodnight. Bonkers entered the room as Tracy was leaving it, so she gave the pooch a smooch too. She found her husband sitting on the downstairs couch and was grateful when he offered his massage services.

"I don't know if I did the right thing," Tracy sighed.

"You did what you had to do for your client."

"But my client doesn't want me doing what I'm doing."

"He has a secret to keep."

"But what is he afraid of? Does he think Megan will suddenly hate him?"

"His wife might. Maybe he just doesn't want to hurt *her*."

"You're probably right. I wonder what Elaine would do if she found out. I met her today."

"And…?"

"Very nice woman, but I doubt she's involved in this. I'd think any hurt and hatred she would have would be directed at Carrie Wallace, *not* Carl Jeffries."

Brian continued rubbing her shoulders. Her back was to him.

"What are you going to do now?"

"Use my imagination, I guess. That's what El said I should do."

"Imagination?"

"Try to imagine what the killer had to be thinking as he planned this thing out. What precautions did he have to take? How could he have worked everything?"

"I see."

"Take for example Carl Jeffries' return."

"Okay."

"The killer calls him, lures Jeffries back somehow. We know Jeffries came in the back because Corky, the security guard, didn't sign anyone in that night after everyone had left. But how does this work? Does the killer wait outside for Jeffries to arrive and then let him in? Probably not. A passerby might notice him. So that must mean he waits *inside*. So, when Jeffries gets there, what does Jeffries do?"

Brian kissed her neck.

"Stop that."

"Sorry."

"No, you're not."

"I am though."

"Where was I? Oh, what does Jeffries do? Does he knock on the door? Is the killer standing right inside the doorway?"

"I thought there was tape on the door."

"There was. But that was— Hey, that's right. Maybe there *was* tape put over the catch." She turned suddenly and faced Brian. "I thought that a piece of tape was just placed there as part of the frame. But maybe there was tape put there so that Jeffries could just come right on in. The killer waits inside; he's told Jeffries that the door will be open; then Jeffries shows up and goes on in. Neither person needs to loiter in the parking lot."

Brian smiled. "Sounds good to me."

"But then how do things play out? I need to think about that too."

"Does what you just said help you at all?"

"Not really. The killer may or may not have had keys to the studio. So, everyone is still in play."

"What about cars? Didn't that guard see cars arrive?"

"No. The desk is too far away from the main doors to have a good view of the parking lot, unless you're parking very close to the building. Our players would have made a quick right and parked in the back. The killer may have even parked his car on the street and hoofed it."

Brian kissed her lips.

"Stop that."

"I'm sorry."

"No, you're not. Where was I?"

"Hoofing it."

"Oh right. If he did hoof it, I bet he had a disguise on."

"In case he was seen."

"Right."

"What kind of disguise?"

"I don't know. Something innocuous."

"Jogger, maybe."

"Maybe."

"Let's go upstairs."

Tracy smiled. "That's a good idea. I should look at the video again. Thanks, Brian."

"But I wasn't—"

Brian didn't finish his sentence. Tracy was already trotting up the steps. When he arrived in the home office, Tracy had already opened the email with the video footage.

"Come watch with me," she said cheerfully.

"Okay," Brian responded glumly.

"Maybe I missed something."

"How many times have you watched that thing?"

"Brian, remember the one case where I noticed something in a video, and it led to the solution?"

"Oh, yeah. Right."

"Maybe magic can happen again."

"Speaking of magic…"

"Stop that."

"I'm sorry."

"No, you're not."

Brian shrugged his shoulders. After a few minutes he asked, "What exactly is it you're looking for?"

"Don't know. I don't see anyone using any studio phones, do you?"

"I…"

"Look," Tracy ordered, pointing at the lab table. "There's the tape that was used on the door. It was still on the table at three in the afternoon. Unfortunately, this is the last time we get a clear look at the table. So, who knows when the tape was taken?"

"Right. Who knows?"

"Here's my big scene."

Brian chuckled. The camera focused on the skeleton that was mostly concealed behind the coffin.

"Say everyone, how do skeletons get to work every day?"

"Oh no," Brian groaned.

"Quiet, Brian. This is kinda cute."

"They carpals."

"Groan," Brian announced.

"Shush," Tracy ordered.

"I guess that's a keeper," Jeffries called out.

"Don't you mean crypt keeper?" Honeywell asked.

After a few minutes of silence Jeffries said, "Leave the jokes to me, sonny boy."

"Deal. And you'll leave the directing to me."

"This is where Jeffries leaves the stage," Tracy whispered.

Andy Honeywell looked at his watch. "All right folks it's after 6:00 p.m. Let's call it a day. Everyone did really well today. Enjoy tomorrow and we'll see each other on Monday."

"And make sure you put everything back where you found it!" Larry Peachtree called out. "I still am missing one of my paint brushes."

"I'll buy you a new one," Topolski could be heard grumbling.

Honeywell sighed. "Larry's right. Let's not leave everything a mess."

As the camera panned to Larry Peachtree, Tracy could be seen briefly.

"There I went," Tracy said.

The voice of Ned Topolski said, "And I want some interviews if I didn't talk to you already."

Peachtree growled, "Get that out of my face. I'm still at work here."

"Just some positive words for our potential audience," Topolski pleaded, as Peachtree continued loading various items in drawers.

"Not now; maybe later. Find someone else."

"Megan won't be happy about this."

"What, you're going to *tell* on me?" Peachtree snorted as he slammed a metal drawer closed. He then turned and moved quickly elsewhere.

"What is it with people around here?" Topolski could be heard asking. Then the screen went blank.

"And this, dear Brian, is when the killer must have found a phone and called Jeffries. I'm not sure yet if Jeffries was in or out of the building when he got the call on his cell phone."

"But he was seen leaving."

"Yes. Corky the guard was pretty sure he saw him exit."

"Okay."

"Did you notice anything, Brian?"

"No. But people were sure snippy, weren't they?"

"Poor Ned," Tracy chuckled.

"I guess. If only he had kept the camera going a little while longer, he may have gotten something."

"Want to see the rehearsal footage of Dr. Mort that Ned filmed?"

"I—"

"Supreme! Just give me a second."

"Great."

"HELLO ONCE AGAIN MY FRIENDS! It is I, Dr. Mort Itchin, coming to you once more from my House of Funerals. We've been quiet but very busy all these years!"

"This looks and sounds great," Andy Honeywell interrupted. "I don't think we need to go through the whole script right now."

"But I memorized everything," Richard George protested.

"Sorry, Mr. George. But I have some rewrites to show you anyway."

"Rewrites? Can't you get it right the first time?"

Tom Kramer came on to the stage. "How much longer are we doing this today?" he asked Honeywell.

"I think until around 6:00."

"That sounds okay I guess." Kramer looked at George. "Your wig's crooked."

"I don't care."

"Let me fix it."

"It's not necessary. *Herr Direktor* won't let me run all my lines."

Kramer looked at Honeywell. "Should I fix his wig or what?"

"No. Why don't you instead help him off with his coat and just put it on the table? Richard and I are done for now."

"The coat helps me stay in character!" George protested. "And I want to practice."

"We're not ready to do a full-dress rehearsal, Richard. There will be time to get you all dolled up next week and we'll rehearse to your heart's content."

"FINE!"

Tom Kramer chuckled as he removed the lab coat. "Just wait here and I'll help you off with your makeup." Kramer started towards the table.

"You do that. And this time I'd like to keep my skin if you don't mind."

"Hey that's a great one, Richard!" Carl Jeffries announced as he came on the stage. "I can use that." Ned Topolski's camera was now focused on Jeffries.

"You use everyone else's lines. Why not mine?"

Jeffries ignored the comment. "I'd like to keep my skin…I'll have to find a way to use that."

"You'll stick to the script, Carl," Honeywell said sourly.

"Hey, just work that into your rewrites Andy, my pal."

Honeywell frowned. "We'll see."

"We have plenty of time to get things right," Jeffries said enthusiastically. Then he looked at George. "Don't we Richard? We have plenty of time left for lots of things, don't we?"

George said nothing. He marched past Jeffries as he exited the stage. Tom Kramer soon followed him.

"That's quite a gift you have there," Honeywell said. "I hope you don't clear out audiences the way you clear off stages."

"Very funny," Jeffries snorted. He looked towards Ned Topolski's camera, squinting. "Hey! Are you filming this?"

"What?" Topolski could be heard asking.

"Turn that damn thing off before I turn it off for you!"

"*You?*" Topolski asked incredulously. "Why don't you come over here right now and try it. I'll wait."

Jeffries raised a fist and shook it. "You damned punks have no respect for anything or for anyone!"

Jeffries turned and left the stage. The image went black.

"This is exciting stuff," Brian murmured.

Tracy sighed as she stopped the video. "Fine, Brian. You can go."

"Are you coming with me?"

"Not right now."

"Tracy, there's nothing there."

"I guess not."

"So come to bed."

"I'm not tired and I'm not in the mood for what you want."

"I want you to get some rest. That's what I want."

"No, you don't."

Brian sighed. "Fine. I'll leave you then."

"Sorry, Brian."

"No, you're not."

Tracy slid under sheets at almost 1:00 in the morning. Her eyes were tired, but her brain was refusing to let the rest of her shut down.

She closed her eyes nevertheless and images immediately appeared in her mind's orb: Dr. Mort Itchin; bloody skeletons; video cameras; candy corn; a mallet pounding a stake into a horrified Carl Jeffries; his cries of "No, Richard!"; Carrie Wallace's cold stare; Tom Kramer's demonic masks; "Pumcans!"; a ticking clocking with a skeletal face; Brian Shane starring in *The Magic Wand!* Wait. What? Tracy sat up.

"God, I'm losing it," she whispered. "Now I'm making Brian a porn star."

She threw herself backwards violently, her noggin nearly hitting the headboard. This case: absolutely insane. A brutal murder where all clues point to one and only one person. And he was willing to take a plea. Why? To hide that he was Megan's father? Maybe. Maybe he didn't want to risk losing his wife Elaine. Or maybe there was something else. Maybe there was something else going on here that Tracy hadn't considered. It was time to use the imagination again; time to try and step into the killer's mind as he worked everything out. When exactly did he plan all this? During the filming? As soon as the reunion was announced? And why did he pick that particular Saturday? Was that part of the original plan? Had rewrites been necessary? Tracy turned on her side forcefully.

That video. Those cries of "Richard." Jeffries called out "Richard" after he had been struck with the mallet. Would he do that if he originally thought this was just some audition or rehearsal of a new scene? The strike would have given away that this was no play acting. Would the blow have scrambled his mind so that he still would say her client's name? It would be tough convincing anyone of *that*; impossible, really. *She* didn't even believe it.

Tracy returned to her back, and she covered her face. She had dealt with some tough cases before. But this one just may have topped them all. She had two days; she had a client who didn't seem to care what happened to him; she had a bunch of alternate suspects whose motives were weak or seemingly nonexistent; and she did not have a freaking clue as to what she was going to do next. Where was that luck of hers? Where was that seemingly innocuous comment or observation that ended up leading to the solution? No way could this be the perfect crime. There had to be a very good reason why someone would do all of this. Money? No. That nearly $100,000 wasn't going into anyone's pockets. And the whole thing was too elaborate to be a paid hit or something. Jealousy? Who could possibly be jealous of Carl Jeffries? He was a laughingstock, a butt of jokes. Revenge? That was possible. But she couldn't fathom Carrie or Megan — the people who probably hated Jeffries the most — framing Richard George for it. That just didn't track, unless this professed love for George was a lot of bull, a part of the plan. Tracy sighed. This was getting her nowhere.

Maybe she was wrong thinking only one person was involved in the murder. Maybe two people conspired to get rid of Carl Jeffries. That actually made more sense. No, actually, that didn't make *any* sense. If two people committed the crime they could alibi each other. And nobody seemed to have an ironclad alibi. Megan and Andy had fought and weren't together. Everyone else was single or not with their significant other that night. A joint effort seemed unlikely in this case.

Megan and Andy. Tracy twisted her lips. They *should* have been together that Saturday night. They each *should* have had an alibi. Megan: a person everyone seemed to like, and the person Richard George had been most worried about; the person he thought would be arrested for the crime. Kill Carl and frame Richard, all the while protecting Megan. Is that the key to this whole thing?

Carrie Wallace. She fit the keyhole. She hated Carl and Richard knew her secret. With both out of the picture it would be just her and Megan. She knew Richard George would keep quiet as long as he didn't suspect her involvement. But how could she have done this? Nobody saw her at the studio, and she wouldn't have known all the details of the coffin and the lab coat and the stake. An accomplice? No. If the motive was to eliminate those who knew her secret, she wouldn't very likely commit an even worse transgression that yet another someone would know about. She'd be right back in the same position! So, if Carrie Wallace is involved in this mess, there's some other factor Tracy couldn't at present figure out.

Elaine George. Did she find out about her husband's infidelity and want to punish him for it? She would have to have had help. But who would help her and why? A mutually beneficial crime, perhaps? She wanted to punish her husband and someone else wanted to hurt Jeffries. So, they came together. But how could that have happened? Elaine had no cause to visit the studio since her husband retired. To whom would she reach out? Besides, she was at a pumpkin patch with her family that evening. No. Tracy couldn't see Elaine George being a part of this either. It was even more unbelievable to her than her husband being guilty.

But that damned video! It kept coming back to figuring out how the damned video came about. How'd the killer pull *that* off? The police insisted the video was genuine. So, if it had been altered in any way, it would have to been done so by an expert. Ned Topolski had won an award in school for his filmmaking skills. But if he were *that* gifted, why would he be working for some local station like WMFT? And what reason would he have for killing Jeffries anyway? The only link they had was college. And Topolski was constantly laughing off Jeffries. The video footage and Tracy's own eyewitness accounts showed that. Topolski didn't seem to care one iota about Carl Jeffries.

But Jerry Debusey seemed to care about what Jeffries was doing to his station: pissing off staff, making his superiors miserable, and threatening lawsuits. But kill Jeffries over all that? Over a local show that may have actually benefited from the free, albeit negative, publicity a whiny Jeffries might cause? That didn't make any sense. And why frame the star of your show for the crime, thereby no longer having a show to publicize? No sense to that at all.

"Keep thinking simple, Tracy," she told herself. "Use the imagination and focus on that video; *that's* where you're going to find your answers. If you wanted someone to say you were someone you weren't, how would *you* do it? Write your own script. Start back in 1986 or so, when Carl Jeffries and Carrie Wallace started seeing each other."

So, she thought, and she thought, and she thought, until finally, the thinking had tired her brain. Nothing was coming to her. Nothing until…

"HOLY CRAP!" she shouted. She sat upright and tore away the covers.

"What?" Brian asked, stirring. "What's wrong?"

But Tracy didn't answer. She was already moving towards the home office. Brian soon also headed in that direction. Tracy already had the computer in the process of starting when he found her.

"What's going on?"

"Oh. Hi, Brian."

"Hi. What were you yelling about?"

"Nothing. I just want to see something."

"That damned video footage again?"

"Yes. Have a seat."

"No, thank you." Brian watched as his wife studied the screen. "What is it?"

"Nothing yet. I just want to check something."

"Oh."

"I need to zoom in here."

Brian decided to sit down.

Tracy pointed at the screen. "What does that look like to you?"

"Not sure. A hammer grip, maybe."

"How do you shift this thing so I can zoom in here?"

"Let me do it."

And when Brian clicked his last mouse click, his wife screamed.

"What is it?"

Tracy was covering her mouth, stomping her feet merrily on the floor. "The answer. I know the who and I think I know the why. I just have to figure out the how."

"The how? He drove a stake into the man's heart."

"That's not what I meant." Then her enthusiasm left her. "But even if I'm right, I can't see how I can prove it."

"I thought you just found the proof."

"Not proof of murder, Brian. Just a lie."

"I'm confused."

"And I'm tired. I need to get some sleep. Tomorrow I can refocus now that I have a clear target to focus *on*. That's *not* a hammer grip. Goodnight, honey."

Tracy kissed Brian's cheek and headed back to their bedroom.

Brian, still dazed, remained seated.

"My wife is officially nuts," he mumbled.

It wasn't too long before he decided to return to his bed, and the woman he shared it with. Tracy was sound asleep, until the next outburst at least. Better get some shut-eye while the shut-eye getting's good.

CHAPTER 14

"I can't believe it," Megan Wallace said in tears. Then she embraced Richard George tightly.

Steve Dante looked at Tracy in shock. "The charges have been dismissed?"

"Yes," Tracy said. "Richard is a free man."

Andrew Honeywell was practically laughing. "This is *great*! We still have time to pull this thing together!"

"But tomorrow's Halloween," Dante said. "Is that enough time?"

"Richard's a pro," Megan said. "He'll be fine."

"I want to try," George said.

Dante folded his arms. "Well, we do have the movie itself ready to go. What the hell? Let's move on."

Megan grabbed George's arm. "Let's go to the studio, Richard.

She left Dante's office. Honeywell followed.

Now that he and Tracy were alone Dante asked, "How on earth did you do it?"

Tracy smiled. "You'll find out tomorrow once the police have finished some tests they're running."

"Tests?"

"I wish I had a more exciting answer for you, Steven. But it all comes down to science."

"Science?"

"All will be made clear tomorrow. In the meantime, I want to watch Richard in action for a little bit."

"Okay."

Dante watched Tracy leave. He twisted his lips as he found his seat. He was no longer sure a live show tomorrow was such a good idea.

When Tracy entered the *House of Funerals* studio people were already gathered around the returning Richard George. They were trying to learn all the details they could. But George could tell them little.

"Tracy knows the answers," he said when he caught sight of her entering. "Ask her. I have work to do."

Tracy saw all heads turn in her direction. She smiled and waved.

"Hi, everybody."

Ned Topolski spoke first. "How the hell did you pull it off?"

"Sorry, Ned. Still a thing or two being worked on. But I think we'll have all the answers tomorrow."

"*We?*" Tom Kramer asked.

"Me and the police."

"Oh."

"YOU!" Larry Peachtree shouted as he approached Kramer. "You have my staple gun!"

Kramer looked in his hand. "I was just bringing it back to you."

"Back to me? You never asked to borrow it in the first place!"

"Easy there, Peach," Topolski said.

Kramer handed Peachtree his tool and said, "Thanks just the same."

Peachtree just snorted.

"Hey, Larry?" Tracy asked.

"What is it?"

"Can I bum a cigarette?

"A what?"

"A smoke; a cancer stick; a charch; a ciggy; a—"

"I get it, I get it…I don't smoke."

"Know anyone who does?"

"No! And there's no smoking in here anyway. Don't you dare smoke in here!"

"I won't, Larry. Sorry I annoyed you."

"You and everyone else!"

Peachtree turned and moved hastily toward the stage.

Kramer shook his head. "I'm going to staple that guy's yap before this over."

"Tom," Tracy began, "why did you need the staple gun?"

"Oh, put some staples on one of my masks. Kind of a man-made monster deal."

"Ah."

"Want to see it? It's just over—"

"No, thank you."

Kramer chuckled. "Oh, right."

"Do you have a cigarette, Tom?"

"Sorry. Don't smoke."

"Does your girlfriend?"

"Huh?"

"Aren't you dating a rock star or something? I thought if she smoked you might carry cigs for her."

"She doesn't smoke either."

"Oh. Do you know anyone around here who does?"

"No. But I've been here only a few weeks."

"That's true. I should let everyone get back to work. You guys have a pretty intense day coming."

"Intense is my middle name," Kramer grinned as he left the attorney. Tracy grinned in return.

"You think you made the killer nervous?" Detective Deborah Price asked.

"I don't think there'll be a confession, Detective. But the oven's been turned on."

Price chuckled. "I have the lab report back. You will like what I have to tell you."

Tracy smiled. "Does this mean you won't wait until tomorrow?"

"I shouldn't. But…"

"You'll let me do me my thing?"

"Tracy," Price said sympathetically, "with what you went through — what you put yourself through — over the last the few weeks, I can't refuse you. Besides, you may do better getting a confession with your usual…theatrics. I'll never forget your performance during the Montado case."

"Thanks, Debbie."

"You're welcome."

On Halloween night Brian, holding Peter, came into the dining room. Tracy was seated clearly enjoying *something*.

"What do you have there?" he asked her.

"A muffin," she answered.

He sat down next to her and smiled. "Wait a minute. That's a cupcake."

"No, it isn't."

"It is. Your mom made them earlier today."

Tracy pointed at her consumable. "Do you see any icing on this?"

"No."

"Then it very well can't be a cake, can it?"

"Huh? Plenty of cakes typically don't have icing; pound cake, for example."

"No icing, no cake. It's a muffin."

Brian started chuckling. "Call it anything you want, love. The sugar is still there."

"Mind over matter, honey."

Nicole came running into the room. "Mommy! Mommy! Mommy!"

"Whaty whaty whaty?"

"I want to go now!"

"I have to fix your costume."

Nicole looked at the muffin. "I want another cupcake."

"You already had one," Brian told her. "That's enough for now."

Tracy was now trying to tie her daughter's sneakers. But Nicole wouldn't stand still.

"Nicole, honey, you need to stop hopping so I can tie your shoes. You don't want to trip and fall while you're out, do you?"

"I wanna leave now!"

"In a few minutes. It's not quite 6:00 yet."

"I want candy!"

"I know that. Be still."

Brian chuckled. "You're the most beautiful ballerina in the world," he told his daughter.

"I wanna dance!"

"All right," Tracy said standing up. "Go show Grandma."

Nicole started running towards the kitchen shouting, "GRAMMAW!"

The parents started laughing. They stood and started moving towards the living room. Peter reached for his mother.

"Maybe next year you can come with us," Tracy told him.

"How long will you be?" Brian asked.

"About 35 minutes or so. I'm not sure how much Nicole will be able to stand. Plus, we have to motor to the studio."

Brian sighed. "Are you sure you're not in any danger?"

"Yes, Brian. I'm sure. This case isn't like most others."

"I guess not."

Nicole came running into the living room with Bonkers right behind her.

"Mommy, let's go!"

"All right, honey. Let's get the flashlight and your plastic pumpkin."

Tracy handed Peter back to his father.

"Bye, Daddy!" Nicole wrapped her arms around her father's legs.

"Bye, sweetheart. Have fun and bring me some candy."

Tracy opened the front door and she and Nicole were soon holding hands, the latter hopping along the walkway.

"The *last* thing that kid needs is more sugar," Brian thought.

They made it with 12 minutes to spare. Tracy and Brian exited their vehicle at 7:48 p.m. and moved quickly toward the front doors.

"Hi!" Corky said when he saw Tracy.

"Hi, Corky. This is my husband, Brian."

Corky offered his hand. "Nice to meet you."

Brian smiled as they shook. "Good to meet you too."

"Your wife's a real nice lady."

Brian grinned. "So, she keeps telling me."

Tracy elbowed Brian's ribs.

"You two go ahead. You know where you're going."

"Thanks, Corky. See you after the show."

"Sure!"

There were more introductions made as Tracy and Brian moved towards the studio. As they entered Megan Wallace approached.

"There you are! I was worried."

"Had a kid with more stamina than I thought," Tracy explained.

"I have seats for you upfront."

"Supreme!"

Tracy bore a broad smile as she and Brian took their places. The first row was far enough away from the stage so that everyone would have a clear view of the show. Tracy looked around and spotted the plainclothes officers that were scattered about. There were also uniformed persons there to protect the cast and crew from any overzealous fans. And Tom Kramer's masks were being put to good use. The masked attendees sitting on end-row seats were getting curious stares from their neighbors. The stage itself was, at present, shielded by large, black curtains.

"I've seen the set and it's incredible," Tracy told Brian. "It's really going to be something with all the light effects."

"I hope I can enjoy the show."

"Brian, don't worry. There are police everywhere. And I don't think anything will happen. After the show is another story."

"Marvelous."

Tracy took Brian's hand. "Try to have fun, honey. *I'm* going to."

At 8:00 p.m. sharp, the studio went dark. Suddenly the familiar strings of generic spooky music could be heard. Thunderclaps boomed throughout the studio while lights flickered. The audience started applauding.

When the curtains were lifted, smoke crept across the bottom of the stage. Green and black and purple lights moved wildly over the backdrop. The larger-than-life image of Dr. Mort Itchin that topped the makeshift lab's center brought "oohs" and "ahs" from the onlookers. Suddenly, the center doors were pulled back, accompanied by creaking sound effects. And when Dr. Mort Itchin emerged, the crowd stood and applauded. Tracy had tears in her eyes.

""HELLO ONCE AGAIN MY FRIENDS!" Richard George greeted in a confident, booming voice. "It is I, Dr. Mort Itchin, coming to you once more from my *House of Funerals*." The applause continued. "We've been quiet but very busy all these years!"

The audience finally returned to their sitting positions as the doctor moved towards his lab table.

"Tonight's feature is *Abbott and Costello Meet Frankenstein*, a classic homecoming of your favorite fiends. And here, tonight, right before your eyes, we will have a homecoming of sorts too." The doctor let his head fall backwards as he cackled madly. "For tonight, after so many — too many — years, I am going to bring my beloved bride back from the dead!"

The lights started flickering and the thunder resumed booming. The audience clapped loudly. George moved towards the edge of the stage.

"Yes, my dear friends! Tonight, you will meet the Bride of Itchin!"

And as the doctor resumed his maniacal laughter, the lights dimmed, and the curtain fell. The large video monitors that had been placed on either side of the stage now came to life. The Universal-International globe appeared as the film's soundtrack could now be heard throughout.

Tracy squeezed Brian's left arm with both her hands. Even Brian had to admit that Act 1 had gone very well. He started to relax. And by the time Lou Costello was doing his scaredy-cat routine to a moving candle, Brian was laughing along with the audience. When the lights came up for the first commercial break, Tracy turned to Brian.

"Isn't this the best?"

Brian put his arm around her. "Enjoying it are you?"

"Oh, my yes!"

"Maybe I should call home and see how Nicole's doing."

"She's fine, Brian. Mom can handle things."

"I know that."

"Stay here with me, Brian. We're on a date, remember?"

"Sure."

He kissed her quickly. It wasn't long before the lights dimmed, and the curtains started rising again to thunderous applause. The spotlight shined on the doctor.

"And now, my friends, let me direct your attentions to the coffin on your right." The spotlight moved and settled on a coffin. Tracy hadn't expected this. A new one must have been assembled. "In this coffin— "

The doctor's words were interrupted by the sound of laughter and applause, as a boney white object started to rise from behind the coffin. It stopped after about its ribcage cleared the casket.

"Oh, hey doc," the voice said.

Tracy pressed her fingers into her throat. The voice certainly sounded like Carl Jeffries. But she knew it wasn't really his. They must have found someone who could imitate him. And Tracy thought they had done well.

"What do *you* want?" Dr. Mort asked in typical exasperated fashion, which delighted the gathered.

"I heard you say your wife's coming home."

"Yes! I, Dr. Mort Itchin, will bring my beloved back from the grave!"

"You will huh?" Nagging Skeleton asked skeptically. "Are you cervical about that?"

The audience howled at the badness.

"I, Dr. Mort Itchin, have discovered the secret of immortality!"

"You, Dr. Mort Itchin, have finally gone completely mandible." More badness, more laughter.

"Get out, you jabbering jukebox of junk!"

"All right, all right, doc. I'm going. I have an appointment to make anyway."

"An appointment?"

"Yeah. I'm getting a phalange-icure."

"OUT!"

And then the curtains came down on Act 2 of the Dr. Mort show.

Tracy felt a bit apprehensive as the break before the big finale was coming to its end. Surely, they were not going to have Dr. Mort drive a stake through the vampire bride's heart. That would have been beyond bad taste. So, what did they have up their collective sleeves?

"And now the moment we have all been waiting for," Dr. Itchin said as soon as the curtains were raised. He pointed to a tube of colorful liquid. "When I pour this into my bride's…well, what used to be her mouth, she will live again!"

Dr. Mort moved quickly towards the casket and lifted the lid. Thankfully, the audience had full few of the coffin's contents as the casket was sufficiently propped up. Tracy covered *her* mouth as the doctor poured the tube's contents into his wife's mouth.

"This is it!" Dr. Mort said excitedly. "This is the moment I've waited my entire life, or afterlife, for!"

He looked at his audience. He looked back to his bride. He looked back to his audience. He looked back to his bride. He scratched his head and shrugged his shoulders.

"LIVE! LIVE AGAIN, I SAY! I SAY: LIVE AGAIN!" He looked back to the audience once again.

Thunder boomed throughout the studio. There was complete darkness except for the light that shined on the bride and her groom. He leaned in close to her.

"LIVE! Please live. There are people here. Please live. Pretty please. COME ON, *LIVE*!"

Suddenly, the corpse's arm slowly started to lift. The hand reached out in the darkness, finally grabbing the edge of the coffin.

"SHE'S ALIVE! ALIVE!"

Dr. Mort Itchin turned to the audience. And then 77-year-old Richard George started jumping up and down like an excited child.

"I DID IT I DID IT I DID IT!"

A drumbeat started sounding and the doctor put his hands on hips, his bent arms flapping like duck wings. He bent his knees slightly and started prancing around the stage to the rhythm of the bass-heavy thumps.

"I did it! It's my birthday! It's my birthday!" he started singing.

The crowd roared with laughter and the applause began. Eventually everyone came to their feet, clapping along with his rap.

"It's my birthday! I'm the doctor! It's my birthday! Who's your daddy? I'm the doctor! It's my birthday!"

Suddenly he stopped.

"Oh, dear me! My bride!"

The music ceased and he moved quickly back to his immobile spouse. He looked down into the coffin.

"Speak to me, my love. It is I, your love doctor; your schnooky; your pooky bear; your stud stack. I have brought you back to me, back from the dead. Speak to me! Tell me how you feel! *SPEAK*!"

There was quiet in the studio. Everyone's eyes were on the stage. The doctor moved his face closer and closer to his beloved, his expression one of anticipation and excitement.

And then…and then the bride spit out the liquid contents so that they sprayed and covered Dr. Mort Itchin's puss. The audience went wild. The bride then rose; slapped Dr. Mort across his moistened mug; and laid back down while pulling the coffin lid shut, almost smashing the doctor's fingers in the process.

Dr. Mort looked at the audience, which was applauding and hollering. He stood tall and cleared his throat.

"Well, I guess she still needs a few more years of beauty rest. She never could get up before 10:00 p.m. on a weeknight anyway."

The audience clapped as the curtains fell. When the movie's credits had finished, Dr. Mort Itchin was standing proudly at the stage's center. The rest of the stage was dark. Richard George waited patiently for the crowd to settle.

"Well, my fellow seekers of knowledge, the funeral parlor above me is about to open, which means I must say—"

"Oh, hey doc," a voice announced. Another light now illuminated the closed coffin and the form behind it.

"I thought you had an appointment," the doctor snapped.

"You can't trust those bone joints, doc." The audience groaned. "Say doc, sorry your bride didn't want to come back."

"She was always headstrong," Dr. Itchin lamented to scattered chuckles.

"That's too bad. Say doc, what's a skeleton's favorite rock band?"

"I don't know. The Rolling Bones?"

"No."

"Radius Head?"

"Nope."

"Ped Zeppelin?"

"No, doc. Give up?"

"Yes."

"The Beatles."

"The *Beatles*?"

"Yeah. They sing the classic *Baby You Can Drive My Carpals*."

The crowd laughed and applauded as the doctor pointed to the right stage exit and shouted, "*OUT!*" Then, once again, it was Richard George in the spotlight.

"Thank you all so much for coming out tonight. You chill my heart. Perhaps, we will meet again sometime. But until then, remember…"

George leaned towards his audience while placing his hand behind his ear.

"KEEP YOUR LABS CLEAN!" they shouted.

And at this point, Dr. Mort Itchin started his familiar maniacal laugh while leaning backwards. He pointed to the audience as the curtains came down for the final time of the evening. The video monitors started showing the *House of Funerals* credits as the lights came up.

"Ladies and gentlemen," a voice announced. "For those who would like to meet the bad doctor to have pictures taken or get autographs, please form a single line in the center aisle. Please follow all security instructions."

"Come on, Brian."

"Where to?"

"It's my turn now. But this is a by-invitation-only show."

"Ah."

Tracy left the studio with Brian trailing behind her. She navigated the halls without any difficulty and then entered Megan Wallace's office. She closed the door after Brian entered.

"Make yourself at home, why don't you," Brian commented.

"I have permission," Tracy said snapped.

"I was just kidding."

"No, you weren't. Now, listen. We have a while to wait until Richard is done with his fans. Then we're going to regroup in the studio."

"And then you take center stage."

"More or less."

"At least I get to watch this time."

Tracy smiled. "Did you like the show?"

"I did. I managed to enjoy myself despite it all."

"Me too. I wonder who did Carl Jeffries' voice. He was great."

"I thought the Nagging Skeleton jokes were above average, which isn't really saying much."

Before the couple could discuss things further, Megan Wallace entered. She had a washcloth in her hand but was no longer wearing her Bride of Itchin outfit.

"Hi, Megan."

"Hi Tracy!"

"Everything was supreme, Megan. You all did a great job."

"Thank you. I think everyone is happy with how it went. There were a few glitches, but I don't think anyone noticed."

"I sure didn't. And you were a great bride."

Megan laughed. "That came off very well."

"Whose idea was all that?"

"Andy's of course. I wasn't sure if it would work. But the audience really responded."

"Great stuff. Who did Carl's voice?"

"Oh, that was Ned. He won the voice addition we held yesterday. I never realized what a good imitation he could do of Dad's voice."

"I think it worked. It wouldn't have been quite the same without Nagging Skeleton."

Megan nodded. "Richard is so happy right now. All the people he's meeting have been so nice and enthusiastic. He really needs something like this given what's he's just been through."

"I agree."

Megan embraced Tracy.

"And it's all thanks to you. Thank you."

Tracy pulled back. "Listen, Megan. I have to warn you that tonight is going to get rough."

"Rough?"

"The reason for Carl Jeffries murder…it's not what a lot of people might expect it to be. I need you to remember that when things start happening, I'm not trying to hurt anybody. I'm just trying to get to the truth."

"About who killed my father."

"The truth about your father will definitely be a topic of discussion."

"Okay. I guess there's no way to pleasantly deal with a murder like this anyway, right?"

"Right. I hope when this is all over, we'll still be friends."

Megan looked at Tracy curiously. But she decided not to ask any more questions. Instead, she sat down and continued removing makeup. It was another half hour before Megan's phone started humming. She answered.

"All right," was all she said. She looked at Tracy. "That was Detective Price. They're ready for you."

Tracy rose and looked at Megan.

"Okay, Megan. It's time to bring down the curtain on a killer."

CHAPTER 15

The cast and crew had been assembled in the studio: Richard George, Steve Dante, Andy Honeywell, Larry Peachtree, Ned Topolski, Tom Kramer, and Jerry Debusey were seated as Tracy entered. Megan Wallace soon sat next to Honeywell and the two held hands. Tracy looked around. Someone was missing.

Tracy was about to call Detective Price when the studio door opened. Tracy turned to see Price escorting in the missing guest star: Carrie Wallace.

Megan stood. "Mom, why are you here?"

"I don't know," was all Carrie said as she sat on an outer seat. She looked at the floor.

"That just leaves one more person," Tracy told Price.

"He's coming," Price grinned.

Again, the studio door opened and in walked a demonic beast from the imagination of Tom Kramer.

"This way, Brian," Tracy called out.

The masked, horned figure gave Tracy an upwards thumb and then sat down.

"Okay. We're ready."

Tracy moved down the center aisle and sat on the stage, facing the small group.

"I just want to begin by saying how wonderful tonight was. You all did a great job and really captured the magic of those Saturday nights I used to snuggle next to my father. After the ugliness that happened here a few weeks ago, I wondered if I could ever watch one of those videotapes again. Thanks to tonight, I think I can. So, thanks again."

Most smiled at her.

"And you were great, Ned. Nice job on Nagging."

He smiled and nodded.

"So, I hope I can express my thanks to you all by sorting through the murder of Carl Jeffries. I know not too many people here cared for him. But what was done to him — and subsequently to Richard George — was an even greater evil than anything Carl ever did. I know he hurt a lot of people. But he didn't act alone in that. He had help, even if that wasn't the intent of various parties here. But the truth needs to come out. The killer's motive makes that a must."

Tracy sighed. "Let's begin with the Saturday of the murder. We know that production shut down shortly after 6:00 p.m. We know around that time Carl Jeffries received a call on his cell phone from a phone somewhere in the station. We know that Carl must have come back and entered through the rear door of this very studio. The police found tape that someone borrowed from Larry Peachtree on the latching mechanism. We know the murder occurred at 8:37 p.m. based on the video that was taken; the police assure us that no one tampered with the video. We know Corky the security guard found the body less than two hours later. And we know that Carl called out Richard's name twice during the attack, which is why, of course, Richard was arrested in the first place."

Tracy tossed her notebook to her right. "The assumption is that whoever called Carl had him return to the studio surreptitiously and enter through the back. I'm willing to bet the killer put the tape on the door so that Carl could just come right in, and neither of them would have to hang around in the parking lot waiting for the other. But as to what the caller said to get Carl to come back, we may or may not ever find that out. I think though the offer of a large sum of money is a good bet."

Tracy hopped down from the stage. She looked at Ned Topolski. "Ned, did you interview Carl for that pseudo-documentary you were making? I don't recall seeing any video of him."

"I guess I didn't get to him yet."

"I of course saw the footage you shot. You really didn't *interview* too many people. It was more filming people in action."

"So?"

"On the day of the murder you had footage of Richard George, Carl, Andy, Tom, and Larry."

"Sounds about right."

"Did you interview Jerry Debusey or Steve Dante or Megan Wallace?"

"Not yet. They didn't really have the time."

"And it was Megan who asked you to shoot the footage?"

"Yes."

"Did you give the police everything you shot or just what you shot on the day of the murder?"

"I gave them everything since they asked for it. I don't understand where you're going with this."

"You don't do any freelance work, do you Ned?"

"What do you mean?"

"Filming weddings, birthday parties; that sort of thing."

"Oh, no, I don't do any of that."

"You won an award for a short film you made. Are you making any other films outside of work?"

"I don't really have the time."

Tracy twisted her lips. She looked at Tom Kramer. "Tom, when you were working out in California, did you ever meet a man named Oliver Culp?"

"Oliver Culp? I don't think so. Who is he?"

"We'll get to him later. Did you know Carl Jeffries was in Hollywood for most of the nineties?"

"I heard he went there."

"When you were out in Hollywood, did you ever hear his named mentioned?"

"No. I understood his career was a bust anyway."

"Funny you should put it like that."

"Huh?"

"Did Carl ever try to kiss up to you by trying to talk about your career? I remember you telling me he wanted you to make him up like Dr. Mort."

"…Which I refused to do."

"But he was a charmer. Didn't he try to cater to your ego before asking his favor? That's how guys like that work. They butter you up before coming to their true point."

"I never talked to him about his or my career."

"Okay. So, you never heard anything about Carl's west coast work?"

"No."

"You told me you were busy this time of year working on Halloween attractions."

"True."

"How about outside of Halloween season. What kinds of projects do you work on?"

"I do special effects for some local filmmakers. I also do similar work in Delaware, Virginia, and DC."

"Just scary movie type stuff?"

"Yes, pretty much."

"Ever work with Ned on any projects?"

Kramer and Topolski looked at each other. Then Kramer looked at Tracy. "I met Ned for the first time a few weeks ago."

"I see."

Tracy looked at Steve Dante.

"How about you, Steve? Did you know about Carl's work in Hollywood?"

"What work?"

"I guess you didn't. It was you that hired Ned Topolski, right?"

"I recommended he be hired."

"You thought he would be a good fit for the documentaries you wanted to make."

"Sure."

"Was he working on a documentary at present?"

"No, not really."

"This footage he was shooting for Megan, was that going to end up in a documentary about the making of the live show?"

"I never got a chance to see any footage."

"Ah." Tracy looked at Jerry Debusey. "Mr. Debusey. You were the one who actually hired Ned, I take it."

"Yes."

"Did you two ever talk about the trouble Carl Jeffries was causing on the set?"

"No. Steve told me about that."

"Did he tell you voluntarily or did you have to go to him?"

"I went to him. I heard Megan yelling at some point and went to find out what was going on."

"And Steve told you all about it."

"More or less."

"What does that mean?"

Debusey cleared his throat. "Steve tried to downplay it. But that's not unusual to do in a situation like that."

"Like what, exactly?"

"He was the one who wanted this thing. He told me he'd take care of everything. I doubt he wanted me finding out one of his cast members was causing problems."

"I understand you called a meeting with Steve and Megan about Carl. What brought that on?"

"Continued complaints about Jeffries. I'd had enough."

"Were people coming to you and complaining?"

"No, but when people are gossiping on the lunch breaks, I hear about it."

"And what happened during this meeting?"

"I told Steve and Megan they needed to get Jeffries to act like a professional. If they couldn't do that then he had to go."

"And how long was it after this meeting that Jeffries was killed?"

Debusey thought a moment. "Maybe little less than a week."

"Thank you, Mr. Debusey." Tracy turned her eyes to Larry Peachtree. "Larry, you and Carl go way, way back."

"Huh? What does that mean? We weren't pals."

"You've been here the longest. You knew Carl back in the day. Hear any rumors about him after he left?"

"What rumors?"

"*Any* rumors."

"No."

"Nothing about his Hollywood career?"

"I told you: no."

"You remember Oliver Culp? He used to work here."

"He got fired — that's what I remember about *him*."

"He knew Carl, I understand."

"Hardly."

"They *weren't* buddies?"

"Of course not. Culp was just a cameraman; Carl was a *star*. And the *star* didn't want anything to do with the likes of *us*."

"Us?"

"The crew."

"Ah. But Oliver did know that Carl went to California because he went there looking for him."

"Well, every once in a while, Carl's name would come up, just in conversation though. It was well known he left in hopes of becoming an even bigger star."

"But nobody here kept in touch with him?"

"No, I don't think so. Why would they? He didn't get along with anybody."

"You didn't like him either, I take it."

"What is this?" Peachtree growled. "So, what if I didn't like him?"

"Easy, Larry," Tracy said. "That's kind of what my point has been by asking everyone these questions. Nobody seems to know or care what Carl did when he left here. They just heard he wasn't likeable and when he showed up, he did nothing to disprove the rumors. He came here and caused problems and some people just ignored him, others threatened to fire him, and others just didn't really care one way or the other. Nobody here admits to knowing Carl outside the studio. Furthermore, Carl Jeffries didn't seem to have any kind of job until this reunion came along. It's curious that he seemed to have so little contact with people, and yet someone spent so much time plotting his vicious murder. So, somebody here isn't being quite honest when they say Carl Jeffries was little more than a pain in the ass. Obviously, he was much, much more than that."

Tracy looked again at Steve Dante. "After Jerry Debusey said he was willing to fire Carl Jeffries, you told Megan to make her father behave. Is that right, Steve?"

"Not exactly."

"But that was the gist of it, right? You let her produce this thing practically on her own because she had some kind of control over him."

"I guess that's right."

"Even though this was a pet project of *yours*, you stayed pretty much hands-off."

"I trusted Megan could handle things."

"But you had to have known by bringing Carl Jeffries on board that it might feel more like the Fourth of July rather than Halloween here, Steve."

"Everyone's a professional here; everyone's an adult. That's what *I* counted on."

"But adults can have scars too, Steve."

"Well…"

Tracy sighed. "One of the saddest days of my life was realizing that adults are nothing more than kids with responsibilities. They can still pick on others, be cruel to others, and behave like spoiled brats. Wouldn't you agree with that, Steve?"

Dante stared at her. "I guess so."

"There are just some people, no matter how old they are, who enjoy making others miserable." Tracy moved towards where Megan Wallace and Andy Honeywell were seated. "How about you, Andy? Do you agree with my cynical summary of adulthood?"

He nodded without hesitation. "I deal with those kinds of people all the time. It's part of my job."

"By 'those kinds of people' you mean cruel brats?"

"Yes."

"And Carl was one of them."

"Most certainly."

"And how did he treat Megan here?"

Honeywell looked at the woman seated next to him. "Not like a father should treat a daughter."

"What do you mean, Andy?"

"He never showed her any affection — any *real* affection."

"But she didn't want his affections."

"Okay, that's true. But the only time he ever brought up being her father was if he wasn't getting his way about something. He used him being her father as a threat of sorts, as if that entitled him to something. He may have well just said he was her boss."

"Ah." Tracy looked at Megan. "Is that true, Megan? Did Andy pretty much nail it?"

"Pretty much."

Tracy pointed to Richard George, who was sitting two chairs over on Megan's right.

"Richard George was more a father to you than Carl ever was."

"He *was* my father in a lot of ways."

"And that made Carl very angry."

"I guess."

"You're not sure?"

"We never talked about it. I tried to avoid talking to my father at every opportunity."

"There wasn't anything meaningful between the two of you? Anything at all?"

Megan shook her head. "No. I didn't trust him. I didn't like him. I certainly didn't love him. I never understood what my mother saw in him."

"And you never wanted this reunion, did you Megan?"

She looked at the ground and shook her head.

"I'm sorry." Tracy looked towards rear of the studio. "How about you, Ms. Wallace. How did you feel about this reunion?"

"Just leave me out of things, please."

"Why? You knew Richard and Carl. You were here when they worked here. You know your way around the studio. And you are the only person here who not only tolerated Carl but claim to actually love him."

"What does that all mean, exactly? You can't always help loving the person you love."

"It means you knew him better than anyone. If something was bothering Carl, you, as someone who claims to love him, should have known about it. I certainly want to know when something is troubling my husband, even if it's just a mild tummy ache. Care to offer any reasons why someone would want Carl Jeffries dead?"

"NO!"

"Okay. Just one more question. Is it true you didn't want your daughter to come work here?"

"Maybe," Carrie answered after a few quiet moments.

"Why wouldn't you?"

"Huh?"

"Why wouldn't you want her working here? Carl wasn't here anymore. Both you and Richard worked here so that could work to her advantage if she needed a reference. She was a creative, imaginative person who wanted to work in television. Just like her father. Wouldn't you agree, Carrie?"

Carrie Wallace just glared at Tracy. Tracy held the stare a few moments before continuing. She looked back at Honeywell.

"Andy, as a director, has your work always been in television?"

"Yes."

"You never worked on a short film like Ned did?"

"Oh. In school I made films."

"Avant-garde type stuff?"

Honeywell smiled. "Some of that. But I shot quite a few short documentaries — in black and white, as a matter of fact. There's something about black and white that seems more truthful than color, as strange as that may sound."

Tracy nodded. "I do prefer black and white myself."

Steve Dante frowned. "What does all of this have to do with Carl Jeffries death?"

"Sorry. I was just making sure nobody knew Carl outside of WMFT. Being he was a local celebrity of sorts and longed to be back in the spotlight, I thought he might have done some work with some of the people here before this October."

"So, what if he had?"

"Well, if he had, and no one admitted to that fact, wouldn't you wonder why?"

"I guess."

"And then there's the possibility that maybe he worked with more than just one person here. Maybe this murder involved not just the person on camera driving the stake into Jeffries heart. You see there are all kinds of tricks you can play with audio and video."

"Tricks?" Kramer asked.

"Sure. Aren't sometimes audio and video recorded on separate tracks, and then they are brought together for the finished project?"

"Sure," Topolski called out in agreement.

"So, is it possible the voice we heard on the video — the one that called out Richard's name — was someone other than Carl Jeffries'? The only time you get a good look at Carl is when he rises from the coffin after being shown the stake. Did maybe someone figure a way to manipulate the audio while recording the murder? Or is it possible that the murder we have on video isn't even the real murder, but instead an elaborate special effect? What if two people made the video using special effects magic? What if what the video shows is not the murder of Carl Jeffries but instead a performance? Someone could have recorded this earlier, setting the clock ahead in the recorder, and then reset it to the proper time before leaving it for the police to find. Perhaps if we compare the coffin in the video Ned took the day of the murder to the footage the police have, we may notice something. Remember: Carl Jeffries' stunt of kicking the table leg ultimately damaged the coffin that day."

People started looking at each other. Tracy started pacing in front of the stage.

"Oh, yeah. I came up with this elaborate theory that maybe two people came back to the studio the Friday night before the murder and played out that scene the police have on video. They used makeup and blood packets and whatnot. Then they lured Carl back on Saturday, knocked him out with the mallet when he arrived, carried him over to and put him in the coffin, and then killed him. In other words: maybe more than one person was involved in this." Tracy stopped and looked at Steve Dante.

"All right; fine," Dante grunted. "You've made your point. But can you please move this along?"

"Sure." Tracy cleared her throat. "I think I'm ready to move on. Ultimately this is going to come down to science anyway."

Tracy looked at Detective Deborah Price, who was seated on the furthest seat to Tracy's right.

"The police will need to get a warrant when I'm finished here. I've just basically taken us all through a process of elimination of sorts. So, let's move on to the next phase: figuring out which one of you did indeed have reason to want Carl Jeffries dead. As it turns out, more than one of you has just been less than honest with rest of us."

Tracy took a deep breath. "Now, to understand *why* what happened, happened, we have to go back to the mid-eighties. As previously mentioned, Richard, Carl, Steve Dante, Larry Peachtree, and Carrie Wallace all worked here. As all of you know, a romance developed between Carl and Carrie. Soon after Carl left for Hollywood, Carrie told Richard she was pregnant. Not wanting to have Carl involved in the baby's life, she never tried to contact him. And he never contacted her either. Richard helped take care of Carrie and Megan in many ways. Carrie meanwhile told people Carl was the father, at least people assumed that to be the case and Carrie didn't deny it. No father's name was listed on the birth certificate. But all of this was more or less kept a secret among the staff of WMFT. It couldn't really matter to anyone except Carrie and Megan anyway. Slowly, the staff that knew this secret left the studio for other things. And that should have been it. That is, until a former employee named Oliver Culp went to California and tracked down his old 'buddy' Carl. But not real buddies. Oliver wanted something. He told Carl he had some information Carl might be interested in. According to a woman named Wendy Rakowski — the woman Carl was living with at the time — Oliver said he'd share what he knew with Carl if Carl helped get him work. Wendy told us Carl got Oliver an interview for a cameraman's position. And then Carl learned he was a father. A short time later, Carl came back to Maryland."

Tracy blew out a sigh. "There's no easy way to say this, although quite a few people here are already aware of what I'm going to say. Carl showed up at Carrie Wallace's. He had some news for her, and if she didn't want him to share it with others, she had to make him happy. He wanted room and board and he wanted money. So, Carrie again turned to Richard for help. And he helped her, helped her to the tune of at least $350,000."

There were some murmurs now from the cast. Tracy went to Megan Wallace and knelt if front of her, taking her hands.

"Megan, you need to know this. I've tried in my own clumsy way to prepare you for it. But there was a very good reason why Carl never really treated you like a daughter." Tracy took another deep breath. "Megan, Carl Jeffries was *not* your father. He couldn't have children."

Megan Wallace's expression was one of confusion. "I don't understand," she murmured. "Mom told me he was."

"Your mother will have to explain her motives to you. I'll leave it to her to tell you when she learned the truth about your father."

Megan looked around. She was still in a mild state of shock. Everyone was looking at her. She looked at the sympathetic attorney.

"Who then, Tracy? Do you know who my father is? If you do, please tell me." Megan now looked at Richard George. He would not meet her eyes.

Tracy sighed. "Yes, Megan. I do."

Tracy released Megan's hands, stood up and returned to the center aisle.

"The police learned the truth about everything, more or less, when they were building their case against Richard George. But they initially made one assumption — one that I made too — that was a mistake." She looked at Richard George. "We all assumed that Richard paying the money to Carl meant *he* was Megan's true father." She looked back to the audience. "But he wasn't. I'm guessing he did what he did to protect Megan. I'm sure Carl probably threatened to make a scandal out of the whole thing; report how Richard and Carrie lied and covered things up; paint them as horrible people and play the victim. And Megan would get caught in the middle. Maybe Richard and Carrie were afraid Megan would hate them. Maybe they were afraid what Megan's real father would do when he learned the truth. Again, only they can tell us what their motives were. And such motives aren't really any of our business. What's important to understand is that this lie laid the groundwork for what happened here a few weeks ago."

Tracy folded her arms. She looked around. "All of you disliked Carl, some more than others. But of course, dislike is hardly a motive for murder. But hatred is. You see, the motive for what happened was indeed hatred; an intense hatred that's been building ever since Megan Wallace came to work at WMFT."

Tracy started pacing. "I ultimately came to this conclusion when I tried to imagine a distraught Carrie Wallace all those years ago. She was hurt badly by Carl Jeffries' abandonment and was now feeling lonely. Whom would she go to for comfort?" Tracy stopped in front of her client. "Richard George and his wife Elaine were and still are devoted to each other. His interest in Carrie had always been fatherly — a man who acted as a protector when he warned her to stay away from Carl."

Tracy now walked to where Dante was seated. "Steve Dante here was young and new to the station. But he was also a newlywed married to a former Miss Maryland; things were probably still hot and heavy. He didn't seem like a likely candidate. And most of the other people vying for Carrie's affections probably looked to her like alternate versions of Carl Jeffries."

Tracy approached Ned Topolski. "Ned, can you please help me? Can you please cue up the video on the monitors?"

"Sure."

Ned stood and moved towards the DVD player connected to the left-stage screen. Meanwhile Tracy continued.

"I'd like you all to watch this. This is some of the aforementioned footage that Ned shot the day of the murder. I promise it won't take long." Tracy looked at Topolski. "Whenever you're ready, Ned."

Topolski handed the player's remote to Tracy after he started the video. The crowd was now watching a point of view shot of Topolski approaching Larry Peachtree.

"Get that out of my face," Peachtree growled. "I'm still at work here."

"Just some positive words for our potential audience," Topolski pleaded, as Peachtree continued loading various items in drawers.

"Not now; maybe later. Find someone else."

"Megan won't be happy about this."

"What, you're going to *tell* on me?" Peachtree snorted as he slammed a metal drawer closed.

Tracy pressed the remote's pause button.

"I must have watched that video more than two dozen times trying to find *something*. Since the murder was premeditated, I hoped maybe the guilty party had been caught on video doing something: making that phone call that presumably summoned Carl back to the studio; stealing the tape off the table; placing a video camera under the lab coat. Anything." Tracy looked away from the video and at the crowd. "I was always looking in the background for this *something*. But I was looking in the wrong place. Now I'm going to replay this, this time zooming in on the drawers. I'd like everyone to watch just once more." Tracy fidgeted with the remote until she found the scene she wanted.

"What, you're going to *tell* on me?" Peachtree snorted.

Tracy pressed the pause and zoom buttons. "There, what does everyone see in Larry's hand?"

It was Steve Dante, as the one closest to the monitor, who volunteered, "Hard to tell."

"My husband thought it was a hammer grip." Tracy looked out in the audience for the masked attendee. "Doing okay Brian?" The beast raised his thumb upwards.

"Can you zoom in a little more?" Andy Honeywell asked.

"Glad you asked, Andy. That's just what I planned to do." Tracy quickly pressed the zoom button twice.

With the item of discussion now much clearer, Dante again spoke. "It looks like a roll of black electrical tape."

Tracy shut off the video and looked at Dante. "Yes, Steve. That's *exactly* what it is."

"Wait a minute," Megan said. "I thought Larry left that on the lab table and someone else put it back for him."

"That's what Larry said — screamed, actually." Tracy was looking at Larry Peachtree. "Want to explain this to us, Larry?"

Peachtree gulped. "Explain what?"

"Explain why you carried on about misplaced tape when it was *you* who put it in that metal drawer yourself. That's what we all just saw, isn't it?"

Peachtree looked around. "I was upset; I was confused. I just made a mistake."

"You, Larry? Mr. A Place for Everything and Everything in Its Place? I don't think so."

"What does it matter anyway?" Peachtree challenged. "*Tape* didn't kill Carl Jeffries."

"It matters, Larry. You made a big production out of that tape in front of the police and everyone else. Why? I'll tell you why. You needed to draw attention to it being missing so when the police found the tape you *deliberately* left on the door, they would make the connection and have a way to explain how Richard reentered the studio. You just didn't realize Ned had captured what you did on video."

Trying to remain calm and unworried Peachtree said, "You're crazy, lady. I didn't kill Carl Jeffries."

Tracy, also calm, said, "Yes, you did, Larry. You did indeed kill Carl Jeffries."

As all eyes were now fixing on Larry Peachtree, it was Ned Topolski who called out, "Wait. Wait just a minute here. Are you implying that *Peachtree* is Megan's father?"

"Why not? Who better for Carrie to approach for comfort than a man who had suffered terribly? He was the one person working here who didn't treat Carrie like an amusement park prize when she arrived. He was still grieving the death of his wife and son. Is it so strange to assume that Carrie might think she could find comfort in such a person? They were two hurting people who could console each other, even if just for a brief time. That was Carrie's original intent, anyway."

Everyone was now looking at Peachtree with mixed expressions of horror and amusement.

"I just can't believe it," Topolski murmured.

"When I allowed my imagination to consider such a possibility," Tracy continued, "I re-watched the video footage focusing on Larry. As I watched I wondered what some of the items being put away were. I mean if I was right about him, the whole tape story was made up. And then I saw the electrical tape."

Megan Wallace was staring at the floor. Andy Honeywell had his arm around her. Tracy looked at her sympathetically before continuing.

"I still wasn't sure if my guess was correct. And then I saw this."

Tracy tuned the video monitor back on, and then pressed the remote's 'skip' button. There was now the image of an attractive young woman on the monitor.

"Who's that?" Honeywell asked. Then he frowned. "She looks like she could be Megan's sister."

Tracy nodded. "Actually, this woman is Larry Peachtree's younger sister. She lives in Chicago now. This photo is several years old, but my PI was able to pull it off a social media website." Tracy started moving towards Peachtree. "That must have been quite a shock for you the day Megan Wallace walked in here looking like your sister, Larry. All these years you had heard the stories of Carrie Wallace's baby girl being Jeffries.' You had no reason to doubt the stories. Despite her mother's wishes, however, Megan came to work here. And as soon as you saw her, you knew the truth."

Peachtree too was staring at the floor. He was starting to weep.

"I suppose you confronted Carrie about it. Carl may have even been there. At some point, Richard must have stepped in and pleaded with you to keep it all quiet. Megan was beginning a promising career; telling the truth could hurt her deeply; other people's reputations might be hurt; and who knows what other reasons they gave you. I guess you thought they made sense at the time. And you got to see Megan almost every day as things stood. Maybe you were afraid that if the truth came out, she'd be so upset she'd leave the station and vanish from your life. Is that what you were afraid of, Larry?"

Peachtree just shook his head as she continued.

"And how, during these past nine years, you grew to hate them for what they did; *all* of them. Carrie lied; Richard helped cover it up; and Carl was living on easy street. Instead of exposing the lie, Carl kept quiet about it and pocketed some cash for his silence. Together they effectively stole from you your second child. I feel so awful for what happened to you, Larry. I really do. I can't imagine losing a child and then my spouse. And then, when you have another chance to be a father, these people collectively deny you that opportunity. And you must have hated them for it."

"YES!" Peachtree shouted suddenly as he jerked his head upwards. "I HATE THEM! So what? You can't prove anything. Jeffries called out *Richard's* name, not mine!"

"Right. It's Richard you hated the most, I bet. He was the one paying the blackmail money and keeping Carl comfortable. He was the man who you respected and liked, relatively speaking. You never liked nor thought much of Carl. But Richard was a beacon of respectability. He was kind to you when you lost your family. To have him involved in something like this, must have really pissed you off; you felt betrayed. Then, Steve Dante came up with the idea for this reunion. All the people you hated most in this world would be gathered together for several weeks. The thought of seeing them day after day was just too much. And there, Carl would be, knowing the truth about everything and making his little jokes. So, you started planning. But since everyone loved Richard and hated Carl, it was Carl who would die and Richard who would take the fall for it. You'd punish both of them. If you had gotten away with it, I wonder if you had something special in mind for Carrie Wallace."

"HOW DARE YOU?!" Peachtree protested. "You have NO proof!"

"Oh, I have the proof all right, Larry. I wouldn't dare accuse a person of murder without proof. My reputation means something to me." Tracy again looked at the masked visitor. "Brian, you can take that mask off now so we can all see that handsome face of yours."

But when the concealed guest removed the mask, it was not Brian beneath it. People started looking at Tracy, confused.

"Hey! That's Corky," Tom Kramer said. "What gives?"

"I'll explain my innocent little deception in just a moment," Tracy grinned. "First though, I want to let everyone know what Corky told me. He said that a cleaning person saw him out back sneaking a smoke break the night of the murder. But Megan said Corky was at his station when the cleaning crew was coming in for the night. They would still have been here at the time of the murder. But of course, this particular studio was locked so they couldn't come inside here. And that is what led to the proof Larry is so insistent I provide."

Tracy started backing away from Peachtree and was soon again near the stage.

"When Larry, pretending to be Richard George, called Carl Jeffries, he told Carl to enter through the back. He had taped the catch so it wouldn't lock. He did this, we now know, both to make it easy for Carl to come in and to provide a means someone without keys could gain entry. But what about Larry himself? Would he just reenter as Larry Peachtree? Not likely. He may have been recognized. So, he took the precaution of borrowing one of the studio's security guard outfits, complete with hat. He must have parked his car within walking distance of the studio but out of sight, and came back here almost immediately after having left, wearing that uniform the whole way. He needed time to prepare after all. So, it was Larry whom the cleaning person saw in the parking lot. And because this supposed guard was walking with his head lowered to hide his identity, the crew member just assumed having a cigarette was the reason."

"But once Carl got there, he'd know it was Larry and not Richard," Honeywell challenged. "Why in the hell would he say Richard was the one who was killing him?"

"Well, Andy, sometimes when all is said and done, the explanations are ridiculously simple. In this case, for example. Carl just assumed it was Richard."

"*Assumed?*"

"Carl couldn't see Larry, because Larry was wearing a mask."

Tom Kramer started laughing. "Are you telling us that Larry here made a mask of Richard's face?"

"Oh my no. Larry's creative and all, but masks are your thing, Tom, not Larry's. No. Larry just borrowed one of your masks and used some simple psychology."

"Psychology," Ned Topolski repeated.

"Yes. In fact, I've already demonstrated it. I introduced the person wearing Tom's demon mask as Brian. You all assumed I was telling you the truth. Nobody challenged me on it; nobody insisted Corky remove his mask to prove my claim. And consider that some of you mistrusted me since I was looking for someone else to accuse of murder. But you all nevertheless accepted my word.

"Now let's imagine the night of the murder. Carl arrives thinking he will be meeting Richard. That's who the caller claimed to be. When Carl gets here the door is open as the caller told him it would be. Eventually Carl sees a person in a uniform and wearing a mask. There's nobody else here. Isn't it a logical to assume that Carl *assumed* it was the man who called him? Can't you all imagine Carl saying something like, 'Richard, is that you?' And this masked man just nods, like Corky giving me a thumbs up when I called him Brian. Then, the false identity established, Larry pulls out a gun and motions for Carl to get inside the coffin. Larry taunts him by showing him the stake. Carl panics and, just as Larry hoped he would, calls out the name of the man he *thinks* is about to kill him. In the video, once Carl says 'Richard' Larry strikes Carl with the mallet. And Carl cries out Richard's name a second time before being killed. I know you've all heard stories about the video. But what you may not have known is that the killer's face is never seen. I think we all now know why that was."

"You have no proof of this," Peachtree said weakly. "You can't."

Tracy sighed. "I've seen the video of the murder. Even if the police would have allowed me to include it on my video compilation, I wouldn't have. Just trust me when I say it was shocking, violent, and bloody — *very* bloody. Larry put on the lab coat to both implicate Richard and protect his own costume. But I still believed that blood would have likely gotten on *some* part of the uniform. And I was sure Larry here would have returned the costume to its original location because Larry believes that everything should be in its proper place. He wouldn't have wanted someone to realize it was missing. And he certainly wouldn't have rented or purchased a costume. That would leave a paper trail. It was less risky to keep everything here. If the items were found, it would show only that someone at the studio wore them.

"You see understanding how a person's mind works can sometimes lead to the solution. And most people tend to ascribe traits they possess themselves to other people. A person who lies a lot will assume others are lying to him. A person who is very punctual will expect others to arrive timely. And a person who is very particular about his things and knows where they should be at all times will assume others to be the same way. So, I thought it was perfectly reasonable to assume that Larry would return whatever items he borrowed to their original location, lest someone started pitching a fit.

"So, after I told Detective Price here my *ridiculous* theory last week, I also told her there was one sure way to prove whether or not I was on the right track. I asked her to round up any security guard- looking uniforms they could find in the studio and test them for blood. If my theory were wrong, they wouldn't find anything." Tracy, once again, started moving towards Peachtree. "But they did find something on the collar of one of the outfits tucked away in wardrobe. Namely, Carl Jeffries' blood."

"It proves nothing," Peachtree challenged. "Anyone could have put on that uniform."

"It's not the clothes that I was truly interested in though, Larry. It was the *mask* you wore that would have the proof. So, after the police found the blood on the collar, I had their attention. I next suggested they grab a bunch of cotton swabs and little bottles of luminol and check out Tom Kramer's mask collection. They're the only masks here. Tom's masks of course have blood all over them — fake blood mostly.

So, the killer figured if he missed cleaning some blood off the mask, who'd notice? I think you can all guess that Carl Jeffries' blood was indeed found on one of Tom's masks."

"*SO?!*" Peachtree screamed.

"Well, Larry, it's not really the outside of the mask that's the important thing here. It's the *inside*. You see you were probably wearing that mask for quite a while — 20 minutes, half an hour maybe, as you waited for Carl and then murdered him. And that means you'd most likely be sweating, just like poor Corky here. Even though sweat does not contain DNA, skin cells can be shed when you sweat — and they *would* have DNA. The interior of the mask would have made contact with your sweat-covered face as you removed it, the latex dragging across the skin and hair. Maybe some saliva would escape too, or hair could get yanked if you hurriedly pulled off the mask. And since Tom's masks were all virgin masks, meaning they had never been worn before, they should have been completely clean on the inside. The one with Carl's blood on it was *not* clean on the inside. You with me now, Larry?"

He was shaking his head.

"When the police compare *your* DNA, Larry, to what they found in the mask, it will match; I have no doubt about that. Your lie about the tape will give them probable cause to do so, that and a hell of a motive. And since that mask has Carl Jeffries' blood on the *outside*, the killer *must* have been wearing that mask as he was driving that stake into Carl's heart. How else would the blood have gotten there? Is that proof enough for you, Larry?"

Larry Peachtree, having now heard the case against him, stood up with enough force that the chair he'd been sitting on fell backwards, clanging loudly as it hit the ground.

"HE WAS A *MONSTER!*" he shouted. Peachtree looked around the room. "YOU'RE ALL *MONSTERS!* YOU ALL PROTECTED HIM AND KEPT MY LITTLE GIRL FROM ME!" Then Larry Peachtree's eyes met Megan Wallace's. Tearfully he said, lowering his voice, "My daughter…my baby girl doesn't even *like* me."

Megan looked at her father, salted water coming down her face also. At the moment, she felt Larry Peachtree was more right than wrong in what he had said, even if she couldn't fathom what he had done. But he had been wrong assuming she didn't like him. She had liked him fine. Now, she felt a great pain knowing that she never had been, nor would be, given the chance to love him too.

Nobody else present however could meet his eyes. They all looked at their own hands or shoes, or to the floor. The room was now completely silent.

Larry Peachtree finally broke eye contact with his daughter and then let out a few more sobs before straightening his body. To no one in particular he said, "I'm not so funny now, AM I? I won't be the butt of your cruel pranks anymore, *will I?*"

Tracy, filled with both great disgust and even greater pity for Larry Peachtree, shook her head.

"No, Larry. No one will ever laugh when they hear or say your name again."

Peachtree stared at the attorney. When he told her, "I want a lawyer," Tracy just nodded.

It wasn't much longer before two uniformed officers approached the now calm and quiet Larry Peachtree. He moved towards them and gave them no trouble as he was placed under arrest. Soon he was exiting WMFT for the very last time. He did not even try to take a last look back. If he had, he would have seen Megan Wallace watching him leave.

But the show wasn't quite over for Tracy Brubaker Shane; Carrie Wallace was soon in the attorney's face. Her contempt for Tracy was obvious.

"How could you do that? You didn't have to say all those things. You deliberately made me out to be the bad person here. You deliberately tried to humiliate me in front of my daughter and poison our relationship. Well, I won't let you get away with it; *any* of it! I don't *care* what your reputation is. I'll sue you for ethical violations!"

Tracy shook her heard. Her contempt for Carrie Wallace was even greater than Carrie's was for her.

"You can't, Carrie. Everything I said here was from the police files, which are public records: Megan's paternity, the money found in the safe deposit box — all of it. And I was able to convince Richard this all needed to be done anyway. I wanted you to witness first-hand what your lie caused. As for bringing all this out into the open, well, it's *going* to come out. If I were Larry's attorney, I'd play up how you hid Larry's child from him. And I know *you* knew that Megan wasn't Carl's because I had my PI call Wendy AKA Amber Hardshoe a second time to get some further details. According to Amber, Carl told *her* that he had told *you* he couldn't father a child. And *that's* why you left the father's name on the birth certificate blank. I didn't talk about *that* up there, now did I? If I *really* wanted to humiliate you and expose you, I could have. But I didn't for Megan's sake. You knew all along Carl wasn't the father. You just didn't want Larry Peachtree in your life; he had served his purpose. You thought you'd never see Carl again, so you let everyone think Carl was the father instead of who it really was. I imagine after Carl dumped you, you vowed never to be used again. *You'd* be doing the using in the future. Richard told me he really did think Megan was Carl's as you told him, until Larry showed up claiming otherwise. So, you lied to and used Richard too.

"And *I'd* use all of this in my imaginary defense of Larry Peachtree. I'd draw a picture of a pitiful man who finally snapped when all those who conspired against him came together. Believe me Carrie, this *will* go to trial, and everything said here today *will* be said at the trial. The very thing you tried to conceal will be fodder for the press in the not-too-distant future. So, I suggest you concern yourself with explaining things to your daughter. You let her believe a lie not for her sake, but for yours. And I told Richard all of this so he could see the person you really are. He knows you lied to him. So, you see, you have no basis for a suit. *I* told no lies and violated no ethics. Now, get out of my face."

If Carrie Wallace had been a man, Tracy would probably have spat on her. Carrie continued meeting Tracy's stare for several seconds. She looked at her daughter, who was being consoled by Andy Honeywell. Again, she looked at Tracy, and then she turned abruptly and left the studio without saying another word.

Steve Dante slowly approached Tracy. "Don't you think you were a bit hard on her? You weren't there. How can you be so self- righteous?"

Tracy glared at Dante. It was his turn now. "No, I wasn't hard on her. And I wish I could prove what I suspect about *you*."

"What does that mean?" Dante asked, narrowing his eyes.

"You led me to believe you had been here only six years when we first met. I have to wonder why."

"You misunderstood me."

"No, I didn't. I think you knew or suspected the truth about Megan's real father. Maybe you saw a picture of Larry's sister like I did. Maybe Carrie came on to you before she did Larry and you eventually figured things out, or at least suspected something was going on. I don't know. But I *do* know Megan asked Ned to shoot documentary footage about the making of this show. I *do* know you won awards for your documentaries. Maybe you got bored with making those types of documentaries — *respectable* ones. Maybe *you* suggested to Megan she ask Ned to film what he could. I think you brought Richard and Carl together hoping that something would happen, and you wanted it captured on video when it did. You wanted fireworks but I doubt you envisioned all of this. But who knows? I just feel you had ulterior motives for organizing this whole thing. You figured at the very least you'd have a unique Halloween program. But I think you wanted something more. And your little misdirection about your personal history was just to keep yourself off the radar if Carrie's name started being tossed around. I wouldn't bother you about her if I believed you'd only been here six years. What reason would I have to dig into your past, right? And that's why I think you were interested in some tabloid-type thing instead of what Larry ultimately did. You *did* come from a New York station that specialized in tabloid topics, didn't you?"

Dante continued looking at Tracy. Then he shook his head. "I really wish you worked for the law firm that the station uses. You've got one hell of an imagination."

"Yes, I do. I find it helps me in my work. And it helps me catch killers once in a while too."

Dante just nodded. Then he too quietly left the studio. In fact, the only people left now were Tracy, Detective Price, and the lovebirds.

"This has got to be one of the most bizarre cases I've ever worked," Price told Tracy. Both women were looking at the seated couple. Megan had her head on Honeywell's shoulder.

"I'd rank it pretty high on the weird meter," Tracy agreed.

"That was a hell of job you did, Tracy. I just can't believe it."

"Thanks, Debbie." Tracy sighed. "I'll never understand why people do the things they do to each other sometimes. There are a of lot people responsible for what happened here, Debbie. Larry will just be the fall guy."

"Yeah. I hear you."

Tracy looked around. "Where's Brian, I wonder?"

"He got tired of peeking from the behind the curtain," Price grinned. "He went to Megan's office to call home. I think he may have fallen asleep though."

Tracy chuckled. "Poor Brian. I exhaust him sometimes."

"I can believe that."

"Hey, I may be stubert and I may be imaginative. But I find it all works for me."

"There's that word 'stubert' again…"

"My daughter's word for stubborn. I'll spare you the details."

Price smiled. "You should go home, Tracy. You should take a long weekend."

"Right now, I'm just hoping my daughter is in a sharing mood; she scored some really good stuff tonight."

The detective laughed as she lifted her coat off the chair. "Let's go, Tracy." Price looked at Megan and Honeywell and added, "They can lock things up when they're done."

"I really hope Megan's going to be okay."

"I think she'll be fine."

"You sound sure of that, Detective."

"I am. I realize now who Megan Wallace reminds me of."

"Oh, really?"

Price looked at Tracy. "Yes. She reminds me of you."

CHAPTER 16

"You don't owe me any apologies," Megan Wallace told Tracy. "A lot of *other* people do though. But I really need time to wrap my head around all of this."

Tracy sighed. "I'm still sorry."

"Thanks. I have Andy by my side right now. He's all I want and need right now."

"Are you going to stay here at WMFT?"

Megan pursed her lips. "Just between you and me, I'll be looking for a new place of employment very soon. I can't stomach this place anymore."

"I can understand that."

"Steve Dante wants to do a documentary about all of this. He's seen all of Ned's footage and thinks we can use a lot of it. Bootlegs of the actual murder have started appearing online. This story has gone national now and he wants to strike while the story's hot. I told him to shove a fire poker up his ass."

Tracy started laughing. "That's supreme! You're my kind of lady."

Megan chuckled. "Well, at least I got to make a new friend because of this." She smiled at her visitor.

"Shucks," Tracy grinned.

"I don't know what to do about Larry, about Dad, I guess. I can certainly understand where his anger came from. I'm not mad at him for killing Carl. I guess that sounds rather cold. But I can't help wonder how things would have been if we both had been told the truth."

"I feel for him too, in spite of what he did."

"The way he looked at me yesterday…He certainly would have been a better father than Jeffries. Now, I'll never know."

"I'm really sorry, Megan."

"Thinking back on things, I can now see he was always nicer to me than he was to anyone else. But I thought that was just because I was a woman. Now I know the real reason."

"I really wish he had just told you," Tracy sighed. "That's a preferable option to killing someone. But I guess whatever means were used to keep him quiet worked. And all the hurt and hate really did twist his mind."

"And my mother did most of the twisting. She's the one I'm *most* angry with. I understand Carl hurt her and she was pissed off. But she dragged other people into things and kept up the lie. I feel like I suddenly don't even know my mother anymore."

"Well, for what it's worth, she did raise a strong, gifted daughter. I know that you'll figure out how to deal with all this crap and move on."

Megan smiled. "Thanks for coming, Tracy. I'm very glad you did."

"And I'm glad at least one person here doesn't hate me after last night."

Megan shook her head. "Nobody hates you, Tracy. You were pretty amazing last night: the way you figured things out; the way you believed in Richard even though he wasn't honest with you about everything. Even Steve Dante made some comment about you being as sharp as a blade and willing to cut with it, or something bizarre like that."

Tracy chuckled. "I guess that's a compliment of sorts." Tracy rose from Megan's office chair. "I'll let you get back to your post Halloween show activities. You really did pull it all together despite everything."

"The reviews have been very good. People want us to do another one. But it won't be coming from me."

The women shook hands and then Tracy left her doppelganger to consider her future. Tracy felt it would be a bright one, no matter how and where Megan Wallace chose to live it.

"I wouldn't worry about Carrie bothering you," Richard George told Tracy. "She has other concerns right now, including making statements to the police. I think she's finally realizing how all this is going to play out. And Megan isn't returning her calls."

"Megan needs time."

"Yes, she does."

Tracy sipped her iced tea. The Georges had invited her to lunch, and she was sitting across from them.

"You've been getting rave reviews, Richard. People loved you."

George smiled. "It's flattering, of course."

"People have recognized him already," Elaine said proudly. "He gave some autographs in the parking lot and lobby."

Tracy chuckled and nodded. "Are you going to do another one if it can be arranged?"

George shook his head. "No. Don't get me wrong. I *did* enjoy it. But it was exhausting. And given what happened, I just have no interest in it anymore. It's time to bury Dr. Mort Itchin once and for all."

Tracy sighed. "That's too bad. I think last night proved there was still life in Dr. Mort."

George crossed his arms and leaned forward. "Sometimes, Tracy, I think it's better to just leave things alone. I understand why people want to escape to their youth and return to a time when things *seemed* a lot simpler. I get that. But there's so much going on *now* that needs our undivided attention. And I'd rather perform for my grandchildren anyway." He leaned back. "I've taken my trip, and helped others take theirs, down memory lane and I've no interest in taking another one."

As the waiter placed their lunch entrees in front of the trio, Tracy said, "I still have the tapes and the memories, thankfully. And I have my own children to make memories with — to make memories for."

George nodded. "That is exactly what you *should* do. It's funny how one forgets so many of the bad things about growing up and remembers instead the good things, *if* there are enough good memories, of course. So, creating happy memories for one's children is perhaps the greatest gift a parent can give a child."

Tracy nodded. "Are you and Megan going to be okay?"

"Yes. We've already talked briefly, and I assured her I'll always be here for her. But of course, she's struggling with her feelings right now. I should have made Carrie come clean when Larry confronted her; I should have ended it there and then. I did wrong even though that was never my intention. Carrie lied to me about Megan right from the beginning. But I had a chance to make things right and I didn't. And look what happened."

Tracy sighed. As she had the same thoughts about the whole ordeal as George, she would make no further comments on the matter. "Thanks for lunch, you guys."

"It's the least we can do," Elaine smiled.

"…Other than pay your bill on time, that is," George added. Everyone laughed. "You know this may sound weird. But you actually remind me of Megan."

Tracy grinned. "Some people have told me that."

"I can see her, in a few years, having a family and doing well in her career. She's so imaginative and creative."

"Family? Do you know something I don't?"

George grinned. "Andy's a fine young man; a talent. He's imaginative and creative too. I gave him a tough time in the beginning, but he proved himself. I like him."

"And Megan loves him."

George smiled. "Yes, I guess she does."

Elaine George raised her water glass. "To imagination and creativity," she declared.

Tracy raised hers. "To happy memories," the attorney added.

Richard George frowned. "And to the memories that were denied the chance to be made."

The women just looked at him. Then they all sipped quietly from their glasses.

"Thanks for all your help, El. You broke the case."

"Amber will be so pleased," Tanner said flatly.

"Did you guys get a lot of trick-or-treaters?"

"For a non-Friday weeknight, we were pretty busy."

"I'll have Brian make a copy of the show for you, El. He recorded it."

"There's no hurry."

"But it was very good, El."

"It's just not my thing."

"Good grief. You and Brian…"

"Me and Brian what?"

"A couple of Halloween Scrooges."

"I didn't say I didn't like Halloween."

"Oh. Well, okay, then."

Tanner chuckled. "Are you guys planning on coming over for Thanksgiving dinner this year? You've missed the last couple."

"I have to talk to Brian. I think he wants to have it at our house; maybe you and Rita and El-J's family can all come over there."

"Elias, Jr. wants everyone over at his and Crystal's."

"Oh. Brian hasn't said anything."

"Tracy, this may be none of my business. But are Brian and Crystal getting along? Elias made some comments."

Tracy sighed. "They just need a break to appreciate each other. Crys picks on Brian and Brian has stopped taking it good naturedly. I'm sure they'll be fine."

"Okay; I guess that can happen."

"Brian is dealing with other things too. I don't want to say anything further but that could be part of it too."

"All right. I hope he's able to work through whatever it is. You guys okay?"

"We're fine. Don't worry on that point."

"Good; very good."

"I guess I'll talk to you later. Thanks for helping me pull another rabbit out of the hat."

Tanner chuckled again. "Sure. Let me know the next time your hat is giving you trouble."

"Oh, you're cute. 'Bye, El."

Keandra Moore entered the boss's office. "How was the show last night?"

"Supreme, Keandra. How was your party?"

"Don't ask."

"Too late. I just did."

Keandra laughed. "A couple of the husbands started fighting over some nonsense."

"Nonsense?"

"Fantasy football league nonsense."

"Oh."

"Is Brian in one?"

"Oh my, no. His sport is baseball and he's not even hardcore about *that*."

"You are *so* lucky."

"I don't mind it so much until he starts acting like those players are his pals or something. 'My boy' did this or 'we' did that. I want to pour a bucket of cold water over his head and bring him back to reality."

Keandra laughed louder. "Try listening to men arguing about teams that don't even *exist*."

"Well…"

"Well, what?"

"I can't really comment on that."

"Why not?"

"Don't ask."

"Too late. I just did."

"Good one, Keandra."

"Well?"

"I did some role playing in my youth. I had a male friend who was really into it, and I played with him and his friends."

Keandra's laugh filled the office. "What happened?"

"Why do you think something happened?"

"Because you keep avoiding the subject."

"It was such a sad sight, Keandra."

"What was?"

"Watching a young man cry over the death of his Bluckensnup."

"His *what*?"

"I don't remember what it was called exactly. I just remember the Dungeon master rolling a fatal series of roles and Brad's Flippensmaugdoodle was no more.'

Keandra Moore now had tears in her eyes and Neal and Rebecca had joined the party.

Neal asked: "What the heck is a Flippensmaugdoodle?"

Tracy shrugged her shoulders. "I don't know, Neal. Cousin to the Nuckmuckwump or something."

Rebecca, Keandra, and now Tracy were all laughing. Neal wasn't.

"You know, being a Dungeon master — especially one who comes up with their own campaigns — takes a lot of imagination and creativity, a lot of hard work. You all obviously have no clue about any of it."

Tracy covered her mouth. "Oh, Neal. I never realized you were a Dungeon master. I didn't mean to hurt your feelings or put you down."

"You didn't hurt my feelings."

"I didn't? Then why are you acting like the Igmunch of Jalahopscotch stole the sacred Crunchberry of Whoopiehops?"

Both Keandra Moore and Rebecca Dietz had to sit down. The latter was grabbing her side.

Neal folded his arms. "The next time any of you need my help, *don't* bother asking."

Tracy, gasping for breath, assured him, "Don't worry, Neal. We'll just summon the Dingledoodle of Scratchycrack for help."

Neal gave Tracy a fake smile and turned. After the women finally stopped laughing, Tracy, feeling a little guilty, said, "All right. Each of us should bring in some leftover Halloween candy on Monday for Neal. We were all bad."

Keandra Moore folded her arms. "Tracy, in my house there is no such thing as 'leftover Halloween candy'."

"Mine neither," Rebecca agreed.

Tracy pursed her lips. "You know that goes for my house too. I guess I'll bring him some of my mother's vegetables instead."

"Vegetables?" Keandra asked.

"Yes. Fresh from the garden of Tushyworm."

And then the laughter began again, while Neal wished he could banish all of them to some imaginary, faraway land — one filled with monsters bearing very sharp teeth.

"You have that ghost on," Brian frowned.

"The lights too," Tracy added.

"But Halloween is over."

"Good grief, Brian. Relax."

"We should take down that stuff this weekend; get the house ready for Thanksgiving and Christmas."

"I'll take the stuff down Sunday, Brian, okay? Jeez."

"I'll help."

"Don't bother."

"Now don't be like that."

"Keep your mitts off my monsters, Brian, or else."

"Fine; fine. I just took Bonkers out so I'm heading up to brush my teeth."

"You do that."

Tracy grinned as Brian twisted his lips. She then looked at Nicole, who was making a pile of candy for the evening's dessert. The pile consisted of at least six treats.

"Nicole, honey," Tracy said. "One candy bar is enough."

"I want two."

"Grandma let you have extra last night because it was Halloween. So, one piece of candy is enough."

"I want another one."

"Nicole, just one. If you can't decide then I'll decide for you."

Nicole Shane frowned. Then she smiled and grabbed a peanut butter bar. "This one!"

Tracy smiled. "A fine choice."

The mother started putting the treats back into the plastic pumpkin.

Violetta came into the dining room.

"Look, Grammaw!" Nicole shouted while victoriously holding up her candy. The grandmother leaned over and pretended to take a bite. Nicole giggled. "You can have some Grammaw."

"No thank you, dear child. Grandma is all full from dinner."

"Okay!"

"You have to scrub your teeth tonight though."

"I will, Grammaw. Daddy will help."

Violetta smiled. Then she frowned at Bonkers, who was sitting by Nicole waiting for *his* bite. "Go away," Violetta ordered.

"Easy there Gram*maw*," Tracy grinned. "Bonkers is growing into a fine attack dog. You better be careful how you talk to him."

"Bah!" Violetta grunted as she headed toward the stairs.

Tracy chuckled and leaned in close to Nicole. "Did you have fun last night trick-or-treating and playing with Grandma and Peter?"

"YES!"

"Supreme!"

Nicole looked at Tracy, confused. "What's 'supeeme,' Mommy?"

"It's *supreme*, sweetheart. And it means better than great. It's a much nicer word than stubert."

"I love you, Mommy. You're sup-reem."

Tracy smiled and kissed Nicole on her cheek. "I love you too, Nicole. You're pretty 'sup-reem' yourself."

On her way back from Nicole's room after the tuck-in, Tracy stopped to look at several of the pictures that adorned the second-floor wall. Framed memories of her and Brian's family members stared back at her. Wedding photos of Tracy's and Brian's parents sat atop a photo taken at the Shane's civil ceremony. Below them were multiple pictures of Nicole and Peter at various ages. Tracy smiled at the photo where a newborn Peter rested on his sister's lap, a big smile on big sister's face. Another part of the wall had pictures of Crystal Shane and her family, as well as photos of her with Tracy, Brian, and her niece and nephew. There was plenty of wall space left for future captured moments — images that would spurn still more remembrances. But it was rather bittersweet since the display would serve as a constant reminder that time was passing — quickly. Still, she felt grateful for everything. She was grateful she had such a wall and the memories to fill it. Not all people were so fortunate. The story of Larry Peachtree and Megan Wallace had made that all too clear. It would haunt her, which was appropriate given the time of year.

"It's all relative, isn't it Brian?" Tracy asked her husband as they readied themselves for slumber.

"What is?"

"One's problems. We think we have it so bad and then we meet someone who has it a lot worse."

"What are you talking about exactly?"

"Larry Peachtree. He lost a lot more than 10 years, Brian."

"Oh. I get it."

"He was never given a chance to step up. And when a second chance presented itself, he let himself get talked out of it. And it festered. Now…"

"I get it, Tracy."

"I'm not saying this is going to make you feel better when you start beating yourself up again over our 10-year separation. But there are people dealing with worse things than the two of us are."

"I suppose so."

Tracy sighed. "Still no word from Ben or Lisa?"

"No. And I'm not really expecting to."

"Why? You were close at one time after all."

"Ben likes his life the way it is. He has Lisa and he has his drink. I'm not essential to any of that. In fact, I'm probably something of a buzz killer now."

Tracy forced a smile. "Not to me, you're not. You're my honeybee." Tracy moved close to Brian so she could kiss him.

"I do like my hive."

"Even though your queen can be a pain?"

He chuckled. "You're not a pain. Challenging, maybe."

"Challenging?"

"In a good way."

"How am I challenging in a good way, Brian? Am I like an obstacle? Am I like a super-huge jigsaw puzzle? What?"

Brian frowned. "You're pulling a Joe Pesci on me again."

"Tell me how I challenge you, Brian."

Brian wrapped his arms around Tracy's waist and pulled her closer. "How do you challenge me? Well, practically every day you present me opportunities to grow; to learn something. You remind me that there will always be things to learn about each other. You're always doing something constructive: working, cooking, taking care of the kids, taking care of me, or wanting to help other people. You just never stop. You can be hard to keep up with. But you do it all with the best of intentions and biggest of hearts. I want to be like that too but it's difficult, maybe impossible. You're a tough act to follow, Mrs. Shane. You're one of a kind."

Tracy kissed him. "Actually, several people think there are others out there like me. You met one of them last night."

"I think I like you better though."

She chuckled. "Very good answers tonight, Mr. Shane."

"Do I get any treats for my answers, Mrs. Shane?"

"You made it clear Halloween was over, Mr. Shane."

"Treats aren't just for Halloween, Mrs. Shane."

"Very well. What treats would you like, Mr. Shane?"

"Just one."

"Just one?" she whispered.

"One's enough…"

Their foreheads were pressed together. "Hey Brian…"

"Uh-huh…"

"I have a riddle for you."

"Oh boy…"

"Up for the challenge?"

"Sure."

"Why couldn't the lady skeleton fall in love?"

"That's easy: because she had no heart."

"Nope."

"You're kidding."

"Nope. Give up?"

"Yes."

"She couldn't fall in love because Brian Shane was already taken."

He laughed softly. "Very cute."

"I love you, Brian. You're 'sup-reem'."

"Is that like stubert?"

"Better than stubert."

"I love you too, Tracy. You're everything and a bag of chips."

"Did you just call me a bag?"

He laughed again. "A goodie bag."

"Nice recovery. You *do* seem up to the challenge."

"I'm feeling *up*, all right."

"Oh, good grief. Come here, you."

Brian was now asleep, and the Shane family had the entire weekend to look forward to. What memories could they make? Tracy decided she wanted to watch another Dr. Mort Itchin tape. If she waited too long, she might never be able to do it again. She didn't want that to happen. Why let the present negate the past? And of course, the holidays and the children's birthdays were on the horizon; all good memory making opportunities. Nicole would be three and Peter would turn one. Her children: thinking of them would sometimes bring tears to her eyes. She loved them so much; more than anything else in the world, save for Brian. They were her family, something she had always wanted. And she couldn't imagine life without them. She couldn't imagine not knowing them. She didn't want to try; she had better things to do with her imagination. Better to imagine Nicole growing up to be a strong person and finding someone to share her life with, if that's what she wanted; better to imagine how handsome Peter was going to look standing next to his prom date someday; better to imagine her grown children would still keep in touch with their mother because she was open and honest with them in all serious matters; and better to imagine that in 40 or so years Brian would still be sleeping next to her at day's end. She suddenly giggled at her next thought: the wand may not always be what it is now, but the magic could still be there.

Trying to live in the moment while keeping an eye on the future can be a challenge sometimes. Tracy knew that somewhere down life's road she'd be looking back on this very moment and feeling nostalgic. She was so happy right now, so content. It wouldn't always be so easy to feel this way. Sooner or later, she'd have a new, desperate client who needed her help. And she'd fret and worry and lose her temper and feel bad and struggle and irritate her husband — and hopefully prevail as she usually did. As hard as things had been at times during the last few weeks, she could never see herself refusing a person in trouble; a person who needed her help. Turn such a person away? No. Tracy Brubaker Shane could never imagine doing *that*.